BARONI

Also by Alfred Harris

THE JOSEPH FILE

BARONI

a novel by

ALFRED HARRIS

G. P. PUTNAM'S SONS
NEW YORK

c. 2

M

Copyright © 1975 by Alfred Harris

SBN: 399-11626-5
Library of Congress Catalog
Card Number: 75-24851

For Bettina

1

THE sun was shining the day Evelyn Hawley died—but then it nearly always shines in Southern California.

The sun was one reason why Maria Lehmann happened to witness Mrs. Hawley's abrupt departure. As she told the police later, she was sitting on her tiny fifth-floor balcony peeling potatoes, her stockings rolled down so her rheumatism-laden legs could soak up the warmth, when she had heard the sound of breaking glass and had turned her head in time to see Mrs. Hawley hurtle from the living-room window of her apartment across the street and fall, arms flailing, to the pavement five floors below.

Maria Lehmann had never met Evelyn Hawley, but even so she felt she knew her well. A woman in her fifties, Maria had brought with her from Germany not only five children, but also the habit of watching the world from her windows. As a result, she had seen Evelyn Hawley many times. Especially whenever Mrs. Hawley had been in her kitchen. Its window was directly opposite Maria's balcony, and Maria, who spent most of the day in her apron preparing a hot, wholesome dinner for her family, had never ceased to shake her head at the way Evelyn would only begin to open cupboard and refrigerator doors a few minutes before her husband came home from work. To Maria, whose world revolved around nourishing schnitzels and stomach-filling knoedel, Evelyn Hawley was what she disparagingly termed a "modern" woman.

Old Harry Trask—thick glasses, wisps of white hair—

7

was also a witness to Evelyn Hawley's passing. He was Maria Lehmann's neighbor, living one floor above, and he was a window-watcher as well.

He had been a salesman until the year before when his birthday had brought on his retirement. At first he had luxuriated in so much free time, but then, as the months passed, everything began to pall, especially daytime television. Now he spent most of the day on his balcony with a book in his hands. But his eyes and interest invariably wandered to the events going on in the street below or in the windows of the apartment building opposite.

He didn't know the Hawleys by name, but he knew their routine. Especially Edward Hawley's. As he told the police, it wasn't uncommon for Mrs. Hawley to begin haranguing her husband the minute he returned from work. In the past Hawley had always accepted the tongue-lashing meekly, but this time, Trask reported, he had yelled back at his wife, startling her so much that she had simply stared at him in surprise, at first, and then had become absolutely furious. Speechless with rage, she had stormed out of the living room into the kitchen.

Trask had had to crane his neck to see her through her kitchen window—he had admitted this—but he did catch glimpses of her now and then, and judging from the rapid movement of her mouth, he was certain she had continued her harangue.

He had had a much better view of Edward Hawley, for he had gone into their bedroom and stood near the window, his hands pressed tightly to his ears, a look of anguish on his face.

Trask's phone had rung then and he had been forced to leave his chair to inform a young lady that free dance lessons were the least of his desires. It was an unfortunate interruption, for when he returned to his balcony the sound of shattering glass had already been heard and Evelyn Hawley was already airborne.

Laurie Knight occupied the apartment next to Maria's on

8

the floor below. An attractive redhead with an intelligent, impish face and a figure that looked good even in jeans, she had come to California five years before when she was nineteen and ever since had been trying to prove to the world what she sincerely believed—that she was truly a great actress. So far she managed to land only bit parts on television—but they did pay the rent.

Often discouraged, but never defeated, she continued to study acting whenever she got the chance. And that was frequent, for people were the subject of her studies: their moods, their movements, their reactions to stimuli of all kinds.

That's why, on that particular afternoon, she had stood on her balcony watching Evelyn Hawley in the apartment building opposite with such intensity.

It was Evelyn's angry gestures as she confronted her husband that had first attracted Laurie's attention. Each movement of the hands, the twist and tilt of the head, the tight lips—they were all the essence of the actor's art. So were the coldness of the eyes, the taut cords in the neck, the rigid stance, vibrant indications of anger, frustration, impotent rage. Laurie devoured it all. If ever she were called upon to play such a role, she would re-create it exactly. It was so perfect!

Edward Hawley's reactions were perfect, too—the stooped shoulders, the air of acceptance, the look of resignation, the sudden outburst of temper as he shouted back at his wife.

Laurie's balcony was perfectly situated. Unlike old Mr. Trask above, or Mrs. Lehmann next door, she could see not only into the Hawleys' living-room window, but also into their kitchen and their bedroom.

When Evelyn stormed into the kitchen, Laurie was not only able to watch her, but also Edward Hawley, who stood at the bedroom window, his eyes closed, his hands pressed tightly to his ears, his face etched with the effort he was making to ignore his wife's voice.

9

Laurie made a mental note of the way a vein seemed to stand out on his forehead against the ashen white of his complexion. Seething anger, she categorized it. No, mounting rage would be better.

Edward Hawley had turned. His face was no longer white but suffused with red. Now, abruptly, he wheeled and moved away from the window.

He appeared in the living room almost at once, yelling at his wife even as he entered "frame," as Laurie thought of it. Of course Evelyn Hawley yelled back, but what interested Laurie most just then was their natural spacing. They stood almost toe to toe. She had never realized before how people in anger often stand as close to each other as people in love.

If only she could see their eyes more closely, she thought. Did the eyelids flutter? Were tears involved?

She ran into her apartment to get her binoculars, but it took her precious moments to locate them buried beneath a pile of books and magazines. And so it was that she too missed the moment of climax—the split second in which Evelyn Hawley shattered glass and began her final plunge to the pavement below.

2

IT was a good thing Detective Lou Baroni liked to drive. Sergeant Steve Perry didn't. Most of the city's streets were too narrow. There were too many crosswalks. Too many stop signs. Too much traffic. He was only happy driving when he was in his own Corvette, racing along a freeway, heedless of the other cars around him.

The bright sunlight, even now at six P.M., annoyed him and it was too damn hot in the prowl car. Now, if he were only in an air-conditioned office in the Police Center, in a supervisory job, it would be different. That's what he felt he was meant to be—a man who managed men. He couldn't understand why his superiors failed to realize it.

Perry was a young man compared to Lou Baroni beside him, young and handsome. He was tall, well-built, broad-shouldered, muscular, dressed in the latest acceptable fashion. His hair was fair, his eyes blue. His smile, when he saw reason to produce it, could be warm and engaging. In fact, he could be quite charming if he so chose. It was an acquired skill he had practiced for most of his twenty-eight years.

Now he was scowling. It was his usual expression—the one that came to his face when nobody important was around.

He glanced at the older man sitting beside him as Baroni pulled the unmarked police car to a stop for a traffic light. He noted with distaste his bulk; his wrinkled, shiny suit; his gray thinning hair; his coarse features. Perry couldn't

11

understand why he had been saddled with such a man. It had been five weeks since his previous partner had been transferred and he still couldn't accept the idea. And he felt a touch of bitterness whenever he thought of the man who had arranged it. He had considered Lieutenant Tate his friend, feeling Tate considered him a comer—but then Tate had assigned him Baroni. It wasn't fair.

The light changed and Baroni pulled away from the white line, threading his way smoothly through the heavy suppertime traffic, heading back toward the Police Center.

The radio was on and both men listened to it without seeming to, their minds rejecting the calls that didn't concern them directly.

A car suddenly pulled out of the center lane, cutting directly in front of them. Baroni had to brake hard to keep from hitting it.

"Asshole," Baroni muttered.

Profanity, Perry thought. Baroni's lack of education always showed. A limited vocabulary encouraged the use of street words, and they, Perry felt, made the policeman no better than the scum with which he dealt. He ignored the fact that practically all policemen, including himself, used such words. After all, he didn't—usually.

He sighed. Baroni, plus the trouble he was having with his wife, Shirley, was almost too much to bear. In college, then at the Police Academy, and ever since, he had paid strict attention to all the social graces that meant so much—taking great pains to make himself an acceptable dinner guest, golf companion, and tennis partner—and, at first, it had seemed to pay off. But now here he was stuck with Baroni and, at the same time, with a wife who seemed to think all his free time and effort belonged solely to her.

Damn it, he thought, he would be stuck on the three-to-midnight watch today! If he could get home before Shirley went to sleep—she was a bitch when she was awakened—he knew he could make her see reason. After all, all he'd have to do was feel her up a little, turn her on full, and then

12

lay her from end to end. Afterward, he knew from experience, she'd forget about his latest unfaithfulness. What, he asked himself, did she expect him to do about it anyway? The other woman, this time, had influence with the department. Her old man was a captain. He just couldn't ignore her invitations, could he? A man didn't get ahead that way, did he? Anyway, why shouldn't he play around a little? It kept a man young—and a man like Steve Perry certainly needed more than one woman.

Baroni swung the car around a truck and asked, without taking his eyes off the road, "What are you gonna tell Tate?"

Perry, his thoughts interrupted, queried, "What about?"

"Zakos. We drew a blank."

"No," Perry answered, annoyed, "we didn't draw a blank. We found out a piece of vital information. If Spiro Zakos ever did maintain a mistress in that hotel, it was long ago."

Baroni's grin annoyed Perry. "All right, it's negative information. But it's still information."

Baroni shook his head. "They lied through their teeth."

"Who did?"

"The jerks we talked to."

Perry sighed. "We have no legal reason to assume that."

"We got all the reason in the world," Baroni told him. "Those pricks hate cops. They'd lie to us about the weather."

"Lou," Perry said firmly, "it's that kind of old-line thinking that promulgates the hatred those people feel for the police."

"Promulgates!" Baroni exclaimed, glancing at Perry. "They didn't even have that one in the dictionary when I went to school."

"Yes, they did." Perry smiled now. He enjoyed putting the older man down. "You just didn't go long enough to get to it—and a great many others."

Lou Baroni didn't bother to reply. He didn't think much

13

of Steve Perry or what he had to say. He'd seen too many others like him during his long years in the department. Eager, overly ambitious young men who saw their police work only as a stepping stone to something else. And, of course, they always resented the real policemen, the plodders, who did the real work.

But Perry was right about his lack of education. He couldn't deny that. He should have taken more extension courses. He regretted now that he hadn't. But he had married young, started his family young. And there had never been a day made that was long enough.

Of course, that was long ago. Now, with retirement only fourteen months away, it was much too late for schooling.

They were nearing the Police Center when the radio crackled loudly.

"One-Baker-Seven, One-Baker-Seven. Possible homicide, twelve-twenty-four Barstow. See the patrolman."

Perry cursed silently. It was a long way back to Barstow. He had hoped to chat with Lieutenant Tate for a while before he left for the day. Now Tate would be gone by the time they got in. Reluctantly he reached for the microphone. "One-Baker-Seven. Roger."

Originally Barstow Street had been occupied by small, inexpensive homes, but nearly all of those had been replaced years before by small apartment buildings. Most of the palms that had once lined the street were gone too. Only a few scraggly ones remained.

As Lou Baroni wheeled the car around a corner and onto Barstow he had no trouble identifying the site of the investigation. A black-and-white was parked in front of a five-story building and a small crowd of people clustered near it.

Lou pulled to a stop behind the patrol car and saw that a uniformed policeman was holding the crowd back, not from the entrance to the building, but from an object on the sidewalk. Perry saw it too, and came to the same conclusion.

14

"A jumper," Perry said, a note of distaste in his voice. He disliked suicides.

Lou grunted and got out of the car. Perry hung back, allowing the older man to clear a path for him through the crowd. Lou was polite enough when he told the people to move on, but just barely. There was a harshness in his voice that belied the "please" he spoke. The spectators parted, some actually moving on, but most simply moved back a step and stayed. Among these Lou noticed a young redhead in jeans. Unlike the others, she seemed more interested in the people around her, and in him, than in the shapeless object that lay covered on the concrete.

Another spectator who caught his eye was a stunned old man with wisps of white hair. He seemed more than normally upset. So did a third person—a motherly woman. It was her apron Lou noticed first. Few aprons were seen on the street these days.

The uniformed policeman, a young man named Willis, seemed to be enjoying himself. His instructors at the academy, Lou thought, would be proud to see the "professional" way he "jollied" the crowd—the firm but friendly policeman.

The young officer turned as they approached and his face broke into a pleasant grin when he recognized Steve Perry. Lou knew he had recognized him, too, but Perry was the sergeant.

"Hi, Sarge," Willis said cheerfully, "how are you?"

"Fine, fine." Perry smiled slightly to let Willis know he was pleased to see him, but not so much that the spectators would think him callous in view of the corpse at his feet. "What's gone down?"

"She lived on the fifth floor," Willis replied. "Apartment 5-D. Hawley, Evelyn." Then, leaning closer, he added, "She came down too quick and stopped too fast."

Perry frowned. Willis was too flip. He hoped nobody in the crowd had heard the remark. A policeman's image was important. "Ambulance?" he asked loudly, professionally.

15

"On its way," Willis replied.

"Talk to anybody yet?" Lou asked.

"Nearly all," Willis said. "Nothing much yet." He answered Lou's question but he looked at Perry. "My partner's upstairs with the husband."

Perry nodded. "The lab boys on their way?"

"They're here already," Willis answered. "They were in the neighborhood. How's that for service for a change?"

Perry frowned. He'd have to speak to Willis about a policeman's proper demeanor. "Where are they?"

"Upstairs. They got all the pictures and measurements they need down here."

Lou knelt beside the body and raised the blanket. The face of the victim, he saw, bore an expression of outrage.

Perry gave it only a cursory glance and then turned away. Death didn't disturb him, but corpses were the coroner's job.

The sound of a siren filled the street as an ambulance sped around a nearby corner. Perry, Willis, and the crowd turned to watch it as it came to a stop at the curb.

"Shall I let them take her away?" Willis asked.

Perry looked again at the victim and then up at the window from which she had fallen. Then, after a suitable moment, he nodded. "Yes, go ahead."

The ambulance attendants took the stretcher from their vehicle and carried it toward the body, but they had to pause before putting it down on the sidewalk because Lou Baroni was still kneeling beside the corpse, examining fragments which lay near it.

"What are you looking at?" Perry asked.

Without rising, Lou replied, "Glass."

Perry shrugged. "Forget it. The lab boys have seen it already."

Lou straightened, then moved aside. The ambulance attendants began their grisly task of transferring Evelyn Hawley's remains to their stretcher. The crowd of onlookers seemed absolutely fascinated—all except one, Lou no-

16

ticed—the redhead. Instead of staring at the body, she watched him as he followed Perry toward the entrance of the apartment building.

The foyer was empty. Originally it had been meant to be impressive, and it might have been years ago. Now, the floor tiles were discolored, the sofa against one wall was worn, and the mural of palm trees and desert mountains that occupied another wall was faded.

They crossed to the elevator. Neither man spoke. Lou was thinking about the dead woman outside, Perry of the well-built redhead. He wondered what she'd be like between the sheets.

The small elevator arrived and the two men entered. Perry glanced at his watch and Lou pressed the button for the fifth floor.

"Six thirty," Perry reported. "We should be able to write this up in a couple of hours."

Lou, leaning against the wall, said, "Don't count on it."

Perry turned toward him quickly, making no attempt to hide his annoyance. "Look, Lou, don't start making waves. The lieutenant will want this thing cleared up fast and you know it."

Lou looked back at him steadily. "He wants everything—fast," he said derisively.

"We've got more important cases," Perry said. "We've got to practice expediency."

Lou snorted. "Expediency!" The word obviously left a bad taste in his mouth.

Perry controlled his temper with an effort. "That's right—expediency. It's a word you should have learned long ago. Maybe if you had, you'd be a sergeant by now."

That said, he turned his eyes toward the front of the elevator and deliberately changed the subject. "Anyway, with any luck she left a note."

"No chance," Lou said flatly. "It wasn't suicide."

"You know that already?" Perry commented sarcastically.

17

Lou nodded. "There was broken glass all over the street. Suicides open windows."

Perry turned away. Why, he asked himself, did Baroni always have to make things difficult for him?

When the elevator reached the fifth floor, Perry stepped out first, then turned back to Lou. "I'll handle the investigation up here. You go back down and talk to the crowd."

Lou started to protest—Willis was already questioning the spectators—but the door closed and the elevator began its descent, so he simply shrugged.

Outside, the ambulance had gone and the spectators had dispersed. Willis was standing beside his black-and-white.

"Hiya, Lou. Thought you went upstairs."

"So did I," Lou replied. "Perry figured you might need some help questioning the lookers."

"Hell," Willis said, "that's all done. Most of 'em didn't see a thing till it was over, but I took down their names and addresses anyway."

"Most of them?" Lou asked.

"Yeah. Three did say they saw the whole thing go down from over there"—he indicated the apartment building opposite—"an old lady, an old man, and a real built chick."

When old Harry Trask saw Lou Baroni's badge, he said nothing. He backed into his apartment, and Lou followed, closing the door behind him.

Lou remembered seeing the old man on the sidewalk. He had looked stunned then. Now he seemed confused and distraught.

"I went down hoping she wasn't dead," Trask said abruptly as he sat down heavily on the sofa.

Lou looked down at him. "Tell me what happened."

Trask looked up imploringly. "I don't want to get him into any trouble. He's had more than enough already. That woman must have been hell to live with. It's a wonder he didn't kill her long ago."

"Are you saying he did kill her?"

18

Trask was startled by the question. He stared at Lou, try-ing to grasp its implications. Then a look of relief came into his eyes. "Are you saying he didn't?"

"I'm not saying anything. I'm just asking questions."

"But I thought it was obvious—" Trask began. "I mean, I assumed—" New life seemed to flow into him as new ideas came to his mind. "Yes, that's it. I just assumed." The con-fusion vanished from his eyes. He smiled. "But I have no reason at all to assume he killed her."

Lou looked down at him steadily. "Haven't you?"

"No," he replied, looking back just as steadily. "No—not at all. The phone rang. I heard the window break while I was answering it. I really didn't see what actually hap-pened at all."

Lou sat down and took out his notebook. "All right, tell me everything you *did* see."

Mrs. Maria Lehmann was ready for Lou when he knocked on her door and flashed his badge. Her eyes were red but there was a defiant look in them, a resolute set to her chin.

"You can come in and ask all the questions you want," she said belligerently, "but I have nothing to tell you."

The apartment was filled with the smells of a magnificent meal cooking. Lou deliberately mentioned it, flattering her, but she wasn't fooled like so many others would have been.

"You didn't come to talk about food."

Lou was forced to nod. "You're right. I came to talk about what happened across the street. You told the officer you saw what happened."

"No," Mrs. Lehmann declared firmly, "I did not see it. I made a mistake. I spoke without thinking. My sons, they al-ways say, 'Mama, you talk too much without thinking.' They are right."

Mention of her sons seemed to remind Mrs. Lehmann of the time. "They will be home soon. They will want their supper."

19

"I won't keep you long," Lou promised. "Just a few questions."

"What for?" she demanded. She faced him, feet flat on the floor, her eyes on his. "I saw nothing."

"You said you were on your balcony—"

"Yes—but I saw nothing. And I take back everything else I said."

"Mrs. Lehmann," Lou asked softly, "what made you change your mind?"

"I didn't change it. I was upset before. Now I'm not."

"And so you decided not to tell the truth?"

"The truth!" she exclaimed, moving her hands as if to wave it away. "I have heard too many truths!"

"I'm only interested in one," Lou prodded gently. "The truth about what happened across the street."

"Why?" Mrs. Lehmann demanded. "Why? Will it bring that poor woman back to life again? Will sending somebody to jail make her breathe again?"

So that's it, Lou thought, the decision she's made since talking to Willis. She's decided, since we can't bring back the dead, there's no reason to prosecute the living.

Maria Lehmann waited for an answer. "Well, will it bring her back?"

"No," Lou replied, "but if she was murdered, her murderer must be caught and punished. That's the law—"

Mrs. Lehmann interrupted, actually snorting as she said, "The law! Don't tell me about the law! It changes! It's always different for different people in different places in different times—but it's still the law, the law!"

"Mrs. Lehmann—" Lou started to say, startled by her outburst. She went on, ignoring what he was going to say.

"Let me tell you, Mr. Policeman, something about the law. When I was still a young girl a young man came to me and he talked about the law too—and he seemed just as nice, just as friendly—and he was such a good-looking boy—so I listened and I learned all about the law—only the uniform he was wearing was black and it had a swastika on it!"

20

* * *

Willis was right, Lou thought, when Laurie Knight answered his knock. She was built. And, what's more, she was the same redhead he had noticed on the street—the one who had seemed more interested in the spectators than in the corpse.

"You're a detective?" Her voice was pleasant, well-pitched.

"That's right. I'd like to ask you a few questions."

"Sure," she said, stepping back to allow Lou to enter. "That policeman downstairs said somebody might be along."

The apartment was cluttered with books and magazines but it was still nice. Not overly feminine, like so many others Lou had seen in which a woman had lived alone, but still it left no doubt that it was a woman's home.

Laurie sat down gracefully on an ottoman, cross-legged. Lou chose the sofa opposite her, aware that she had been taking inventory of him just as he had of her.

"You're old to be a detective, aren't you?"

"Not too old," Lou answered, slightly annoyed at the question. "Why?"

"I always picture detectives younger."

"They come all ages—and all shapes and sizes."

She laughed, pleased. "It's so easy to get the wrong idea, isn't it? Are you married?"

Lou found himself saying no.

"But you have been?"

"Yes," Lou said and then added, bluntly, "I didn't come here to talk about myself. I came to talk about the woman who was murdered."

"Murdered?" Laurie exclaimed, her eyes wide. Lou saw they were hazel. He wondered how old she was.

"Was she really murdered?"

"Don't you know?" Lou asked.

"No. How could I?"

"You said you saw her fall from the window."

21

"No, I didn't. I said I saw her falling. I saw her land."

"Damn!"

"I'm sorry."

"Just what did you see?"

She got up and began to pace. She was quite tall for a girl. "I've been thinking about that. I mean, about the answer I'd give to the question. I really didn't see much—just two people arguing—but then, they, always argued so that doesn't mean much, does it? Yet, this time he yelled back at her. I've never seen him do that before."

She walked across the room. She turned now to face Lou. "What's he like?"

"Who?"

"The dead woman's husband."

"I don't know. I haven't met him."

"You haven't?" She was genuinely surprised. "But you've already decided he killed his wife. You said 'murdered.'"

"That's right."

"But how? Why? I mean, without even talking to him—"

"It's the odds. People just don't fall through closed windows that often."

Officer Vernon Johnston was just coming out of apartment 5-B when Lou Baroni got off the elevator on the fifth floor of Evelyn Hawley's apartment building. He wasn't young like Willis downstairs. He was closer to Lou's age. He remembered the "good old days" and that created something of a bond between them.

He waited until Lou joined him and then, together, they walked toward the Hawley apartment, 5-D.

"Hi, Lou. How's it going?"

"A broad just told me I looked too old to be a real detective."

Johnston laughed.

"Been talking to the neighbors?" Lou asked.

"Yeah."

"Get anything?"

"Three things." Johnston held up his hand, ticking off each item on his fingers. "One—Evelyn Hawley would die before she'd kill herself."

Lou nodded. He had gathered that impression.

"Two—everybody felt sorry for the husband. She never stopped yelling at him. And—three—this was the first time he ever yelled back."

"Yeah, I heard about that," Lou said.

"Sort of supports his story, doesn't it?"

"What story?"

"Haven't you been inside yet?" Johnston asked.

Lou shook his head. They had reached 5-D and stood in front of the door.

"The husband admits yelling at her. He says she was so surprised she took a step backward, tripping over a vacuum cleaner hose, and went out through the window."

A vacuum cleaner hose, Lou thought. No, it didn't figure. Not for a woman like Evelyn Hawley. The way she'd been described, it wasn't likely she'd trip over anything.

He opened the door to the Hawley apartment and went in.

The living room was like a hundred others Lou had seen. The furniture, the drapes, the pictures on the walls were all typical of a lower-middle-class, middle-aged woman who had lost her imagination along with her youth. Most of it was old, but too well taken care of to replace. The only relatively new object in the room was a color television set. It sat against one wall, opposite a sofa, which occupied another wall. An armchair, a china cabinet, a coffee table, and a bureau comprised the rest of the furniture.

The scene that met Lou's eyes was a familiar one too. The lab boys had their gear spread all over the room. One man was measuring the broken window. Another was taking pictures of a canister-type vacuum cleaner that sat on the floor in front of the window.

Perry stood near the bureau, talking on the phone, probably to his wife, Lou thought. He had that half-impatient, half-imploring look on his face. A small man sat on the

23

sofa—at least he seemed small at the moment, with his head bent, his shoulders stooped, his expression numb. The husband, Lou guessed—slightly overweight, slightly worn, tired, his brown hair touched with gray and thinning. Yet, unlike most other husbands Lou had seen in similar situations, this one didn't really seem overcome with grief—just slightly bewildered, apparently not sure, just yet, how he felt.

Lou walked over to him and Hawley looked up. It's not just his stooped shoulders that make him look tired, Lou thought. It's his eyes, too.

Lou indicated the vacuum cleaner behind him. "Is that how it happened? You yelled, she backed off, tripped?"

Hawley nodded. "I might have done more than yell. I might have taken a step toward her. I don't know."

"Or raised your hand to her?"

"No."

"Or shoved her a little?"

Hawley didn't answer that one right away. Instead he looked at Lou for the first time. "No," he said calmly. "No. I'd remember that."

"What were you fighting about?"

Hawley shrugged—a gesture that seemed a natural part of him. "Everything, nothing. The minute I got home she started complaining. You know, I didn't care how much dirt I tracked in. I didn't care how hard she worked. I didn't—"

Lou cut in. "Like she's always done?"

Hawley nodded.

"Only this time you yelled back?"

"That's right. This time I yelled back."

"Why?" Lou asked. "Why this time and not before?"

Hawley was about to answer, but Perry, who had put the phone down, spoke across the room to Lou, not attempting to hide his annoyance.

"Lou, leave it alone. We've been over all that already."

Lou glanced at Perry, then back at Hawley, his expres-

24

sion impossible to read. Lou crossed to Perry. Keeping his voice low he asked, "Homicide?"

"No way," Perry replied. He was watching the lab boys, waiting for them to finish so he could leave.

"What then?"

"Death by misadventure."

"You're kidding!"

"Lou," Perry said warningly, "it's open and shut."

The scorn in Lou's voice was unmistakable. "Sure, it is—if that's how you want it."

Perry held his temper in check only with effort. "Look, Lou, it's not how I want it. It's how the lieutenant wants it. Anyway, you haven't got anything that says it wasn't misadventure, have you?"

"No," Lou had to admit, "not yet."

"Exactly."

"What about motive?"

"There is none."

"Insurance? Savings?"

"I've seen his bank book and his policies. Forget it."

"There could be others."

"Sure—and I'll check, but I'll come up empty."

"What about girlfriends?"

"Girlfriends—him?"

They both glanced over at Hawley, still seated on the sofa. The idea didn't seem likely.

"He must have looked good to his wife once," Lou pointed out.

Perry nodded. "Precisely—once."

Lou couldn't argue the point. "It could be something else."

"I wouldn't bet your pension on it if I were you."

For a moment Lou stared at the younger man, wondering if there was a double meaning to that remark. Deciding there probably was, he said, "Maybe that's just what I *will* do."

As he moved slowly around the room, he noted the carefully arranged bric-a-brac, the shelf of women's magazines, the slipcovers, the doilies.

The kitchen was immaculate, too—the plastic counter-tops, spotless; the electric stove, shining. But only three items really caught Lou's attention—two TV dinners thawing on the table and an unopened can of soup near the range.

He turned to the refrigerator and opened its door. There was very little in the lower half, but the freezer section was full of frozen meals.

Back in the living room he saw Perry talking to one of the lab men. He knew with certainty that they weren't talking about the case. Not in that conspiratorial manner. They were discussing angles. The lab man was as deeply involved in department politics as Perry was.

Lou walked back to Hawley, who still sat on the sofa, his eyes on the floor.

"Work around here?" Lou asked.

Hawley shook his head. "Downtown."

"Where?"

"The Acme Credit Company."

"A bookkeeper?"

"I used to be, before they put computers in. Now I work in delinquent accounts."

The thought came to Lou unbidden: after years of experience, the experience no longer mattered. "Did you like making the change?" he asked.

Hawley shrugged. "I had no choice."

Lou nodded. "None of us do." He indicated a door. "Bedroom in there?"

There wasn't much inside except a double bed, a woman's dressing table, a nightstand, and a closet. Lou opened it knowing what to expect—90 percent of it was occupied by Evelyn Hawley's clothes. Only two or three hangers held Edward Hawley's suits.

Lou closed the closet and walked over to the dressing table. Besides makeup, it held only one item that interested him—a framed photograph. He picked it up and carried it over to the window where the light was better. The picture showed two young people. One was obviously Edward Hawley, but much younger, handsomer, more virile. He stood with his arm around a very lovely young woman. Both were smiling and both seemed very much in love.

"That was taken twenty-five years ago."

Lou turned to see Edward Hawley in the doorway. "On your honeymoon?"

"That's right."

Lou put the picture back on the dressing table. "A long time, twenty-five years." For a moment he looked down at the photograph. "I was married for twenty-seven years." Hawley said nothing. "Everything changes in that time." Indicating the picture, Lou went on. "A man thinks he's got it made at that age. Cock of the walk—that was me. I was gonna remake the world."

Edward Hawley sat down on the edge of the bed. "My ambitions were never that extensive."

Lou looked at him. "But you did have ambitions?"

"Sure."

"And your wife was part of them?"

"Of course. She was the main part."

Lou walked over to the bed. "When did you decide to kill her?"

Hawley looked up at Lou to answer. "I never really did decide—one way or the other."

3

THE suppertime traffic had begun to thin out when Lou Baroni and Steve Perry left the Hawley apartment and drove back toward the Police Center.

They spoke little. Each man was wrapped up in his own thoughts. Lou felt more tired and depressed than usual, and he knew the reason. It was the photograph he had seen of Edward Hawley and his wife when they were young. It had brought back memories of his own marriage. His wife had been dead for eight years, and ordinarily he only thought of her as she had been during the final years of their marriage, not the way she was in the beginning. He found it hard to picture her now as she had been then, not only young and beautiful, but adoring. Or, he suddenly asked himself, had she ever really been that way? Was it, in truth, simply something he had read into their relationship because it was supposed to be that way? Certainly there was no "adoring" during their later years together.

And what of her? Had she once thought him to be something he wasn't? Had she only gradually realized what he was really like? Is that why she had turned sour? He shook his head. Such thoughts led nowhere.

He wheeled the car around a corner, heading west. The sun was still up, but low on the horizon. Perry, beside him, put on his sunglasses. They weren't really needed, but Lou knew he felt the dark lenses gave his image a lift. Lou grinned ruefully to himself. Had he postured in ways of his own when he had been Perry's age? Probably.

Steve Perry was tired, too—tired of what he considered menial chores, tired of Lou Baroni, tired of the problems he had with his wife, and tired of trying to impress superior officers who refused to be impressed.

Well, he decided, there was nothing he could do but go on trying. For, he felt, promotion was the answer to everything. He wouldn't have to work with old cruds like Baroni, and Shirley, he was sure, would get off his back if he could stuff her hands full of money.

His thoughts turned to Lieutenant Tate. Maybe, he reasoned, if he could find a way to make Tate feel indebted, he'd open a few doors for him, bring some clout to bear, get him a promotion to some job where his abilities would finally be recognized.

Yes, he thought, he'd have to go on pleasing Tate—even if he had made Baroni his partner. Tate must have had his reasons and he'd just have to accept them and show him he could handle the situation. That was the answer. Show Tate he was willing to go along—with anything. And, he decided, he'd make sure Tate understood that fact. He'd do it by simply saying as much to him—obliquely, of course. He glanced at his watch. Too bad, he thought, it was so late. He was in the mood to talk to Tate right away but it wasn't likely Tate would still be in his office. Tate had so many social obligations that he usually left early.

The police building was a modern structure with a large outdoor parking lot and, even at this hour, Lou had to hunt for an empty stall. When he finally found one, Perry's mood rose. There was a cream-colored Eldorado parked nearby—Tate's.

The police building had been built with an eye to economy. Inside, the walls were painted concrete block. The doors were steel where it mattered, Masonite where it didn't. The floors were covered with linoleum tile. If the architect had set out to create a cold, unfriendly atmosphere, he had succeeded admirably. Lou often compared it to the older, smaller building it had replaced. That one had worn

29

wooden floors, varnished wooden bannisters, cracked plaster, and chairs and desks with carved initials and cigarette burns. It had been dirty, it had smelled of perspiration and disinfectant, but, somehow, it had lived, flourished, and grown old. This one seemed stillborn.

It was quite late, but because crime is a thriving business, the place was as busy as ever. As Lou and Perry walked along the wide corridor, a number of uniformed policemen, plainclothesmen, and just plain citizens moved by. Most of the citizens were handcuffed. Only a few of the officers or detectives knew Lou or Perry well enough to greet them. It was a large police department.

As soon as they left the car, Perry had begun to urge his point of view on Lou. He did it as a father tries to coax a recalcitrant child.

"Look, Lou, if we go into Tate's office and tell him this Hawley thing is a possible murder-one, he'll have to instigate a complete investigation."

"Let him," Lou answered.

"But there's hardly a chance it was premeditated. And, anyway, the case just isn't that important, is it?"

Before Lou could answer, two men left an office and walked into the corridor. One was a uniformed officer, the other a tall, bony, emaciated Negro wearing a huge overcoat. His thin, knobby wrists were in handcuffs. As soon as he saw Lou his face broke into a grin.

"Lou, baby!" he exclaimed as they passed each other. "How's it going, man?"

"Same as always, Wally," Lou answered. "Hanging in there."

Perry didn't let the meeting interrupt his argument. "You see, Lou, you act as if Hawley and his wife are somebody important. They aren't. You've got to admit that."

"Yeah, sure. They're just 'people.'"

"Lou, stop it! You know what I mean. They weren't involved in anything big. The woman's death won't lead us anywhere. Take the Spiro Zakos murder, for example. Now,

30

if we can tie Nick Pappas in with that, Papa Pappas and his whole operation goes down—pushers, pimps, numbers."

They stopped at Tate's doorway. Before knocking, Perry paused for one further remark.

"To put it another way, Hawley's life and his wife's death affect nobody but themselves. That's right, isn't it?"

Lou studied Perry's face. It didn't seem possible, but it was. He really meant what he was saying! "Yeah," Lou said, "that's right. It doesn't affect anybody but them."

Perry knocked on the door, opened it, and entered. Lou followed.

Lieutenant Harold Tate was a tall, handsome man in his early forties with prematurely silver hair that made him seem very wise for his age. Well educated, highly trained, he was conscious at all times of his public image. That explained the thin waist, the expensive clothes, the deep tan, the manicured nails.

He was standing before a series of charts lined up on easels around the room, and as Steve Perry and Lou Baroni entered, he turned from them with a satisfied smile on his face.

"Steve, Lou—glad you got back. I was just about to leave. I'm speaking to a Citizens' Action Committee tonight."

He stepped aside to allow Perry and Lou to receive the full impact of the array of bright-colored graphs, an expectant look on his face. Perry rose, dutifully, to the occasion.

"They look good, sir, really good. They tell the department's problems clearly and concisely—and emphatically."

Tate smiled, pleased. "They do, don't they? I really believe they're worth all the effort I put into them."

"Oh, they are, sir!" Perry replied. "They are!"

Lou, watching, wondered how in hell two grown men could get so worked up about such crap.

Lieutenant Tate swung a beautifully gold embossed, genuine leather portfolio onto his desk and began placing the art work inside. "How did your investigation go?" he asked Perry.

31

Perry seemed to square his shoulders before he replied. "Splendidly, sir. We've added a decisive factor to the general workup we have on Spiro Zakos. We know now that if he ever did maintain a mistress, her nature was such that nobody remembers her. In other words, if Spiro Zakos was ever interested in women, he chose a plain, nondescript one—obviously because she offered no threat to his ego."

"He means we screwed up," Lou said disgustedly.

Perry turned to Lou angrily. "I happen to think our questions were answered factually."

"Pimps and pushers never answer factually!"

Lieutenant Tate closed his portfolio with a decisive sound. "In any event," he said, "I'll read the report with interest. Circulate copies to Narcotics and Vice. They may be able to apply a little pressure to those pimps and pushers."

Perry's face beamed. "A good idea, sir. If they were holding out on us, a little pressure might help."

Tate started for the door. Lou turned to Perry, amazed. "Aren't you even going to tell him about the Hawley murder?"

"It wasn't a murder!"

Tate paused, then turned back to them. Before he could question them, Perry said, "I didn't want to waste your time with it. I felt a report on your desk in the morning would be sufficient."

"Waste his time," Lou suggested bluntly.

Tate glared at Lou, then said to Perry, "Tell me about it now, briefly."

"Yes, sir," Perry said, holding in his anger. "I'll read you my notes." He took out his notebook, flipped it open with a practiced flourish, and began to read.

"Six ten, this date. Evelyn Hawley, housewife, age forty-six, fell five stories from the window of her apartment to her death."

"Fell or was pushed," Lou added.

Perry ignored him. "Twenty minutes earlier, approximately five fifty P.M., her husband, Edward C. Hawley,

32

came home from work and a domestic quarrel ensued."

"A routine quarrel?" Tate asked.

Perry looked up from his notebook to reply. "Yes, sir— according to all the neighbors. They quarreled often."

"She was a bitch on wheels," Lou said.

"Go on," Tate said to Perry.

"According to her husband's statement"—Perry referred to his notebook again—"the quarrel ended when he lost his temper and yelled back at his wife—something he rarely did. He also admits to possibly even taking a step toward her. Apparently she was so startled that she took an involuntary step backward, tripped over a vacuum cleaner hose, and fell through the window, breaking the glass in so doing."

Lou snorted. Tate ignored him and asked Perry, "What does the lab have to say about it?"

"They claim it could have gone down that way. They couldn't find anything to indicate it happened differently."

"What about motives?"

"None," Perry answered. "The preliminary investigation indicates no inheritance, no vices, no extramarital affairs. I'll run a complete routine check, of course, but there's no doubt in my mind it was just a domestic quarrel that ended in death."

"Death by misadventure?" Tate asked.

Perry nodded, closing his notebook. "That's how I see it."

"Bull," Lou said.

Lieutenant Tate turned to Lou and regarded him patiently. "Lou," he said, sincerity dripping from his voice, "no one values the intuition of the old-line policeman more than I do. But intuition isn't enough anymore. The courts won't accept it as sufficient probable cause to even investigate—"

Lou interrupted. "A woman doesn't drop five stories just because her husband yells at her."

"She does," Perry interjected, "if she trips!"

Lou ignored Perry, taking a step toward the lieutenant. "Look—we don't know anything about the guy. Let's find out what he's like at work, where he goes in his spare time—"

"Lou," Tate said, interrupting, "think! Probable cause! You know we can't go around making unlawful inquiries, carrying out unauthorized surveillance, illegal searches—"

"I didn't say anything about searches, not yet."

"All right," Tate went on impatiently. "Let's say we risk a charge of harassment. Tell me this—what for?"

"You know what for."

"I do," Tate said, "but I don't think you do. Even if we do prove he did it, what's the best we could get as a result? A single conviction that wouldn't amount to much. On the other hand, we've got a dozen other cases far more important—"

Lou snorted. "I knew we'd get to that."

Tate went on. It was one of his favorite topics. "Lou, consider this—one drug peddler kills more people in a year than this man of yours even knows. One paid agitator provokes more havoc than this man of yours could create in a lifetime."

"He's still a killer," Lou said stubbornly.

"But even more important," Tate continued, "we don't want to give ourselves a black eye in the public's estimation by persecuting this man when all the hard information you have indicates he's innocent."

"Not in my book," Lou said, still challenging his superior.

Tate sighed and glanced at Perry, who felt like smirking but simply shook his head sadly.

"Lou," Tate said patiently, "you've had a hard day. Why don't you go home and rest. Steve will write up the reports."

A scowl flicked across Perry's face in spite of himself. He had planned to tell Lou to do the reports. He was still thinking about his wife, about taking enough time off to

34

hurry home and placate her in bed. Now that was out.

Lou still confronted Tate. "So it's going to be death by misadventure?"

"That's right. And from now on I want you to concentrate your thinking on the Zakos case. We're getting far too much static from the media—"

Lou interrupted. "I'd rather finish this case—"

Tate lost his temper. "It *is* finished!" His face flushed. He liked to be in control, but for some reason, whenever he was with Lou Baroni, that control always slipped. He searched for a way to regain it, but Lou spoke first.

"You'd better get going to your Citizens' Action Committee. You don't want to be late." And then, before Tate could reply, he walked out the door.

Tate stared at the closed door, a vein throbbing on a tanned temple. Finally he turned to Perry. "Steve," he said, his eyes grim, "it's time we talked."

"Yes, sir," Perry replied, wondering what was coming.

"It's about Baroni."

Perry waited.

"You must have wondered why I made him your partner."

"Yes, sir, I certainly have."

Tate walked over to the window and stood looking out, his hands clasped behind his back, a favorite pose. "I have a reason, a very good one."

"Yes, sir," Perry said quickly. "I was sure you had. That's why I didn't complain. I made up my mind to go along with—well—with whatever you had in mind."

Tate turned back to him. "I'm glad to hear you say that, Steve, because that's just what I want you to do—go along with what I have in mind."

Perry nodded.

"I don't need to tell you the department's split. There's the old faction and the new—the 'traditionalists,' to use a polite term—and the progressive, organization-minded cadre."

35

"Yes, sir," Perry said, "I know that. It's obvious to any-one with—" He paused. He was going to say "intelligence" but he wondered if he should give himself that accolade. Tate did it for him.

"Anyone with intelligence? That's what you were going to say, wasn't it? Well, don't be ashamed of the truth. We have to blow our own bugles if we're going to be heard." He paused. "But being heard isn't enough. We have to do more."

Perry raised his eyebrows questioningly. Tate clasped his hands in front of him this time, another favorite pose.

"You realize this conversation is strictly confidential?"

"Yes, sir. Of course."

"Good." He paused again, his eyes drilling into Perry—a mannerism he had perfected with care. "We—those of us who think it's time the old-timers, the so-called old-line po-licemen, moved aside and let the younger, more modern-thinking men take over—have decided to take steps."

"What kind of steps, sir?" Perry asked, eagerly, extremely pleased, aware that he was being let in on the "inside." He was forming an "allegiance." He couldn't wait to tell his wife. If anything should convince her he wasn't a man to be ordered around, this would. And when he got his promo-tion—and he was now certain he would—his life would finally be his own to live as he chose.

Tate began pacing, slowly, each movement measured. "What kind of steps?" he repeated. "Disappointingly small ones to begin with, I'm afraid, but nonetheless important."

"I understand," Perry said.

"But do you understand why they have to be small?" Tate pointed a finger at Perry. "It's because the chief him-self is one of these old-timers!"

Perry nodded again, beginning to see Tate's ultimate goal.

"So we've decided," the lieutenant said, "to start slow-ly—to begin cleaning the old-timers out gradually, one by

36

one, until before too long there'll only be one old-timer left in the whole department—the chief himself."

"And once he's the only one left," Perry ventured, "he won't be hard to ease out."

"Exactly," Tate said. "Now, you know how many of these old-line policemen we have, don't you, Steve? In this division alone?"

"Yes, sir," Perry said. "Besides Baroni, there's Seidler, Miller, Zollars, O'Hare—"

Tate interrupted. "The others don't matter. They never accomplish anything anyway. They can be transferred, one by one, or relegated to some ashcan. But the chief likes him. The chief feels Lou Baroni produces results!"

Perry nodded again.

"Baroni will be retiring soon," Tate said after a moment. "They all will—but we can't wait that long. We've got to make room now for younger, more progressive men."

"Isn't there any way we can move up Baroni's retirement?"

"It's possible," Tate said, "but it wouldn't sit right at all. We don't want to reward men like Baroni. We want to oust them, we want to prove they do more harm than good."

Perry smiled mirthlessly. "We'll just have to find a way to prove that, then."

Tate's smile, in return, was warm. "Exactly." Then he waited for Perry to go on.

"And that's why he's my partner, isn't it? So I can report each infraction of the regulations he makes?"

It was Tate who nodded this time. "But not just infractions. They're not enough. We need something more, something bigger. And I'm counting on you to get it."

"Yes, sir," Perry said confidently, grinning.

Tate moved to him and put his hand on his shoulder. "Not 'sir' when we're alone, Steve. Call me Harold."

Once Lou left Tate's office, he shoved his fists into his

37

pockets and hunched along the corridor. He shouldn't be working wth men like Tate and Perry, he told himself for the hundredth time. They weren't his kind. He didn't belong in their world. It was an alien world that had somehow usurped his own.

He passed an open doorway and a voice called out his name. Al Miller, another detective, only a few years younger, came out into the corridor.

"Got a minute?"

"Sure," Lou replied. He liked Miller. The man tried. In a way he felt sorry for him. He was a plodder, never had made a bust that mattered on his own. And he had trouble at home—a runaway daughter and a wife who drank too much. It showed, too. Miller was grayer than Lou.

"What's going down?" Lou asked.

"We've got a friend of yours inside." Miller indicated the room behind him. "Wally Blue. Can't get anything out of him that counts, but he's got the hots for you. He might snitch if you asked the questions."

"What's the charge this time?"

"Same as always," Miller answered. "Possession—but there's a good chance he might give us a handle on the Zakos killing. He was seen with Nicky Pappas the same day, and some say he was even letting Nicky bugger him now and then for a fix. Want to give it a try?"

"Sure," Lou told him. "Why not."

He followed Miller into the small interrogation room. There wasn't much inside—just four bare walls, a cigarette-scarred table, and two chairs.

The tall, emaciated Negro who had greeted Lou in the hall earlier sat in one chair, behind the table, an expression of pain on his face. He wore a huge, old, ragged overcoat even though it was quite warm, but even in it he seemed to be shivering—a typical hype reaction. His shoulders were slumped, his eyes watery.

"Lou baby!" he exclaimed when he saw Lou walk in. His wide grin revealed broken, stained teeth.

38

Miller stopped near the door. Lou perched himself on the edge of the table and faced Wally. In spite of his years as an addict, Wally's skin was still a deep blue-black, and it was this color that had given him his street name—Wally Blue.

"Hey, man, how's it going?" Wally asked and Lou knew he really meant the question. He was the kind of hype who cared.

Lou shrugged. "Same as always. It's still dragging and the sidewalk's still rough."

Wally laughed. It was more of a bray than a laugh.

"Lou, you don't change none, ever, man, that's a fact!"

"How about you, Wally—what's new?"

Wally wagged his head. "Hell, man, ain't nuthin' ever new with me. I'm here again, ain't I?"

Miller leaned back against the wall beside the closed door and folded his arms. Lou said to Wally, "It must be a couple of years since I busted you."

"Yeah," Wally replied, "but I ain't been true to ya, baby. Others have busted me since."

He tilted his head back and laughed loudly at his own humor. His Adam's apple bobbed vigorously in his long, thin neck. He sobered, regarding Lou earnestly.

"But there ain't been none like you, that's the truth, man. You done your best for me and I ain't forgot it."

Neither had Lou. It had happened one night on the East Side. Wally had been sucking juice from a brown paper bag in a back alley when some young studs, white, decided to roll him. He must have put up one hell of a fight for when Lou arrived on the scene, one of the four was laid out over a garbage can. But that left three—and Wally wasn't much good for anything by that time.

In spite of the odds Lou went into action. He could have pulled his gun, but he made a mistake—he didn't. He hadn't thought it necessary. And he was angry. It burned him to see four healthy punks picking on a scarecrow wino junkie.

Things had gone bad almost at once. The three meatballs

39

had all jumped him at once, and before he made them scatter, he had a three-inch gash in his scalp.

Wally, bleeding from numerous cuts, sat flat on the pavement, his back against a wall, grinning up at Lou, who was wiping away his own blood.

"Hey, man," he said. "Thanks. That sure was sumpthin' to see!"

Many another man, Lou had thought, would have sat there, whimpering.

Later, both Lou and Wally rode in the same ambulance. But as soon as they reached the hospital, they were separated. A ten-cent bag of heroin had been found on Wally, undoubtedly what the four punks had been after, so he'd been booked on possession and taken to the prison ward.

In his usual perverse way, Lou had felt Wally had gotten a raw deal. After all, he was the victim. He shouldn't have been booked, not that time, not after being cut up. And when Wally came before a judge Lou said as much. Wally had appreciated the effort. The judge hadn't.

Suddenly Wally shuddered, a huge shiver moving him even under the massive coat. "Hey, Lou, make 'em turn up the furnace, will ya? I'm freezing!"

"What are you jobbing these days?" Lou asked.

"Smack, horse, the big H—you know—to make the pain go away."

"You're coasting right now, aren't you?"

Wally nodded. "Yeah, but slow—real slow." Then his expression brightened. "You oughta try it, Lou. It's like Disneyland all over. It's the only way out."

Lou, still sitting on the edge of the table, shook his head. "Not for me, Wally. I've got to find another way."

"But you ain't tried it, man! You don't know! And I'd sure like to do sumpthin' for you, you know?"

Miller, standing at the door, smiled. It was such a perfect setup. Lou saw the smile and played it straight, talking as if Wally's offer hadn't been finessed out of him.

"There is something you can do for me, Wally," Lou said softly, "there is, if you really want to."

Pleasure replaced the pain on Wally's face. "Lou, baby, for you, anything." Then, a look of shrewdness came to his face and he glanced at Miller. "But only for you, Lou. Nobody else. Just you."

Lou glanced at Miller and Miller nodded. A moment later the door closed behind him. As soon as they were alone, Wally said, "Name it, Lou—Bernice, Miss Emma, Horse—name it and I'll get it—and you'll leave all your chickenshit troubles behind."

"Wally, thanks. But that's no way out for me."

"Baby, it's everybody's way out!"

"If you want to, you can help me another way."

"But there ain't nothin' else as good," Wally insisted. "Nobody bugs you when you're high. You ain't ever too old or too tired and you don't hurt anymore, any way!"

"Wally, there's something we've got to know."

The smile vanished. Wally sat straight, wary. "We?" he repeated. "Lou, I said I'd help *you,* not them babyfaced lieutenants you got running this place now."

"You would be helping me, Wally. I've got to work with them babyfaced lieutenants."

Wally wrung his great knobby hands. "Man, don't ask me to squeal—"

"Wally," Lou said earnestly, "you know me better than that. I'd never ask you to squeal on one of your friends."

"Who then?" Wally asked, his eyes troubled, furtive. "The pushers? Lou, look, they ain't been independent ever since Papa Pappas came along years back. They're organized. If I squeal on one of 'em, the rest will find out and I'm all of a sudden a dear-departed."

"Not the pushers, Wally. I don't give a damn about those punks. I've got to have more than that."

"More?" Wally said, alarmed. "What do you mean, more? What do you want from me, anyway?"

Lou said it slowly. "The crud on top. The Big Man. The one who let the contract on Zakos."

Wally began to shake. It wasn't the hype's usual tremor. This time it was fear.

41

"Lou, man, forget it. I don't wanna get ripped off. I wanna go on breathing."

"Who's the big dick, Wally? Who had Zakos killed? Papa Pappas?"

Wally was kneading his big hands now, shaking from side to side. "I don't know, Lou. That's a fact. I swear it. I don't know."

"But you've got some ideas, haven't you?" Lou pressed. "Come on, Wally, it's me, Lou Baroni, asking. You said you wanted to do something for me."

"I do," Wally said urgently. "I do wanna help you—but I can't. I can't!"

"My babyfaced lieutenant is shoving it to me, Wally. He's screwing me hard. I've got to have something to shove back into him."

"Ask me sumpthin' else then. Anything. What else you got going? Who else you want fingered?"

Lou, who had been sitting on the edge of the table, sighed and slowly got up. Softly he said, "Forget it, Wally. If that's how it's got to be, that's how it's got to be."

Wally Blue looked like he was going to cry. "Lou, I'm sorry. Real sorry. I'll help you any other way, honest!"

Lou walked toward the door and paused, his hand on the knob. "Sure, Wally. Sure, I know."

"Lou—wait—listen—ask me sumpthin' else, will ya? Please? Ask me sumpthin'—I don't wanna let you down—just go ahead and ask—please!"

"No, Wally," Lou said. "There isn't anything else. But thanks, anyway." He opened the door and went out. Behind him Wally Blue called out, "Lou, ask me sumpthin' else—please!"

When he closed the door behind him, Miller, who had been leaning against the wall nearby, said, "Nothing?"

"Nothing," Lou replied, matter-of-factly. "But he knows something. I'd bet on that. He might still open up."

Miller shrugged. "Well, we've got him on possession. He won't be hard to find for a while. Thanks for trying."

42

"Sure," Lou answered and started to move down the hall. Miller stopped him.

"By the way"—he broke into a grin—"I promised the wife I'd invite you to dinner tomorrow."

Lou grimaced. "Not another widow?"

Miller laughed. "She says she's perfect for you—about your size and weight—"

Lou grinned and shook his head. "Bull. Even your wife wouldn't do that to me."

Miller nodded, serious now. "That's right. This one's not bad—and the wife's certain you're as lonesome as hell."

"Not that lonesome. Make up an excuse for me, will you?"

"I already have," Miller answered. "Told her you had to have dinner with your daughter on your day off."

"That's no excuse," Lou said, grimacing again. "Every goddamn day off she expects me for dinner. She's certain I'm lonesome too."

4

IT was after midnight when Lou Baroni finally got home. He had eaten alone in a Chinese restaurant that only charged policemen half prices and then he had gone to a bowling alley where he had bowled some practice frames.

Home, for him, was a one-bedroom apartment in a building that sat high on a hill overlooking much of the city. It wasn't a luxurious building, even though the area was now considered high-rent. It was old, one of the first built on that particular side of the hill, but Lou liked it and, even though the rent had gone up steadily over the years, he resisted the idea of moving. He couldn't afford anything better, and the idea of learning to live in something that was less, at his age, was repugnant.

The apartment itself was very much like Ed Hawley's—a living room, a kitchenette with a breakfast nook, and a bedroom—all of which Lou didn't keep as neat as he should have.

As soon as he came in he went from room to room turning on the lights. He did it unconsciously now, but in the beginning, after his wife had died, he had done it deliberately to make the place seem less lonely.

Once the lights were on, he turned on the radio. That was part of the routine too. He enjoyed silence—but not too much of it.

Sometimes he would sit and watch television—mostly news and sports—but it was too late for those now and, anyway, he wasn't in that kind of mood. He went into the kitch-

44

en and took a beer from the refrigerator, pulling the tab as he walked back into the living room where he sprawled in his easy chair.

All the furniture had come from the home he had had when his wife was alive. He had sold or given away most of their belongings, but he had kept his chair and the sofa and other articles that now occupied the apartment. Not for sentimental reasons. He had kept them because they were still serviceable.

The walls of the apartment were bare. His wife had occupied every available square inch of wall space in their home with prints of every shape, size, and color, but he had never liked any of them or the overall effect. Bare walls seemed much more sensible to him. They required less dusting. There was one picture on his bedside table, a photograph of his daughter, Antonia. She had placed it there.

Sitting in his living room now, sipping the beer, he found himself wishing he had asked Al Miller or one of the others at the station to go to a bar with him for a few. He even considered calling Al and asking him to come over, but he knew he was probably in bed, and even if he weren't, his wife wouldn't want him going out again.

He sighed and for a moment thought about turning on the TV, but he had never enjoyed old movies, or new ones, for that matter.

Next he found himself thinking about Ed Hawley. This would probably be the first night in years he had had to sleep alone. That is, if he were able to sleep at all. Maybe, Lou thought, he was pacing, wondering if he had gotten away with it. Or perhaps his conscience was keeping him awake. But no, he decided, that wasn't likely. It was more likely the man was sound asleep, smugly certain he had committed the perfect murder.

The beer can was empty; he got up and dropped it into a wastepaper basket. Then he did something he found himself doing frequently lately. He stood looking around the room, wondering what it would be like to give it up. He

45

wouldn't care at all, he knew, if he were moving on to something better, but that wasn't likely. He'd have to move to something less, and after all these years, that—to his mind—would mean his life had been a failure.

The whole problem was his pension. He knew he wouldn't be able to afford the place on a detective's pension. What he needed was at least a sergeant's pension.

That was obviously the answer. If he could make sergeant soon, his problems would be over. The big question, however, was how could he earn that promotion? It was a question he had asked himself a thousand times lately.

Wearily he went into the bedroom and began undressing, his mind dwelling on the subject of a sergeant's rating.

In the past, he had just assumed he'd be promoted. But old Lieutenant Soble had died and Tate's takeover had changed everything. To make sergeant now he knew he'd either have to force Tate to recommend the promotion or go over his head. But neither was possible unless he had some kind of big stick to back his demand.

He got into bed and lay there, wondering what that lever could be. It was another one of those questions he had asked himself again and again lately. And the answer was always the same—a big bust.

If he could make a big bust by himself, hand over the criminal bundled neatly in conclusive evidence, Tate would almost have to recommend his promotion. And if Tate refused, then he'd have good reason to go to the chief himself.

But that solution only raised another question: Whom could he bust? He turned out the light and pondered the problem, as he had for so many nights before. In the immediate past there had been only one possibility—the Zakos killer. But now there was another—Edward Hawley.

The Zakos killer might be best. There would be lots of publicity there. But, on the other hand, Tate and half the department were working on it already. Even if he did bring in new evidence, the groundwork had already been done by others. Besides, the Pappas family was involved. One man didn't take on Papa Pappas—not if he wanted to live to retire.

That left only Edward Hawley. If he could prove Hawley had killed his wife, with premeditation, he might earn a sergeant's pension yet. Yes, he decided, as he began to doze, it all depended on whether or not he could nail Hawley.

He slept then. And dreamed of the time when he had been a rookie cop, a green beginner, and the whole world had seemed his for the taking.

Lou Baroni wasn't the only one who wondered what Edward Hawley was doing that night. Another was Laurie Knight. Unable to sleep, her mind still racing with all the sudden events of the day, she sat in her pajamas on her balcony watching the windows across the street. Her apartment was dark, but Hawley's wasn't. There were lights on in every window.

She sat, elbows on the railing, chin cupped in her hands, wondering what Edward Hawley could be doing. It seemed very important to her to know the answer. What if sometime she were called upon to play such a role—her husband or lover dead, her first night alone, the double bed they had shared a terrible reminder of the awful absence? How would she play it? What would be her major motivations?

But then she thought of Edward Hawley himself. It wasn't a part he was playing—it was all too real for him. And suddenly she wondered if there wasn't something she should do. His wife had died and his world had suddenly filled with policemen and detectives. But now they had all gone and he was left alone in what could only be a terrible void.

She frowned, displeased with herself for thinking only of reactions and responses. Others might find the transition from selfishness to unselfishness difficult, but not Laurie. Empathy and sympathy were natural to her makeup. She

47

had no need to learn them, not when she allowed herself to be herself, rather than some character she was attempting to play.

Impulsively she got up and went back into her apartment. If Edward Hawley was sitting alone in his living room unable to sleep, he needed company. That, at least, she could provide. It didn't matter that she was a stranger. In times of tragedy, she believed, there were no strangers.

She slipped out of her pajamas and reached for her clothes, but through the open balcony door, she saw the light in Hawley's kitchen go out, followed a moment later by the living-room light. Finally, the bedroom light went out and the apartment was dark. Edward Hawley had gone to bed.

Laurie put her pajamas back on and got into her own bed. When she fell asleep she was still wondering what it must be like to be a man who had just lost his wife, a man who might be suspected of murder.

No one was asleep in Steve Perry's apartment. He had just come home after spending the evening in a bar celebrating what he considered his entry into the inner circle at the department. Of course, he hadn't celebrated alone.

When he finally walked into his bedroom he found Shirley sitting up in bed, her eyes flashing anger. But even that hadn't dampened the glow he felt.

"Where the hell have you been?"

He smiled, removing his jacket and tie.

"I suppose you were with one of your easy lays?"

"Not just one," he told her, "a dozen. They were waiting for me when I came off watch, legs spread."

"You wish!"

Still smiling, he moved toward the closet and began to undress. He could see his wife in a mirror as he did. She was a desirable woman—blond, petite, built. She hadn't been a bad choice, he thought—the daugher of well-to-do, influential parents. But they had spoiled her and now she expected him to spoil her too. Well, why not? That's all it would take to keep her happy—the money to move in the circles she envied.

"What are you grinning about?" she demanded.

"I just feel like grinning," he said.

"If you think I'm going to stay cooped up in this damn cheap apartment while you ball around, you're mistaken!"

He turned to her. "You won't be in this damn cheap apartment much longer."

"I talked to Daddy today," she went on. "He wants to take me to Europe."

It was an old threat. This time he chose to ignore it.

"Mother still thinks I should get a divorce. She always said you wouldn't get anywhere."

He was down to his underwear now. He removed it and approached the bed.

"Oh, no! You're not getting any from me tonight!"

He sat down on the bed beside her. She was wearing an almost fully transparent negligee. He ran a finger down her bare arm. She pulled away, but he noted with satisfaction that she had shivered.

"You didn't hear what I said," he told her. "You won't be in this damn cheap apartment much longer."

"What do you mean?"

"And you'll be able to join that club your sorority friends talk about so much."

She looked at him skeptically. "Are you just talking or has something happened?"

He paused for effect. "Tate took me into his confidence today."

She didn't appear to be impressed. He pushed on.

"I'm part of the in-group now. It won't be long before I get a promotion. The way I see it, Tate is angling for captaincy and he's grooming me for his job."

"The way you see it?" The skepticism was heavy in her voice.

Perry felt a flush of anger. Damn her, he thought, must

49

she always doubt me? "He said as much," he told her, exaggerating. "And he made it plain."

The skepticism faltered. "But—how? I mean, why did he say it? What for?"

Perry was pleased by her interest. "He needs me," he said smugly, slipping his legs under the sheets. "He needs my support."

"To do what? What's he need your support for?"

"They're easing the old-timers out one by one, even the chief, eventually. They want men like me—young, aggressive, modern—running the department."

She shook her head. "That's not answering my question. Just what does Tate want you to do? Specifically?"

He placed his bare leg against hers, moved it rhythmically. "I told you about Lou Baroni?"

"That old fart you've got for a partner?"

"Uh huh. He's got to go. Tate wants me to 'find' a reason to bounce him."

"Tate told you that?" she asked, beginning to be impressed at last. "He admitted to you he's maneuvering?"

Perry nodded, grinning.

"If that ever got out," she said thoughtfully. "If the chief heard about it. . . ." Then, smiling, she said, "Tate really put himself into your hands, didn't he?"

Instead of answering, Perry cupped his wife's breast in his hand. She moved his hand away—but only a fraction of an inch.

"Can you find a reason to get rid of Baroni?" she asked.

"Baby," Perry said, "I won't have to find one. He'll hand it to me. Right now he's hungry to make a man named Hawley and he'll break every regulation in the book to do it. I just have to wait and watch."

Shirley allowed her husband's hand to return to her breast. "We won't have to wait too long, will we? For that promotion, I mean."

He shook his head. "If I know Baroni, it won't be long at all. And if it is, I'll hurry it up."

50

Then Shirley helped him remove her negligee.

When Lou Baroni got up the following morning he didn't know what to do with himself. That was the trouble with his days off. He rarely had any way to fill them enjoyably. Most of the men in the department he liked were married and spent their free time with their families. Of course, many of them invited him to their homes, but he rarely accepted such invitations, always feeling in the way, an intruder who was being tolerated only because he was alone.

There was a time when he had tried fishing or sitting alone in the bleachers at a ball game. Once he had even tried golf. But none of those things really interested him.

He scrambled some eggs and opened a can of chili. As he ate, he listened to the news. When he finished, he glanced at the clock. It was still only eleven A.M. He wasn't expected at his daughter's until six. He wasn't anxious to go, but still he was eager for the time to roll around. It was, at least, something that had to be done.

He went into the living room and stood before the window, looking out. In the distance he could see a good deal of the city, hidden under a blanket of yellowish smog. Eight years ago, when he had first moved into the apartment, the smog had been hardly perceptible.

The window in front of him was very much like the window in the Hawley apartment through which Evelyn Hawley had left this life. Looking at it, he thought again of Edward Hawley. Irrationally he wondered how far from retirement he was—and whether or not his pension would be enough.

He lit a cigarette. He didn't smoke much—the cancer scare was responsible for that—but when he did, he enjoyed it. Inhaling luxuriously, he considered the alternatives that confronted him once again. If he could make sergeant before he retired, his pension would be adequate— but, would proving Hawley guilty be enough of an outstanding bust? Solving the Zakos killing would be, but doing it by himself meant withholding evidence from others working on the case and that was a serious breach of regulations. Besides, going up against the Pappas machine could cost him his life.

Yet he felt he couldn't disregard the possibility of making the Zakos killer entirely. He glanced at his watch. It was still only eleven thirty. What the hell, he decided, he might as well ask around. It would help to pass the time. He got his jacket and a few minutes later left to see a snitch.

Georgios Bacopolous was a small, wizened man with a dark complexion, a large nose, a bushy white mustache, and a bald scalp. He ran what he called a restaurant in a section of the city that had yet to make up its mind about which minority group it belonged to. The restaurant was no larger than many living rooms, providing two tables and a counter with five stools, but it did have several attractions which caused it to flourish. One was the food. Georgios Bacopolous made the best delmatoes that Lou had ever tasted.

The other attraction was Georgios' granddaughter, Angelica, who waited on tables and turned a trick or two whenever she or her grandfather needed extra cash.

Lou liked both the old man and the girl and they had always seemed to like him. Lou was surprised when Georgios failed to smile as he walked in.

"Tecanas," Lou said, his Greek pronunciation so atrocious it usually made the old man laugh.

"*Cala Polecala,*" Georgios replied, nervously wiping his hands on his apron.

Lou sat down at the counter. "A plate of delmatoes. A big plate." Georgios was usually flattered when Lou ate a lot of his food.

The old man had trouble meeting Lou's eyes. "I will get it right away." He hurried into the back room.

Left alone, the only customer, Lou wondered what was bothering the old man. He probably thinks I've come to ask questions, Lou decided, and, of course, he was right. But in

52

the past that had never bothered him. Usually he took pleasure in passing along what he heard among the street people. This time, however, Lou reminded himself, he was here to ask about Papa Pappas—another Greek, a powerful one, a "landsman."

Angelica came in from the back. As soon as she saw Lou she smiled, and, as always, Lou was struck by her beauty. She wore a white smock that revealed her long, nylon-clad legs. Her olive complexion was flawless and the bare skin of her arms and throat invited touch.

"Lou, how are you carrying it today, right or left?"

"In the middle. It don't matter so much anymore."

She laughed. "It'll matter the day you die of old age."

Her voice was soft and clear and belied the things she said. Lou had often wondered why some Hollywood producer hadn't grabbed her for a picture. But that kind of thing only happens in the movies. As it was, she had only a few good years left. The beer she drank, the hours she kept, the risk she ran with VD—they'd destroy her beauty before long, Lou knew. And he felt it was a crime, far worse than many that were prosecuted.

She brought him cutlery and poured a cup of the strong coffee. Lou took pleasure in watching her move.

She had offered herself to him a number of times, but he had always refused. Not because he hadn't wanted her, but because he remembered the skinny nine-year-old he had caught stealing fruit from a grocery store and the sullen twelve-year-old he had slapped for smoking grass, and because for a while, long ago, she had called him *"Babo"*— uncle.

"What's the matter with Georgios?" he asked. "He looked like he wished I wasn't here."

"He does," she answered frankly. "We've already had a hundred cops in here asking questions about Spiro Zakos and Nicky Pappas. Now, you too."

Lou sighed and shook his head. She reached across the counter and touched his hand. She was a toucher, a natural

53

trait. "It doesn't matter. We know it's your job. Anyway, we haven't got anything to tell anybody. We haven't heard a thing. That's the truth."

Lou didn't doubt it. He'd never known her to lie to him. "Why's Georgios so shook up?"

She looked at him this time, her eyes level. "He'll have to tell Papa Pappas you were here. He doesn't want to do it to you, Lou, but he'll have to."

She wasn't saying it, but Lou knew she was asking him to say it was all right.

Lou shrugged. "What the hell. Tell him he can tell Pappas anything he has to."

She smiled and went into the kitchen. Lou, drinking his coffee, heard her talking to the old man in his native tongue. Then he came out, beaming broadly, proudly carrying a huge plate of delmatoes which he placed before Lou with a flourish.

When Lou left the restaurant, it was still much too early to go to his daughter's, so he drove over to one of the city's parks, locked his car, and went for a walk.

He didn't walk far. He found a shady place, sat down under a tree, and lit a cigarette.

He was spending more and more time in the parks lately. He had always loved the outdoors, but never as much as now. Before, when he had been younger, he had always had too much to do to spend much time in the country, and, besides, his wife hadn't liked it. City born and bred, she had always felt uncomfortable away from concrete.

A young couple strolled by, teen-agers, holding hands. Nice-looking kids, Lou thought. And then he wondered how the coming years would change them, bringing—perhaps—looks of self-pity, or greed, or anger, or defeat to their faces. If they were smart, he thought, they'd get away now, go somewhere where the competition wouldn't grind them down, where one failure after another wouldn't build an unbreachable wall between them. That's what he would

54

do, he thought, if he were young again. He sighed, thinking about it. It was what he should do now. Go far away. But he knew he wouldn't go—not because he didn't want to, but because there just wasn't anywhere he could go.

He grew tired of the park. The sounds of traffic filtered through the trees and even though he couldn't see them, he knew the buildings were there, on every side, waiting. He got up and went back to his car. When he drove away, he saw the young couple again. They were sitting on a bench passing a butt back and forth—obviously grass. Maybe, he thought, they had already opted for Wally Blue's way out. What the hell, he thought, it's their lives.

He didn't need to drive by Hawley's apartment to reach his daughter's place, but he did. It was still too early for lights to be on, so he couldn't tell if Hawley was home or not. It really didn't matter, anyway, for, as yet, he hadn't really decided what he was going to do.

Lou's daughter, Antonia—Toni—had flatly refused to move into a typical Southern California apartment building. Instead, she and her husband had found a small, two-story house, old by today's standards, with a veranda. From the outside it was simply clapboard and shingles, but inside it was different. To begin with, Toni and her husband, Dave, had knocked out most of the downstairs walls. Then they had gone on to other things.

The door was nearly all stained glass. And the door chimes had been replaced with an old-fashioned doorbell. When Lou twisted it it gave out a raucous clang that caused people on the street to turn their heads.

The door opened almost at once and Toni exclaimed as she wrapped her arms around him, "Hi there, dear old Dad."

Lou, never as demonstrative as his daughter, had never grown used to her greetings. "Hi, yourself."

She was dark complexioned with black hair, but the family resemblance ended there. Whereas Lou was heavy, she

55

was slender; Lou moved stolidly, she was light, and while Lou dressed conservatively, she dressed, in his opinion, outrageously. Tonight, she wore a serapelike garment that reached to the floor.

"Come on in and rest awhile," she said, taking his arm. "And leave all your cares outside."

The large room that made up most of the downstairs caused Lou to pause when he saw it—as it always did. The furniture was the same strange collection of odds and ends it had been the last time he was here, but the walls had changed their character once again. Happy cartoon characters, some small, some large, hung everywhere, and one wall served as a gigantic chessboard, the pieces held in place by tiny hooks.

Lou let his gaze take it all in and then he slowly shook his head. "I never know what to expect."

"Does that mean you like it?" Tony asked, grinning.

Lou sighed. "It's been worse."

Toni laughed and hugged him again. "Dear old conventional father of mine. I love every part of you—your preconceptions, your narrow mind, your flat feet."

"You were such a normal kid!"

Toni began to take off his jacket. Lou protested. "I can do that."

"Then do it," Toni said, "and relax while I go stir the spaghetti. Dave will be home soon."

"I can hardly wait."

Toni laughed as she went toward the kitchen, the only other room on the ground floor. Lou sat down in a chair that had once been a barrel. He knew from experience it was the least uncomfortable chair in the place.

After squirming for a moment, trying to find a position that didn't cut off too much circulation, he looked up to see his daughter standing by the kitchen door, concern on her face.

"You look tired," she said.

"I am tired."

"I mean old-man tired."

56

"I am an old man."

Impulsively Toni bent and kissed his cheek. "Old, maybe—but you're not old and alone. That's the important thing."

Then, before Lou could respond, she hurried back to the kitchen. Lou never ceased to marvel at the fact that he had spawned such a daughter. She wasn't at all like her mother had been, and she certainly wasn't like him.

A huge poster on the wall caught his eye. It was meant to. It bore the words, LUV THE FUZZ. Another, hanging near the window, suggested TAKE A COP HOME TO DINNER. Lou shook his head. Maybe, he thought, hospitals did get babies mixed up.

The front door opened and a young man walked in. He was wearing a conservative business suit and carrying a black briefcase. When he saw Lou he waved to him. "Hi."

Dave Schulman, Toni's husband, was a slim young man, dark, intense and more argumentative than Lou liked. In fact, Lou felt he should become a lawyer and said so once, but Dave had only begun to argue immediately that the whole legal system was hypocritical and cancerous.

Dave put the briefcase down and called out toward the kitchen, "Hi, honey. I'm home."

"Hi," Toni's voice called back. "I'm glad. Love you."

Lou indicated the briefcase. "Since when do you bring work home from a teller's cage?"

Dave laughed. "Toni's idea. She says since I have to prostitute myself to make a living, I might as well complete the disguise."

The "disguise" rapidly vanished. The suitcoat, tie, and black shoes were all removed and replaced by sandals and a long serape which reached the floor. Lou, who had watched the transformation take place silently, now shook his head again.

"I'll never understand either of you."

Dave grinned. "That's going to make things difficult when you move in here, isn't it?"

"I'll never move in here," Lou answered bluntly.

57

Dave pulled a camp stool close and sat down facing his father-in-law. "You'll have to when you retire. Toni and I talked it over. An officer's pension won't even pay the rent on your apartment—and leave you much to live on, I mean."

"I'll get another job."

"Like what? A security guard? You said yourself there are a dozen ex-cops for every one of those jobs."

Lou, who didn't like this conversation at all, lost his patience, as he usually did with Dave. "All right, all right, then I'll find something else to do. Just don't worry about it. I'll work something out."

Toni came into the room carrying a gallon jug and glasses. Putting these down on the floor beside her husband, she said, "Give Dad a root beer. He's had a bad day."

Then she turned and started back to the kitchen. Lou called after her. "I didn't have a bad day! It's my day off!"

Dave opened the jug and poured two glasses. Lou sighed. "Never any bourbon or beer around here, is there?"

"That's right," Dave answered, handing Lou a glass. "No pollutants."

Lou sipped the root beer. "You're sick, both of you."

Dave swallowed most of his and then asked, making conversation, "How's the job going?"

"Routine."

"Something must be happening," Dave insisted.

"You wouldn't need police if there wasn't."

"What's the latest?"

Lou considered the question for a moment. There was the Zakos killing, but that was old news.

"We had a homicide yesterday."

"What happened?"

"A woman fell from her apartment—five stories up."

Dave raised an eyebrow. "Fell? You said homicide."

"Her husband was home at the time."

Dave, sensing a debate, said, "It could still have been an accident."

58

Lou put down his unfinished root beer. "That's what he says."

Toni had entered the room again. As she set the table now, she listened to the conversation. "Why don't you believe him?" she asked.

Lou turned to her. "There's no reason I should."

Dave jumped on that. "That's not the point. It's why shouldn't you?"

"Because," Lou answered a little hotly, "I've seen a hundred others like him and I know."

"But that's not reason enough to arrest him!"

"He hasn't been arrested. They decided it was death by misadventure. The case is closed."

Toni, returning to the kitchen, said, "I think that's fine."

"You would," Lou called after her. "I don't."

"That's obvious," Dave said. "The reason why isn't."

"I don't like the way it was handled," Lou explained. "We don't know anything about him. We don't know where he came from, who his friends are, where he goes when he's alone. Nothing."

Dave drained the last of his root beer. "I've got a feeling you're going to find out."

Until that moment Lou hadn't actually decided. Even now he didn't really make the commitment. "Yeah, I might."

"What about the fact that the case is officially closed?"

"What I do on my own time is my own business."

Dave stared at him. What had started out as casual conversation wasn't any longer. This was one of his favorite topics—justice. He loved to debate it. "What you do on your own time is not your business—not if it infringes upon the rights of another individual."

Toni, returning with a huge bowl of spaghetti, sensed trouble coming and spoke up quickly. "Supper's ready."

But Lou wasn't to be denied his reply. "Rights of the individual are words used by every con in the country."

"Dad, Dave, please," Toni said, standing by the table.

59

"Come and sit down before it gets cold."

They ate in silence. The spaghetti was excellent but Lou longed for a beer to go with it.

"He didn't have any beer in his refrigerator," he said finally, thoughtfully.

"Who didn't?" Toni asked.

"The guy whose wife dropped five stories."

"You think that indicates something?" Dave asked.

Lou shrugged. "It might."

"Maybe he doesn't like beer."

"He seems like he would—once in a while."

Toni had been turning something over in her mind, troubled. "Dad, if you go on investigating after a case is closed, you could lose your pension, couldn't you?"

Dave answered for him. "He could."

"Only if I don't come up with something," Lou said. And as soon as he said it he knew it had been a mistake.

"You mean, persecution's all right if it pays off."

Lou's anger flared. He should have known better, but he said, "Sure, that's what I mean. What do you think this is, a make-believe world where everybody plays by the rules?"

"No," Dave retorted, "but I think they should—especially the people whose job it is to see that they do."

"Well, it's not like that," Lou retorted in turn. "You should know that by now. Grow up!"

"All right, I will," Dave answered. He was in his element now, turning arguments over in his mind, discarding defense for attack. "Let's get down to the nitty-gritty. Why are you so interested in the case, anyway? What's your motive?"

"What do you mean?"

"Just what I said. What's in it for you?"

"Nothing."

"I won't buy that. You've never spent your own time on a closed case before."

Toni, worried, interrupted. "Dad, Dave, please!"

"No," Dave said to her, "I'm just playing the game his

60

way. It's not a make-believe world, he said so." He turned back to Lou. "So I'm asking, what do you get out of it? What's your payoff? What's the big bonus?"

Lou had to force his eyes to stay on Dave's when he answered. "The guy's guilty, that's all."

"Justice for its own sake?" Dave asked scornfully. "Come on, now!"

Toni's anger was directed at her husband. "Don't," she said. "Leave it alone. Maybe this case is just his thing."

But instead of ending it, her remark gave her husband a new line to pursue.

"Yeah," he said. "Yeah, you're right. But maybe not in the way you mean it." He turned to Lou. "It could be a contest with you, couldn't it? A competition. Proving that guy guilty could give you a big thrill."

Lou started to protest but Dave pressed on, thinking out loud.

"No. I take that back. It's not just for kicks. There's more to it. You're going to retire. You want to go out big—one more conviction before you hang up your gun!"

"Dave!" Toni protested.

Dave continued. "It's ego-building time, isn't it? Ego-building at the expense of some poor slob."

Lou slammed his fork down on the table and spoke to his daughter. "Do I have to sit here and listen to this?"

Toni was angry too. "No, you don't!" she told her father. "Dave, talk about something else!"

But the thoughts were tumbling too fast into Dave's mind for him to stop. "Wait a minute," he said. "It's more than that—it's more than just self-aggrandizement. It's self-interest!"

"Stop it!" Toni cried.

"But, honey, don't you see! This is his last chance to make it big—to get those sergeant's stripes!"

Lou interrupted. "Now, hold it—"

"Toni," Dave continued, "listen—all he has to do is persecute that guy, harass him a little, and once he gets a

61

confession he gets the big payoff—a sergeant's pension!"

Toni started to reply angrily, but the possibility her husband had just raised stopped her. She couldn't ignore it. "Dad—is that right?"

Lou found it hard to look at his daughter. "Eat your spaghetti. It's getting cold."

The doubt left Toni's face. Disappointment took its place. "No, Dad."

Lou lost his temper. "All right! All right!" he exclaimed. "Maybe he is right—but what of it? What's so wrong with it? Why shouldn't I want things a little easier? Why shouldn't I be able to have a place of my own after all these years instead of having to live with you in a place like this!" With a sweep of his hand he indicated the posters, the rag-tag furniture, the room, the house. "Anyway, if this guy is guilty he should be convicted!"

Dave answered, quietly this time. "Yeah—but what if he isn't?"

"He is!" Lou answered intensely. "I can feel it inside! He killed her and I'm going to prove it!"

They finished their meal in silence. Toni hardly looked at her father, and Lou didn't like that. But it wasn't a new experience. There was love between them. He never doubted that. But he had known for a long time there was no real communication. He had often wished there were. He had often thought how nice it would be for a man to have a daughter with whom he could really talk.

Papa Pappas ate a silent meal, too. He sat alone at a magnificent table in the dining room of his immense home in his exclusive Hellenic-West Village, located a few miles west of the city.

His house was, in its own way, as unique as he was. It combined, just as he did, much of the old and the new. The ceilings were timbered; the fireplace, fieldstone; the walls, in part, were stucco—all reminiscent of the tiny hovel in which he had lived as a boy in Greece.

But the rest of the house was modern. Entire walls were glass. The furniture was chrome and plastic. The paintings were abstracts. The lighting was electronically controlled. The air conditioning and central humidifier created, at all times, exactly the weather the old man preferred.

As he sat there, barely picking at the splended meal his chef had prepared, his eyes looked out through glass patio doors upon well-manicured lawns and beyond them to calm water. For his home was built on an island in the center of a man-made lake he had caused to be created in the midst of one of Southern California's most exclusive residential projects.

Hellenic-West Village was the crowning achievement of his life, a community a dozen times larger than the village of his birth. None of it was the result of chance. Long ago he had known he wouldn't be able to go on being the West Coast's underworld czar forever. He had wisely foreseen the coming of frantic competition in the sale of drugs and the procurement of prostitutes. He had realized, also, that the burgeoning population would force increased opposition. Police and politicians would no longer be as easily controlled as they had once been. So he saved his money in Old Country ways and gradually relinquished his control, accepting, peacefully, an honorary role and a small percentage. Then he put his money and efforts into the development of a town where none had been before. He named it Hellenic-West, an entire community, complete with shopping malls, schools, clinics, golf courses, tennis clubs and, of course, the lake where only silent sailboats were allowed—because the sound of motors offended him.

In the beginning his minions had predicted financial disaster, but he had never doubted his vision. He had always been certain of success. What did surprise him, however, was the extent of that success. He hadn't dreamed he'd make so much money, so quickly, in a legitimate pursuit.

But his success was, in a way, a bitter one. Hellenic-West was meant to be more than just a monument to his own life.

It was the bequest he had intended to pass on to his son. The problem was, his son wasn't interested in it at all. And lately, he had even endangered it.

"Demetri!" he called out now, impatiently. He was a small man, and since reaching sixty had seemed to shrink even more. But the strength of his voice, like the vigor of his mind, had never diminished.

"Demetri!" he called again, and within a moment a tall, muscular, middle-aged man entered. Trusted body servant, loyal bodyguard, reliable chauffeur, constant companion, Demetri was the son Papa Pappas should have had.

"Nicholas," Papa said, "hasn't he come yet?"

A silent man, Demetri shook his head.

"You told him he was to be here for dinner?"

"I did." Demetri glanced at his watch. The dinner hour, he saw, was over. "He'll be here soon, now."

Papa sighed. "What am I going to do about him?"

"Protect him," Demetri said simply. "He is your son."

They heard a car pull to a stop outside—the island was connected to the mainland by a private bridge—and a few minutes later Nicky Pappas walked into the dining room.

"Demetri," he said before greeting his father, "coffee— laced."

Demetri nodded and left the room.

Nicky Pappas was a handsome young man, almost beautiful. In the beginning the old man had been proud of the boy's beauty. A young Greek god, he told his friends, and he beamed proudly when the most beautiful girls on the West Coast had flocked around him. But the boy hadn't seemed impressed by any of them, and as time passed he had become more and more uninterested. Papa Pappas had begun to worry. But even so, he wouldn't admit the truth to himself at first, and he had deliberately surrounded the boy with rough, rugged, virile men. He realized his mistake when he discovered that the boy had, in short order, seduced four of them, sequentially.

Nicky Pappas sat down at the far end of the table and sprawled languidly. He wore blue, the same cold color as

64

his eyes, setting off his deeply tanned olive skin. His lips twisted into a mirthless smile as he regarded his father.

"You're looking old, Papa." He stressed the word, mocking his father's nickname, knowing that it had originally been given to him with affection.

"I am old," Papa replied, "and you're making me older."

Nicky Pappas sighed. He had no intention of sitting through another lecture. "When Demetri called he said it was important."

"It is. It's about Spiro Zakos."

Nicky got up and began to pace, petulance in every move. "No, I don't want to talk about that. If you do, I'm going to leave."

Papa felt his temper flare. "What do you mean, leave? You should be thanking heaven I'm taking an interest!"

"It upsets me to think about it."

"You should have thought about that before you killed him."

"I had to. He betrayed me. He had another lover."

The old man bolted to his feet. "Don't talk like that!" he screamed. "I don't want that kind of talk in my house!"

Nicky turned toward the door. "I'm going."

"No!" Papa ordered. "Stay!"

Nicky ignored him.

"The police—I think they know."

At the door, Nicky paused. "How could they know?"

"They've arrested a witness."

"Impossible. There was none."

Papa sank slowly back into his chair at the head of the long table. "My contacts told me you and the Zakos boy were with a Negro."

Nicky walked back to the table. He nodded. "Wally Blue."

"Wally Blue?" Papa Pappas echoed in wonder. "What kind of name is that?"

Nicky ignored the question. "Is he the witness?"

"They say he brought you marijuana."

"We made him leave. He left before anything happened."

"No," Papa said. "My informants say he witnessed a quarrel. They say he heard you scream at the Zakos boy. They say he heard you threaten to kill him."

Nicky Pappas no longer seemed disturbed. A small smile flitted across his face.

"Well," Papa demanded, "is it true?"

Nicky shrugged. "It's not important."

Papa jumped to his feet again. "What do you mean, not important? If he tells the police what he heard—"

Nicky shook his head. "He won't talk. Not Wally." There was smugness in every line of his handsome face.

"How can you say that?" Papa demanded. "How can you be so sure?"

"Wally Blue loves me."

Papa felt his gorge rise, but he fought it down. In the Old Country one man did love another—but as men, as brothers. To hear his own son talk of loving and being loved by a man in any other way was too much. It was something he'd never be able to accept.

"Maybe this 'lover' of yours doesn't 'love' you as much as you think," he said softly after a moment, forcing himself to use his son's words.

Nicky Pappas' face clouded. "What do you mean?"

"There's a detective, an Italian named Baroni, who's been asking too many questions. He went to see Georgios Bacopolous this morning."

"So?"

"A few years ago he saved your Wally Blue's life. My informants say the Negro feels indebted. He might tell him what he wants to know."

Nicky shook his head. "No."

"He owes him!" Papa exclaimed. "A debt of honor! To some people it's important!"

Nicky paused, thinking. To Wally, it might be important, and, in truth, he had to admit he had never encouraged Wally's love, had never had an affair with him. For that matter, he really wasn't certain that the tall Negro was actually gay. He could simply be an addict who would do anything at all for a fix. For a moment he frowned, but then he smiled and said to his father, "It's no real problem."

"Isn't it? Believe me, it is!"

"No. If Wally owes a debt, I'll cancel it for him."

"How?"

"I'll have this Italian cop hit."

"No!" Papa screamed. "No! I forbid it!"

Anger flashed in Nick Pappas' eyes. "Don't use that word! Don't 'forbid'! If I want him hit, I'll have it done!"

"You won't! I'll spread the word. Nobody will dare to take the contract!"

Nicky scowled. He knew nobody would. Nobody convenient, that is.

Demetri returned to place a coffee cup on the table. After he left, Nicky, still standing, confronted his father. "All right. If not the Italian, the Negro. I'll have him hit."

"No," Papa said, "not the Negro either." Then, as Nicky began to protest, he exclaimed, "What's the matter with you, anyway? What do you think we are, Sicilian bums who go around having everybody killed? Aren't we any better than that?"

Nicky threw his hands in the air impatiently. "All right, we don't kill the Negro, we don't kill the Italian. What do we do?"

Papa had spent the afternoon pondering that problem. "We have them watched. We watch and wait."

Nicky smiled coldly and picked up his coffee cup. "All right," he said, sipping from it elegantly. "We watch and wait. And then we have them killed."

Later, after his son had gone, Papa stood on the shore of his tiny island, looking out over the lake as the sun set behind the splendid homes and graceful boulevards he had built. Why, he wondered, wasn't he allowed to enjoy it? Why wasn't he allowed to be legitimate? He sighed deeply, feeling a great deal older. He'd probably have to have the Negro killed, and the detective, Baroni, too. Nicky was right about that. But, at least, he promised himself, he'd try to avoid it—for as long as he could.

* * *

When Lou Baroni returned to his apartment that night he sat silently in his armchair. The argument he had had with his daughter and her husband still rankled, but it hadn't been anything new. They had argued many times before. But it had served to drive home the fact he'd never be able to live with them after he retired. He'd have to find a way of being on his own, somehow.

That thought brought Hawley to mind. If he could make him on murder-one, he'd have every reason to expect a sergeant's pension. The only thing he didn't like about it was the point his son-in-law had made. He would be using Hawley for his own advantage. But then, thinking about it, he shrugged and told himself, what the hell, if the man is guilty, what difference would it make? And, anyway, why shouldn't he benefit from his own efforts?

He glanced at his watch. It was ten fifteen. He wondered what Hawley was doing. Sitting in his living room, just as he was, perhaps? Or watching television? Or out somewhere—maybe with a woman. Yes, that was a possibility. A woman could have been the motive, after all. That possibility hadn't really been explored.

He got up and began to pace. He always thought better when he moved. From now on, he decided, he'd have to spend his spare time learning everything he could about Edward Hawley. And tomorrow would be a good time to start. A perfect time, for he had night watch and that meant he'd be free all day. Besides, tomorrow was going to be a big day for Edward Hawley. It was the day he was going to bury his wife.

5

THERE wasn't a single cloud in the sky when Lou Baroni reached the cemetery the following morning. He left his car in the parking lot, stopped at the mortuary office to inquire about the location of Mrs. Hawley's grave, and then walked along a concrete path under weeping willows and towering palms.

There was something very unreal about the parklike atmosphere; the beautifully kept flower beds, the thick green grass, the lush trees, all in brilliant sunshine. It would have been more in keeping, Lou thought, if the day had been overcast, if the grass were withered, if the tree limbs were gnarled and bare—more in keeping with the idea of death, as if the passing of a human being made some difference. It was a feeling Lou had had a number of times before. He had buried his wife and several old friends, and all had gone into the ground to the sound of birds singing, in bright, business-as-usual sunshine.

When he reached the section of the cemetery in which Evelyn Hawley was to be buried, he thought for a moment he was late, for he saw a long column of cars moving solemnly away from a grave site. But then he realized it couldn't be the right funeral, for the cars were Cadillacs, Mercedes, Lincolns—a majestic procession that seemed in keeping with the luxuriant lawns and the marble statues that lined the wide avenue they followed.

It wasn't until the column had passed that Lou saw the Hawley grave. It was in a remote corner of the cemetery, practically adjoining the nearby freeway. Only three vehicles stood near the open grave—an old hearse, a faded Volkswagen, and a '69 station wagon.

There were signs everywhere that said DO NOT WALK ON THE GRASS, but Lou did, moving to stand, unobserved, a dozen yards away from Evelyn Hawley's final resting place.

Edward Hawley stood alone beside the hearse, his eyes on the road, as if watching for somebody.

The others present were clustered in a small group beside the station wagon. Most were women, with the exception of a gray-complexioned little man who was obviously a husband. They seemed to be annoyed about something, especially a tall, thin, angry-looking woman who was doing the talking.

Two other men were also present, but apart—a minister with a wrinkled collar and an undertaker who looked too professional to be bereaved. These two moved to Ed Hawley's side, pointing to their watches impatiently. Hawley shrugged helplessly in reply.

Their conversation lasted only a moment, for the tall, thin woman with the angry expression joined them almost immediately and began gesticulating, leaving little for Hawley to say.

Lou, deciding it was time Hawley realized he was there, lit a cigarette and moved closer. Hawley noticed him right away. If he was disturbed he didn't show it. He seemed only mildly surprised. He started to walk toward him, as if glad of an excuse to leave the others. They met beside Evelyn's empty grave.

Hawley was the first to speak. "Didn't expect to see you here."

"Looking over the cast of characters," Lou said.

"Like they do in the movies," Hawley replied. "They always have a scene at the cemetery."

Lou flicked his cigarette butt away. It happened to fall into Evelyn's empty grave. Hawley didn't seem to mind.

70

"Sergeant Perry told me the case was closed."

Lou nodded. "I got a funny curiosity. It won't let me alone sometimes. Like right now. I keep wondering about the motive."

Hawley studied him for a moment. Lou noticed once again how thin his hair was and that his suit, obviously his best one, was long past its prime.

"I could report you, couldn't I?" he said.

Lou grunted and pointed his thumb over his shoulder. "My wife's grave is just over there. I've got as much right to be here as anybody."

Still studying Lou, Hawley said, "You really think I murdered her, don't you?"

Lou nodded and then, because he didn't want to be asked why just yet, changed the subject. He indicated the people standing near the station wagon. "Not much of a crowd."

"No," Hawley replied. "She didn't have many friends."

"Neither did mine," Lou said.

Hawley was suddenly interested. "What did you do about pallbearers?"

"Got some of the guys from work."

"That's what I did," Hawley said. "But they're late. They didn't show up at the chapel. I thought they'd be here, at least."

Lou said nothing.

"They did promise," Hawley said.

"It must have been bad, at the chapel," Lou said suddenly, surprising himself with the sympathy.

Hawley nodded. "It was. Too many empty chairs."

Lou knew what he meant. There shouldn't be empty chairs at a funeral.

Suddenly the mood that had developed between them was broken by the arrival of the tall, angry woman. She ignored Lou. "Ed, you've got to do something!"

Hawley looked at her helplessly. "What can I do? They said they'd come."

"The minister says he's got a wedding to perform, and

71

the undertaker's going to start charging overtime pretty soon."

"Overtime?" Hawley repeated, amazed. He turned to Lou. "Undertakers can't charge overtime, can they?"

Lou shrugged. He didn't know the answer to that one. The woman wasn't interested in the question, anyway. She was suddenly interested in him. "Who's he?"

"This is—" Hawley started to say, then stopped, not knowing how to introduce the detective.

"I'm Lou Baroni," Lou answered.

Hawley was relieved. "This is my sister-in-law, Beatrice Huffaker."

Beatrice glared at Lou. "Well, it's a good thing *you* came, at least."

"Beatrice," Hawley protested, "you don't understand. He's not a pallbearer."

Beatrice snorted. "He's here, isn't he? He's a pallbearer."

"But a stranger shouldn't be a pallbearer!"

Beatrice wasn't listening. She was counting on her fingers. "Five. He makes five. Five can do it."

Hawley seemed defeated. "We need six," he said lamely.

"We'll have six," Beatrice said, moving away. "Come on."

Hawley looked at Lou, embarrassed. "Look, I'm sorry. You don't have—"

"What the hell." Lou shrugged. "Why not?"

They followed Beatrice toward the rear of the hearse where she began ordering the minister and the undertaker and the others about. Lou turned to Hawley.

"Your wife anything like her?"

"My wife was the original. She's only a copy."

It was the answer Lou had expected.

They were already sliding the coffin out of the hearse. The minister and the undertaker took the first pair of handles. Beatrice motioned to Hawley and to her husband, the pale, gray man, to take the middle pair, and then Lou found

72

himself taking the last handle on his side. The sixth pallbearer was Beatrice.

After the funeral Lou followed Hawley as he left the
cemetery in Beatrice's station wagon. She drove belligerently, ignoring the rights of the other motorists. Lou wished
a traffic car would appear and ticket her, but none did.

She left the freeway earlier than Lou expected and he
wondered if she might be taking Hawley home with her to
comfort him, but she swung south on side streets and Lou
realized she was taking him directly to his own apartment.
He shook his head. The least she could do, he thought, was
keep him company on the day he buried his wife. Unless, of
course, it was his choice. Maybe he felt no company at all
was better than Beatrice's. And then again, maybe he had
another reason, a special reason, for wanting to be alone.

The station wagon pulled to a stop in front of Hawley's
apartment building and Lou parked on the opposite side of
the street. He expected to see Hawley get out of Beatrice's
car alone, but Beatrice and her husband got out too, and all
three went into the building.

Maybe, Lou thought, she was going to keep him company after all. But no, that didn't seem in character. It had to
be something else.

He was right. Forty minutes later Beatrice and her husband came out of the building, laden with dresses. She had
confiscated her sister's clothes. Lou grinned. He could just
hear her saying there was no reason to waste them.

After they drove away, Lou slumped down behind the
wheel and prepared for a long wait. If he were Hawley,
he'd let more time pass before he contacted a girlfriend or
made some other kind of move. But maybe Hawley was impatient. Maybe he'd play the wrong card. If he did, Lou
wanted to be there, ready to follow him.

"Hi."

He was startled by the voice. His eyes had been on the
building opposite, not on the sidewalk beside him. He

turned to see an attractive face framed by red hair peering in the open window of his car.

"Remember me?"

He did. It was Laurie Knight, the girl who had seen Evelyn Hawley fall.

"Yeah. Hi yourself."

"I've been watching you," she told him. "You've been sitting here for almost an hour."

"In my job that's not much."

"You're watching Ed Hawley, aren't you?"

"Maybe."

"You going to watch for long?"

"That depends," Lou answered. "Why?"

"You could watch from my apartment. You'd see more and it's a lot more comfortable."

A few minutes later Lou sat on her balcony drinking a cold beer. Occasionally, across the road, he saw Hawley move past a window. If he had any intention of going out, he didn't show it. If he expected company, there was no indication of it.

Lou glanced back into Laurie's apartment. She was standing at the range making hamburgers. She wore only sandals, cutoffs, and a blouse that left her midriff bare.

Her long legs, her waist, her arms, were all deeply tanned. Unusual in a redhead, Lou thought. Obviously the color of the hair was hers by choice. Anyway, he concluded, it was effective. She'd arouse any man. But she was too young for Lou, so he put the idea away. Youth was a complication he avoided. Anyway, in his work, he ran into lots of available women, the kind that didn't present any problems.

He turned back to Hawley's apartment. He was in the kitchen, probably making lunch. Lou was willing to bet it wasn't a TV dinner.

Laurie came out onto the balcony with their hamburgers. She gave Lou his, then sat down on the floor in front of him to eat hers.

"You really think he killed her?"

74

"It looks that way, doesn't it?"

"I don't know." She frowned. "I've been trying to make up my mind about that—to put myself in his place—then, in yours."

"You don't know enough about either of us."

"You don't know very much about him either, do you?"

"I've got a feeling—it comes with experience."

She thought about that for a while. "How long have you been a detective?"

"Fifteen years."

"And before that?"

"Patrol."

"You mean in a police car?"

"Uh huh—and on foot, walking a beat. I go back a long way."

Lou glanced over at Hawley's apartment. He saw him carrying a plate into the living room. He's going to watch TV while he eats, he thought. Bet that's something his wife never allowed him to do.

"What made you become a cop in the first place?"

"It was my father's idea," Lou said. "In my day you needed a lot of money to go to college, and we didn't have any. So my old man decided the Police Department was the next-best thing. He figured it would give me what he called position. You know, authority, respect—and the one thing that always mattered most to him—security."

"Did it?" Laurie asked.

"In the beginning," Lou answered. "It didn't last."

Laurie regarded him differently for a moment. "You said that sadly."

At eleven Lou left. His watch began at midnight. He had offered to return to his car long before, but Laurie seemed to enjoy having him there. He knew she was studying him, but he didn't mind. Besides, anything was better than sitting in a car. And, anyway, he liked her. For some reason he found it easier to talk to her than to his own daughter.

When he reached the sidewalk he paused before getting into his car, to take one last look up at Hawley's apartment.

75

Only one window was lit—the living room. He's either still watching television or reading, Lou thought, the same thing he had done all evening. He was neither surprised nor disappointed. He really hadn't expected anything. Not yet. It was still too soon.

He got into his car, turned the key, and cursed when the engine failed to start. He tried again. On the third try it caught and he drove off toward the station. He didn't make it. The motor died four blocks away.

Muttering more curses, he found a phone, arranged to have an all-night garage pick up the car, and then walked the rest of the way to work. He got there at two minutes after twelve.

But it was almost one A. M. before he and Perry finally hit the streets. Lieutenant Tate had held a surprise briefing for the night watch: Lean on the pushers, pimps, and prostitutes. Find out if they know anything about the Zakos murder. Coax them a little. Lou had listened silently. There wasn't anything he could say. He thought Tate's suggestions were as helpful as salt in the Sahara.

But Perry, sitting beside him now, didn't seem to feel their mission was useless. In fact he seemed to be in an unusually good mood.

"You know, Lou," he said, as they rolled along night-quiet streets, "we should become closer friends."

Lou's reaction was one of surprise and skepticism. Perry didn't seem to notice it. "A man needs someone to confide in. It's important to his mental health."

"You want to confide something to me?" Lou asked.

The smile vanished from Perry's face, but he forced it back. "Maybe sometime. And I want you to feel you can confide in me too, anytime."

"I'll remember that," Lou promised.

"After all," Perry added, "we are partners, aren't we?"

Lou didn't reply. He knew how loudly Perry had screamed when he had been told they were going to be partners.

76

They turned onto a main thoroughfare and headed south. Perry watched the side streets go by.

"We just passed Main. There's always some hustlers working the corner of Garden, aren't there?"

"We won't get anything from them," Lou replied, still driving south.

Perry tried his best to remain pleasant. "Lou, the lieutenant told us to question—"

"I figured we'd go to the Plush Parrot first."

"A gay bar? Now, Lou—"

"Zakos was gay," Lou said. "Nick Pappas is gay."

"But neither Zakos nor Pappas frequented the Plush Parrot. It's a sewer."

"You never know what you'll find in a sewer."

Perry said nothing. He had made up his mind he'd win Baroni's confidence and he was going to do just that. If the old crud wants to prowl a gay bar, he thought, well, just let him. It's one more disregard of orders he could report to Tate.

Lou wheeled the car around onto Shepherd and headed west along the dark street.

"By the way, Lou, how's the Hawley case coming?"

Lou took his eyes off the road to look at his partner. "The Hawley case? You're kidding!"

"No, I'm not," Perry insisted. "You had a hunch about it. How's it paying off? Making any progress?"

Lou, his eyes back on the road, said, "Tate closed the Hawley case."

"Uh huh," Perry replied and then added, conspiratorially, "but you're not letting that stop you, are you?"

Lou didn't get a chance to answer. Their police radio suddenly squawked.

"Any car in the vicinity. Assault in progress, parking lot, Shepherd and Oak. Code two."

Lou shoved the accelerator to the floor. Perry picked up the microphone.

"One David-seven, responding. We're on top of it."

77

The intersection was straight ahead. A large neon sign depicting a purple parrot spread more illumination on the parking lot opposite than the streetlights did. Even before the car turned into it, Lou and Perry could see two men punching a third.

Lou hit the brakes and then the pavement almost before the car had stopped skidding to a full stop, his gun in his hand. Perry was out his side of the car almost as fast, but as quick as they were, the two assailants were quicker. They dropped their victim to the asphalt and fled. Perry ran after them, twisting and turning through the maze of parked cars. Lou went to where the victim lay groaning, his arms wrapped protectively around his face.

"It's okay," Lou said. "We're police."

The moaning stopped.

"Are you all right?"

"Police? Are you really police?" The voice was high-pitched, almost feminine.

"Yeah, we're really police. Want an ambulance?"

The arms came slowly away from the victim's head and he sat up. "My face," he said, looking up at Lou, touching it gingerly. "What did they do to my face?"

"Nothing that I can see. Tell me what happened."

"It's going to be bruised. I know it is. Black and blue. I'll look hideous!"

Perry came back, breathing hard. "They got away."

Lou helped the victim to his feet. He was wearing basic black—black suede shoes, black slacks, and a black turtleneck sweater with a single strand of pearls.

"What in hell's that?" Perry said, looking at the victim fully for the first time.

The victim had been feeling his nose carefully. "I was afraid they'd break it. I'd die if it was broken!"

"You're lucky it wasn't. It would have been if we hadn't got here so fast," Lou said, deliberately reminding him of his debt to them.

"How did you get here so fast?" the victim asked.

78

"Oh—it must have been Charlene."

"Charlene?" Perry asked.

"He was with me. He ran off. He must have phoned."

"What's your name?" Lou asked.

"Carrol. Carrol Grant."

"Your real name," Perry said disgustedly.

"That *is* my real name," Carrol retorted. "I had it legally changed. It used to be Wannamaker! Can you imagine how dreadful that was? I was teased night and day! 'Wanna-make-her!'"

Perry turned away. Lou ignored it. "Tell me about the beating. Who were they?"

A wary look came to Carrol's face. He didn't want to become involved with the police. "I don't know."

"Yes, you do!" Lou said.

"I don't!" Carrol snapped back, petulantly.

"Is that gratitude?" Lou asked. "We save your life but you lie to us."

"I'm not lying," Carrol insisted. "They were strangers."

"Strangers," Lou said scornfully. "And they just happened to be waiting for you out here?"

Carrol hesitated, confused.

"We can ask inside," Lou said, indicating the gay bar across the street.

"Well, to tell the absolute truth," Carrol said finally, "I did meet them in there, but I don't know them at all. Honestly. Why, I'd never have anything at all to do with sadists like that!"

"Sadists?" Perry repeated.

"Well, they beat me, didn't they?"

"What are their names?" Lou asked.

"I don't know. That is the truth. I swear."

"You talked to them inside, though, didn't you?"

"Yes—but just casual conversation."

"It couldn't have been so casual," Lou said. "They came after you. Why?"

"I made a terribly unfortunate remark."

79

"What was it?"

"It really wasn't anything. Just something about that dreadful Zakos boy who was killed, that's all."

Perry reacted. For the first time he was interested. "What did you say?"

"I said I just voiced an opinion. One of them became awfully upset. He must have loved that dreadful boy a lot."

"Never mind that," Perry ordered impatiently. "Tell me about the murder."

Carrol was shocked. "I don't know anything about it at ·all! Heavens!"

Perry wouldn't be put off. "You must know something. You said you voiced an opinion!"

"About the boy!" Carrol exclaimed. "About the boy! Not his murder!"

"What was the opinion?" Lou asked.

"I just said he was an unfaithful whore."

Perry insisted on taking Carrol Grant in for questioning. He spent most of the night at it, but learned nothing.

Earlier, when Lou left Laurie Knight's apartment, she had gone out on her balcony to watch him drive away. Then she sat watching Ed Hawley's living room window. It was late, but she wasn't tired.

Like Lou, she guessed Hawley was watching television or reading. Her interest quickened now as she saw his silhouette move across the window, going in the direction of the dark kitchen. Then she saw a dim light in the kitchen window—the light from the refrigerator, she assumed. He was getting something to drink, she thought, or ice for a drink. A moment later, the dim light went out and then she saw his silhouette move back across the living-room window.

She began to wonder what he was feeling. Then she wondered if he knew he was suspected of murder, if he knew he was being watched, and if he didn't, how he would react, what his expression, his gestures, would be if he were told.

Her thoughts turned to Lou Baroni. She liked him, but she wasn't entirely sure she approved of what he was doing. She had seen Ed Hawley many times, walking along the street, in a nearby supermarket, in a local public library, and she just couldn't believe he was a murderer. It must have been an accident, she thought, one he must regret bitterly.

That thought led to another. He had just buried his wife. It must be awful to be alive and alone on the day you buried someone who had shared your life. It must be the most terrible, worst possible, kind of loneliness.

She made her decision without really thinking about it. She left her apartment, on her way to offer Ed Hawley what comfort she could.

A few minutes later she was standing in front of his door. The light was still on—she could see it under the sill—but if he was watching TV, she couldn't hear it. She knocked softly, not wishing to disturb the other tenants. There was no immediate response. It occurred to her, while she waited, that she might be walking in on a murderer. But, she reminded herself, she had decided he couldn't be a killer. It didn't seem in character. She knocked again, louder this time. A moment later the door opened and Hawley stood there in his shirtsleeves.

"Hi," Laurie said, smiling. "I'm Laurie Knight. I live across the road in the apartment opposite."

He didn't say anything. He seemed confused. Laurie felt his embarrassment. She spoke quickly, impulsively. "I saw your wife fall. I came to tell you how sorry I am."

"That's very kind of you."

He made no offer to invite her in.

"I saw your light on," Laurie told him. "I couldn't sleep either." And then, because he gave no sign of responding, she went on. "I know the funeral was today. I knew you'd be alone. There are times when I can't stand being alone. That's why I came to keep you company—that is, if you feel like company?"

Hawley seemed to understand at last. He stepped back from the door almost eagerly. "Come in, please."

She walked by him and he closed the door behind her. Looking around the living room, she saw he hadn't been watching television at all. The set was off. He'd been simply sitting in the armchair. There was a half-filled glass and a bottle of whiskey on the end table beside it.

"Please sit down," he said.

She sat on the sofa. "Thank you."

He started to sit down, but remembered his manners. "Can I get you something—a drink?"

Laurie shook her head. "But you go ahead."

He sat down. "It's very warm tonight, isn't it?"

"It is, yes."

He paused, unable to think of anything else to say. "I'm afraid I'm not going to be very good company. I'm not much of a conversationalist."

"That doesn't matter," Laurie said. "We don't even have to talk if you don't want to."

Hawley seemed to be studying her. She still wore only shorts and the blouse that left her midriff bare. "I didn't recognize you at first," he said. "I mean, at the door." Then, because he apparently felt he might have offended her, he added quickly, "But I do recognize you now. I know I have seen you before."

Laurie nodded. "On television maybe. I've played a few bit parts and I've made some commercials."

"No," Hawley said. "I mean on the street or coming out of your building."

He seemed very tired, she thought, not grief-stricken or remorseful. Just weary.

"We should have been friends before, then," Laurie said.

He shook his head. "Evelyn—my wife—" he started to say, but amended it. "No . . . different worlds."

Laurie was interested. "What do you mean?"

He seemed uncomfortable. He tried to change the subject. "You work in television?"

82

"What did you mean—about your wife?" she asked.

"It's nothing."

"I'd like to hear."

"Well," he began awkwardly, "I don't think you and Evelyn would have gotten along. You see—well—she didn't approve of the way you dressed."

"Oh?"

"I don't mean you personally. I mean your generation. Evelyn was very old-fashioned about some things."

"What about you?" Laurie asked. "Do you approve of what I'm wearing?"

She wasn't fishing for compliments. She wanted to know, to understand another point of view.

"You're very attractive."

"That's not what I meant. Do you like it?"

He stared at her for a long moment. "No. It makes me wish, too much, I was younger."

"You're not old."

"I'm old enough to be your father."

"Now that," Laurie said, "is really an old-fashioned concept."

"How do you mean?"

"That age difference prohibits. It doesn't."

"It does," Hawley said firmly. "It increases the possibility of jealousy. It adds to a relationship's insecurity. It makes youth itself a rival—" He broke off, a little embarrassed.

"You must have thought about that a lot."

He nodded. "I daydream a lot. I guess most men my age do."

"About young girls, you mean?" Laurie asked, interested. "I've been told they do."

He smiled suddenly, amused. "Not just about young girls. There's much more to daydream about than just that." He finished his drink and went into the kitchen for more ice. When he came back, Laurie said, "A detective asked me a lot of questions about you."

83

"A detective?"

"Uh huh."

"Stocky, about my height?"

"His name is Baroni."

Hawley nodded, poured whiskey over the ice, and sat down.

"He spent all day watching you," Laurie confided.

Hawley didn't seem surprised.

"He thinks you killed your wife."

"I know."

Laurie had expected more of a reaction. "You know?"

"He told me. He's accused me of it."

There was silence for a moment. The question hung in the air. Laurie decided to get rid of it. "Did you—kill your wife?"

He didn't answer right away. Instead he took a long slow drink. "She tripped."

Laurie nodded. Baroni had told her that was his story.

He looked at her searchingly. "Is that why you came—he sent you?"

"No!" Laurie exclaimed.

"You could be working with him."

"I'm not. I told you why I came. I thought you'd be lonely. I thought you'd like some company."

He still looked skeptical, as though he wanted to believe her, but wasn't sure he could.

After a moment Laurie said, "There is another reason."

"There is?"

She told him of her determination to be a great actress, of her need to study people, a bereaved man, for example, or one suspected of murder.

"But that's only part of it," she said. "I meant what I said. I really came because I knew you were all alone. I'll go right now if you want me to."

He didn't want her to go. Instead, to help her, he told her about himself, filling in the picture. He spoke of his youth in the Northwest. He mentioned the deaths of his parents, his sister's suicide, and his migration away from the snow to the sun and warmth of Southern California. He also told her of the girl he had met while he was still in school, of the long letters they had written, of his proposal by mail, of her acceptance, of their hope-filled beginning.

It was almost three when Laurie left. He stood with her at his door for a moment before they said goodnight.

"You said you saw Evelyn fall," he said abruptly.

She nodded.

"Tell me what you saw."

"Just that—I saw her falling." She wondered if she saw fear in his eyes. She couldn't decide.

"You didn't see what happened before that?"

"No," she answered truthfully. "No, I didn't."

Later, as she lay in her bed, she wondered if he had really believed her.

Barstow Street was busy at eight A. M., the time most people left for work. Some drove, but many walked to the bus stop six blocks away. Usually, because of the heavy traffic, a bus could get downtown as fast as a car, thus avoiding payment of a week's salary for a place to park.

Since Ed Hawley was a bus rider, Lou Baroni waited for him to leave by the front entrance of his apartment building rather than the driveway behind it.

He waited in Al Miller's car, parked a few doors away on the opposite side of the street, a Polaroid Land Camera in his lap. Miller, seated behind the wheel, rubbed his eyes repeatedly. It was a typical Southern California city morning—bright, cloudless, and smog-filled.

"Don't know if my eyes sting because I'm still tired or because of the damn pollution," Miller grumbled.

"It's the smog," Lou said. "Mine sting too."

Miller shook his head. "I think it's because I'm tired. I worked the night watch last night."

85

"So did I," Lou said.

"I don't have to be in court till ten," Miller went on. "I coulda stayed in bed another hour, hour and a half, if it wasn't for you."

Miller liked to grumble. Lou knew he didn't mind doing him a favor.

"What's wrong with your car, anyway?" Miller asked.

"The carburetor. I already told you that."

"See how tired I am? Can't even comprehend."

"You can't comprehend anything anymore, tired or not," Lou said.

"When are they going to have it fixed?"

"Today. You can sleep tomorrow."

"Tomorrow I got early watch."

The door to Hawley's apartment building opened and several people came out. Hawley was among them, but he was alone. The others, two men and a woman, were involved in banter. Hawley walked along the sidewalk toward the bus stop behind them.

"That's him," Lou said, raising the camera quickly and taking Hawley's picture.

Miller started the motor and pulled away from the curb, rolling slowly down the street behind Hawley. Lou held up the snapshot for him to see.

"Don't look like much, does he?" Miller commented. "You really think he killed her?"

"I would have."

They drove in silence, their eyes on Hawley, who walked along the sidewalk opposite unaware of them.

After a moment Miller asked, "What's this gonna get you?"

"A motive," Lou said. "I hope."

The houses and apartment buildings gave way to small stores as they neared a major cross-street. Hawley, apparently with time to spare, glanced in each window as he passed, not really stopping. The others on the street moved right along.

"He likes to window-shop," Miller said.

Lou grunted agreement. "He's stopping. Pull over."

Miller pulled to the curb opposite as Hawley paused before a window and seemed to study its contents closely.

"That's a jewelry store," Miller said.

"Yeah. Can you make out what he's looking at?"

"Jewelry," Miller replied, grinning at his own humor.

Lou wasn't amused. "What kind, men's or women's?"

"Can't tell," Miller said. "Think there's 'another woman' involved?"

Lou shrugged. "Anything's possible."

Hawley turned from the window and went on his way. Miller pulled away from the curb.

A few minutes later, Hawley reached the thoroughfare and turned the corner. Miller made a left turn and swung over to the far curb.

A girl with great legs and long auburn hair was standing at the bus stop. Hawley's step seemed to quicken as he saw her.

"Maybe there's your 'other woman,'" Miller said.

"Maybe," Lou replied, watching.

Hawley walked up to the girl and stood beside her. He glanced at her when she wasn't looking. But if they knew each other, neither gave any sign of it.

"It could be an act. He could have made us."

"Uh-huh," Lou took another Polaroid, this time of the two of them.

The bus arrived then and Hawley stepped aside to allow the girl to board first. A moment later the bus pulled back into the flow of traffic.

"Did you see if they sat together?" Lou asked.

"Couldn't tell," Miller answered. "Maybe they're gonna get off together somewhere."

"Yeah," Lou said. "Damn it, I wish I had my car."

"I've got time," Miller said. "Want to find out?"

"Thanks."

Miller made an illegal U-turn and followed the bus. It

made several more stops before entering the freeway. Neither the girl nor Hawley got off.

Once on the freeway the bus moved steadily along with the rush-hour traffic. Miller and Lou followed silently. Both were used to endless patrols. Both had long ago developed the habit of letting the mind idle.

It was almost a half hour later when the bus left the freeway and began moving along downtown streets.

It wasn't until the fourth stop that Edward Hawley got off, alone. The girl was still on the bus when it went on its way.

Miller pulled his car to the curb in a no-parking zone. His eyes, like Lou's, were on Hawley, who crossed the street toward a coffee shop that occupied part of the ground floor of a huge office building.

After Hawley had gone into the restaurant, Miller spoke. "Now what?"

"How's your time?"

"Gone."

"Okay," Lou said. "I'll leg it from here."

He reached for the door and opened it. He left the camera behind. It belonged to Miller.

"What'll I tell the lieutenant?" Miller asked.

"Nothing," Lou replied. "I'm on night watch, remember?" He started to leave, then paused. "Do something for me?"

"Sure."

"You still got your contacts in the banks?"

"Some. What do you need?"

"Hawley's bank account. All of them, if there's more than one."

"Didn't Perry already do that?"

"Yeah," Lou answered. "Officially." The way he said it made it sound distasteful. "He could have missed something. You won't."

Miller grinned. He liked Lou's backhanded compliments, even if they were meant to con him. "All right, I'll do it, unofficially, but you gotta promise to come and meet one of the wife's widows."

"That's blackmail!"

After Miller had driven off, Lou stood on the corner watching the coffee shop across the street. People of all shapes and sizes shoved by him rudely. It was almost nine and they were all hurrying to get to work on time.

The traffic was heavy too. Cars and buses crawled by. Lou cursed them more than once for blocking his view. He didn't want Hawley to leave the restaurant unseen.

He didn't. Lou saw him come out carrying a small paper sack, about the right size for a cup of coffee and a doughnut. He went directly to the main entrance of the building and began to thread his way through the crowd entering it. Lou lost sight of him almost at once.

Ignoring the traffic, he hurried across the street, pushed his way into the lobby, and watched as Hawley entered an elevator. He had gone to work and, apparently, had spoken to no one, unless it had been in the coffee shop next door.

The place was crowded. Most of the customers were men, obviously from the surrounding office buildings, grabbing a cup of coffee before going to work. Lou found an empty stool at the counter. The waitress, a bosomy blonde, was busy flirting with a number of men at the far end of the counter. More than a few minutes passed before she came over to him.

When she did, she brought a mug and a coffeepot. "Coffee?" she asked, giving him a big smile.

"Sure."

"You're new, aren't you? You don't work around here?"

"No," Lou answered. "Guess you know most of the men who do."

She answered smugly. "I know 'em all, all right."

Casually, Lou asked, "What about Ed Hawley?"

"Who?"

"Ed Hawley," Lou repeated.

The girl shook her head, puzzled. "What's he like?"

Lou laid the Polaroid of Hawley on the counter. She picked it up and studied it. "Nope, never met him."

"He just left."

The girl shook her head again. "One of the other girls must have taken care of him."

For some reason he couldn't explain, Lou was getting annoyed. "He's worked next door for twelve years. He must have been in here almost every day."

The girl shrugged, losing interest. "If he was, I never noticed him."

"You must have waited on him a hundred times. You must have said something to him once in a while—'Good morning,' 'How are you?' "

"I say that to everybody."

"And you remember them. You said you did."

"Sure—if there's something to remember." She was becoming annoyed now, too. "Look, I'm sorry I don't remember your friend. If I did, I'd tell you." Then a crafty look came over her face. "What's this all about, anyway? What's so important—"

She ended her question as a large, football-player-type man wearing a loud sport jacket slid onto the empty stool beside Lou and interrupted. "Hi there, gorgeous."

The girl's annoyance vanished. She grinned back at the newcomer. "Hiya, Charlie. How are you?"

"Wild," Charlie answered. "And you're responsible."

Lou winced, but the waitress laughed, pleased. "I like my men wild," she said.

She placed a mug before Charlie and poured him some coffee. Charlie's eyes fell on the picture of Ed Hawley, which still lay on the counter.

"Say, I know him."

Lou turned to him. "Yeah?"

"He works in my office. His name is Ed something."

Lou looked at the man challengingly. "You work together and you don't know his name?"

Charlie wasn't disturbed by Lou's tone. Lou guessed it would be pretty hard to disturb Charlie.

"Sure I know his name," Charlie said. "It's right on the tip of my tongue."

Lou let it go. "What else do you know about him?"

Charlie beamed. "Everything. Just ask."

The waitress, still wondering what it was all about, stood listening, ignoring the other customers.

"What's he like?" Lou asked Charlie. "Where does he go in his spare time? Who are his friends?"

Charlie frowned in concentration. "Sure . . . let me think. . . ." He paused, his brow furrowed. Then he grinned again. "You know," he said, "I don't have much to do with him, myself. Not my kind. So I guess I can't answer those questions. But if there's anything else—"

"Does he play around with any of the women in the office? Does he play the horses? Is he in debt?"

Charlie's forehead furrowed once again. "You know, the more I think about him, the more I realize he doesn't make much of an impression."

"You mean," Lou said, "he doesn't come on strong the way you do?"

"Yeah, that's it. Just a face in the crowd, as they say." Pleased with the quotation, Charlie grinned. "Guess he's just part of the Great Unwashed, y'know?" The grin widened. "Only way you know he's not around is by his empty chair."

The waitress laughed. So did Charlie. Lou didn't.

"What do you want to know for, anyway?" Charlie asked when he stopped laughing. "What's this all about?"

"Yeah," the waitress said. "That's what I asked."

"What's he done—stole some paper clips?"

"No," the waitress said, "it's gotta be worse than that. I know—he stole this guy's chick."

She and Charlie laughed again. Lou dropped a quarter on the counter and left.

He stood outside on the sidewalk for a moment, looking up at the tall building. Must be forty stories, he thought. A

91

couple hundred people working away on each. Ants! He shook his head. Then he went in and rode the elevator up to the fifteenth floor where Ed Hawley worked.

The Acme Credit Company was one of the city's largest service firms. It manufactured no product, provided no utility. Its only function was to act as a middleman, a collection agency, for which it in turn collected a percentage. Thus, it stood between the mortgager and the mortgagee, between the seller and the buyer, an anonymity that dealt only with numbers and not with people.

Of course, Lou Baroni, as he waited to be shown into the personnel manager's office, neither praised nor condemned such firms, anymore than he praised or condemned the hypes and hookers who also made up an undeniable part of his society. All he knew, for a reason he couldn't define, was that he had less and less liking these days for a society that made firms like Acme possible.

The personnel manager's secretary, a harried middle-aged woman who did her best to look twenty years younger, spoke to him from behind her desk. "Mr. Fisher will see you now."

Mr. Fisher's office was different from most Lou had seen. One wall was a window that looked out, not over the street, but into a large room that must have contained thirty or more desks, with a man or woman working at each. Fisher was obviously in a position to keep an eye on all of them, from nine to five.

Fisher himself was a short, stout man with a shiny pate. Like his secretary, he seemed harassed, and his smile, which flashed perfunctorily onto his face as he greeted Lou, failed miserably in its attempt to be friendly.

"My secretary said you came to make certain—ahem—inquiries about one of our employees?"

"She got that right," Lou said.

"We don't resent inquiries, Mr.—ah?"

"Baroni."

"—Mr. Baroni. We're well aware of the necessity of a free flow of information for a variety of purposes. Our business,

92

in fact, depends upon it. But we must always know the reason for, and purpose of, the inquiry."

Lou took out his badge and laid it on the desk in front of Fisher. Fisher reacted nervously.

"You're a policeman?"

Lou nodded.

"You mean—" He consulted a scratch pad on which he had obviously jotted down notes when his secretary had first announced Lou. "You mean, Edward Hawley is guilty of a crime?"

Lou leaned back in his chair. "Now, I didn't say that."

"But if he's under suspicion. . . ." Fisher was disturbed. The idea that he employed a criminal unnerved him.

Lou leaned forward and spoke earnestly. "Look—why don't we just talk like two old friends, about another old friend? Unofficially, off the record. Is that hard?"

Fisher's hands moved nervously. "No, no, of course not. Old friends, you said? Well, I suppose so, if that's how you want to treat it."

Tired of his ruminations, Lou pressed on. "Tell me anything you can about him. Your impressions. Your reactions. You know, that sort of thing."

"I'll do better than that," Fisher said, back on ground he knew. "I'll consult his file for you. I have it right here." He drew a file folder over to him. "I had my secretary pull it as a matter of course when you inquired about him."

Lou sighed. "I don't think the kind of stuff I'm looking for would be in his file."

Fisher looked at him, scandalized. "Mr. Baroni—everything of importance—his entire work record—is in here."

Lou tried a different tack. "I'm more interested in personal relations—that sort of thing." Then, because Fisher didn't respond, he asked, "You do know him personally, don't you?"

"Mr. Baroni," Fisher replied archly, "I'm responsible for the personnel in four departments. It's impossible for me to know them all personally."

"But he's worked here for twelve years."

93

"There are more than two hundred people in my active files. He's only one."

"You do know his wife just died, don't you?"

"Of course. We're not callous. Such tragedies are always noted. He had, and has, our deepest sympathy. The entire floor sent their condolences. The firm, of course, sent flowers."

Lou snorted. He couldn't help it. Fisher chose to ignore it. "Shall I read you his file or not?"

Lou sighed. "Go ahead."

"'Edward Hawley, born in 1927, Caucasian. . . .'" Lou got up and walked over to the window. As he listened, he surveyed the rows of desks. Halfway down the fifth row he saw Hawley, hard at work.

Fisher's voice droned on behind him. "'Previously employed by Alford Industries as a bookkeeper. Discharged when the firm dissolved. Absences due to illness, three. Compassionate absences, one, five days. Promotions, none.'"

Near the window, in the first row, Lou recognized Charlie, the man from the coffee shop, talking and flirting with one of the women who sat near him.

"'Psychological evaluation,'" Fisher continued, "'conscientious, but not brilliant. Agreeable, but not aggressive.'" He paused. Lou turned back to him.

"That, Mr. Baroni, explains why he's still in his present position—nonaggression."

"I thought that'd be something good. We lock people up who are too aggressive."

"In your, ahem, line of work, perhaps. Not in ours."

Lou indicated the file, which Fisher now closed. "Is that all?"

"Yes."

"After twelve years?"

"The fact," Fisher explained patiently, "that there isn't more is to his credit. It indicates he's reliable, trustworthy, steady, and so on. On the other hand, if he were difficult,

94

troublesome, irresponsible—"

Lou interrupted. "I know. His file would be full."

"Exactly. Now, of course, it will have to contain a record of your inquiry."

Lou responded quickly. "I don't want this held against him."

"Well," Fisher replied, "after all, he is the subject of an investigation."

"But it's my own idea. Unofficial. I told you that."

Fisher seemed pleased now. "Mr. Baroni—really—he has come to the attention of the police, hasn't he? That fact in itself has to be considered. We have to be very careful, you know. We have to deal with all possible problems before they occur. Steps have to be taken as soon as there's even the slightest indication they might be necessary."

Lou stared at him. "You mean he might be fired?"

"That is not up to me," Fisher replied smugly. "I will simply report the incident and then my duty will be fulfilled. I will have done my job."

"But what about his twelve years—don't they mean anything?"

"As I said," Fisher answered, spreading his hands out on his desk, "the disposition of the matter and the considerations thereto are not concerns of mine."

Lou felt like swearing at the man. He turned away, ready to leave. But the room next door full of desks and workers caught his eye. He paused, an idea forming.

Walking over to the window, he asked, casually, "How long has he worked by the window?"

Fisher's eyebrows went up. "By the window? His desk is number twenty-four. That's not by the window."

"I don't care where his desk is," Lou replied, "the man I'm asking about is by the window."

Fisher hurried from his desk to stand beside Lou. Lou pointed to Charlie, who was on the phone now, talking expansively, judging from his gestures.

"But that's not twenty-four, that's number seven!"

95

Lou shrugged. "That's the man I'm interested in. And you better put that in his report."

"Oh, I will," Fisher said immediately. "I will!"

When Lou left, Fisher was already instructing his secretary to bring in file number seven.

Lou didn't permit himself a smile until he was in the elevator, on the way down.

6

LOU didn't get much sleep that day. His phone rang at four. Tate had called a special meeting.

"I'm not satisfied," Tate was saying as Lou walked into the squad room. "Too many days have passed since Spiro Zakos was killed, and we're no closer to making Nicky Pappas for the murder now than we were then."

Nobody said anything. The room was full. They were all there, the day-, mid-, and night-watches—every detective in the division. Miller, at his desk, winked at Lou.

"The media is laughing at us," Tate said, pacing a little at the head of the room as he talked. "The police commission is ready to see some heads roll. The chief is requesting daily reports. And Papa Pappas is sitting on that island of his, thumbing his nose at all of you."

Lou noted the way "us" had changed to "you" but said nothing. He had learned long ago it was always wiser to say nothing at meetings like this. Let the man rave. It made him feel better and usually did no harm. Joe Segel, sitting next to Lou, was new to the squad and not so wise.

"Lieutenant," he said, "maybe we're trying to follow a cold trail. Maybe Nicky Pappas didn't kill Zakos."

Tate stared at him as if he had uttered complete blasphemy. "Negative thinking"—he pointed a finger at Segel—"always negative thinking! Now listen and understand this. We've been waiting for a reason to clout the Pappas family for years, and now we've finally got one. So don't—I repeat—don't ever tell me we haven't."

97

The young detective looked as if he wished he weren't there. But he had to go on. Tate hadn't left him any choice. "But, sir, we haven't been able to turn up anything at all. Just suspicion."

"Not 'just'!" Tate exclaimed. "Heavy suspicion! Solid suspicion! Don't ever forget that!"

Segel was about to say something else in an attempt to salvage the situation, but Lou kicked him gently. He finally shut up.

"Now," Tate said, "if we've finished with defeatism, I'm going to give you some positive thoughts." He looked around the room. "First of all, you're going to concentrate on this case. The daily complaints can wait."

Nobody said anything.

"Secondly, we're going to forget the watch routine for a few days. You're all on duty around the clock until we've broken old man Pappas by making his son. Thirdly, start thinking like detectives. Zakos was an addict. Somebody was peddling to him. Somebody could have been there"— he stressed the words—"before or even during the time the killing took place."

Lou glanced at Perry. He was standing at the side of the room, nodding his head, approving of Tate's sagacity.

A detective named Orwell spoke up. "Pappas still owns shares in a couple of factories. Nicky could have picked up the stuff at any of them, couldn't he?"

Tate glared at the man, twice started to say something but didn't. His anger rose. It was obvious, to Lou anyway, that he hadn't considered that possibility.

Lou spoke up. He knew better, but he just couldn't keep quiet. It was his professionalism that made him do it. And to make matters worse, he spoke to Orwell, not Tate.

"Pappas won't allow Nicky to go anywhere near the factories. And he'd crucify any of his people who gave Nicky a fix. He laid down that law years ago, and nobody's ever had the nerve to go against it."

Tate's face went white, furious at being shown up, but he

98

hid his anger, just barely. "Baroni's right. Nicky Pappas can't get a fix anywhere. Spiro Zakos had to make the buy. I want to know who his supplier was, and where that supplier was the day Zakos was killed."

"Is that our assignment?" one of the detectives asked. "To question anybody's who's holding?"

Tate nodded. "Exactly. And I want full reports covering every pusher talked to. Is that understood?"

The men muttered assent. At least most did. Segel once again insisted on putting his foot into it. He still believed a little of what the academy had taught him. "Can we work with Vice and Narcotics on this?"

"No," Tate retorted. "This is our case, not theirs. If you can't handle it yourself, let me know and I'll find someone to replace you."

Nobody said anything else. Silently, all but Perry, they left the squad room. Tate motioned to him to stay behind.

When they were alone, Tate said, "That Baroni bastard—did you see the way he tried to put me down?"

"Yes, sir," Perry replied, "but I thought you handled it very well."

Tate ignored the bootlicking. "Tell me what you've got on him."

Perry felt a moment of panic. He didn't like direct questions. They required direct answers—usually when he didn't have any. "Got on him?" he repeated lamely.

"I asked you to find me a reason to boot him."

"Yes, sir. I know, sir. " Perry searched for an acceptable answer. "But that was only a couple of days ago."

Tate glared at him. "You're telling me you haven't got anything yet, is that it?"

"Sir, if you give me a few more days—just a few—I'm sure I can promise you—"

Tate walked away. He wasn't in the mood for excuses. He interrupted Perry by asking, "What about Hawley?"

"I'm still trying to win Baroni's confidence, sir, so he'll confide in me about Hawley and his plans—"

In a foul mood, Tate interrupted again. "Screw that! You'll never win his confidence. You'll have to get the evidence another way. Follow him. Or better still, talk to Hawley. If Baroni's persecuting him, and he signs a complaint, we've got Baroni."

"Yes, sir," Perry lied. "I know. I planned to talk to Hawley." The idea hadn't occurred to him before.

"Then why haven't you?"

Lying came easily to Perry once he had begun. "I've been waiting, sir, to give Baroni more opportunity to really harass Hawley. I want something solid before approaching him, something that even the chief will have to acknowledge."

Tate considered this for a moment, then nodded. "All right. Give it a little more time—but not much." He wagged his finger at Perry. "Not much. Clear?"

A few minutes later when Lou drove their unmarked car out of the parking lot and turned east, Perry sat glumly beside him, saying little. For the past few days he had been coasting, pleased by Tate's praise. But now the praise was gone and everything was suddenly sour. Damn it, he thought, why couldn't things go right for once?

Lou was thinking about Tate's orders. First it had been the hookers. Now it was the pushers. Tate was grasping at straws. They'd never get anything off the streets.

He was right. They spent most of the night in bars and all-night coffee shops, and the following day they visited pool halls, massage parlors, and porno houses. But they failed to find even a single real pusher. They found a few kids, a cowboy or two new in town, a number of addicts who were holding nickle or dime bags, but the reliable sources were nowhere.

Around five they called it quits for the day and Lou drove back to the station. When they got there, Perry told him to write up the report and went home to sleep, not bothering to say goodnight.

Lou went into the squad room and sat down at his desk.

He put a report form in the typewriter and then stared at it. A report, he thought. A report of what?

He considered the question for a long moment and then he pecked out the words: *Failed to find pushers. They know the heat's on. They've all gone underground where it's cool. Baroni.*

Then he left the station to grab a bite to eat. And while he ate he wondered what Ed Hawley had in mind for that evening.

It was after seven when he parked on Barstow opposite Hawley's apartment building and looked up at his windows. No light was showing, but that could mean anything. None were on in the other apartments either. The sun hadn't quite set. Still, he wondered if Hawley had already gone out. He left his car and walked to where he'd have a better view of Hawley's window.

The evening was warm, the concrete giving off the heat it had absorbed during the day. It was going to be a pleasant night.

Many people seemed to agree with him. There was the usual automotive traffic, but there were also a good many pedestrians on their way to do some shopping, or going, perhaps, to a restaurant or a nearby movie.

Most were in pairs, engrossed in their own conversations. In a small town they might look at him and wonder what he was doing there, just standing, alone. But in a big city people never seemed to see strangers.

A light came on in Hawley's living room and Lou felt a moment of satisfaction. He hadn't missed him. If Hawley planned to make a move of some kind tonight, he was in time to follow.

He didn't see Laurie Knight approaching because his eyes were on Hawley's window. And when he did see her, he didn't recognize her at first. She wore a long, shapeless dress and a half dozen or more strings of beads dangled from her throat. She was carrying a bag of groceries.

"Hi," she said. "I wondered when you'd be back."

101

"You dressed up for a part or something?" Lou asked. For some reason he had expected her to wear something more becoming when she wore a dress. She laughed at his question.

"I'm going to a party. Believe it or not, this is in."

Lou made a grimace. She didn't mind.

"Going to be here long?"

"That depends on him." He indicated Hawley's window.

"You'll be long," she said. "Come on up and use my balcony."

The idea was appealing. He never did like standing, and lately it really bothered his feet, but he shook his head.

"You're going to a party," he reminded her.

"Not for an hour. Anyway, you can stay after I leave." She smiled. "If you can't trust a cop, who can you trust?"

She made instant coffee and brought their cups to the balcony. They sat sipping in silence for a few minutes. Across the street, Hawley was seen, occasionally moving by his living-room window. He was in his shirtsleeves and his tie was off. There was no indication that he was going out or that he expected anyone to arrive.

"If he did kill her," Laurie asked suddenly, "what was his motive?"

"That's what I'm trying to find out," Lou answered.

"I've been thinking about it." She was sitting on the floor again, her legs—and the long dress—folded under her. "I can't imagine what it would be."

"How about another woman?" Lou suggested dryly.

Laurie shook her head. "No, I considered that. If there was another woman, he'd be with her right now."

"If he's smart, he'll stay away from her for months."

"But that's just it," Laurie said animatedly. "They never do, do they, because they can't. The attraction's always too great, isn't it?"

Lou didn't reply. She had a point, of course. Triangles involving murder also involve passion. And passion rules out common sense. But, still, there were other possibilities.

102

"Suppose," he said, "she's away. Suppose she took a trip somewhere and doesn't even know about the killing. Suppose he's waiting for her to get back before springing the good news."

Laurie looked at him with admiration. "You mean he took it upon himself, hoping the other woman will fall into his arms now that he's free?"

Lou winced. Laurie saw it and laughed. "I've been watching the soap operas. They use actresses, too." Then, more seriously, she asked, "If there is another woman, you think he'll lead you to her, don't you?"

"That's why I'm here."

She shook her head. "There's no other woman."

She said it so definitely that Lou raised his eyebrows. "How do you know?"

"I went over to see him the other night."

"You *what?*" Lou exclaimed.

"I went to see him," she repeated.

"That was a dumb thing to do."

"Why?"

"He's a killer."

"He killed his wife . . . maybe. Anyway, why should he kill me?"

Lou didn't answer that directly. "You never know about people. You can't tell what they'll do. You took a chance you didn't need to take. That was dumb."

"I'm taking a chance with you right now," she said. "You could be a homicidal cop."

He didn't bother answering that one.

"Anyway, he didn't hurt me. And what's more, I'm glad I went. He needed somebody to talk to."

Lou nodded. "Everybody needs someone to talk to. What did you talk about?"

"Everything, nothing," Laurie answered. "He knows you suspect him of murdering his wife."

"Does he know he's being watched?"

Laurie thought it best to lie. "No . . . I mean, I don't think so."

103

Lou glanced back at Hawley's window. "Did he make a pass at you?"

"No. I could have been his daughter."

Yes, Lou thought, that made sense. If Hawley had killed his wife for another woman, he'd be thinking only of her.

"Anyway," Laurie said, "I don't think he killed her. Not deliberately, I mean. I like him."

Her date arrived—a blond young man with a massive beard and steel-rimmed glasses, who wore sandals and a garment very much like Laurie's. He was polite enough to Lou when Laurie introduced them, but he didn't seem real. Fewer and fewer young people did, to Lou, lately. Laurie seemed particularly interested in their reactions to each other, especially Lou's when she told him her date had already graduated from law school.

After they left, he went back to the balcony and sat there watching Hawley's window. Around midnight he fell a-sleep in the chair.

When Laurie came home at two, he was still there. She covered him with a blanket and let him sleep on.

Papa Pappas was up late that evening too. He sat on his bedroom balcony looking out over the lake, watching the lights in the homes on the far hills wink out one by one as the moon rose higher in the clear night sky. He had built those homes, homes almost as grand as his, situated on five-acre lots, high above the avenues and boulevards of Hellenic-West proper. Movie stars lived in those estates; and politicians; a wealthy, world-renowned writer; a Nobel Prize-winning scientist. And they had all bought their homes from him. It was something to be proud of, he felt. Something a man could hand down to his son—if he had a son who was interested. But not Nicky. Definitely not Nicky. Nicky was a throwback to his early days, proud of his father only when he had been truly a crime czar. Nicky wouldn't admit the days of Chicago crime were over.

He sighed and lit a cigar. Of course, his doctors, the best money could buy, had forbidden cigars. But he had no intention of living out the rest of his life in misery. Nicky was pain enough for any man.

The headlights of a car swinging around the curved driveway of his estate attracted his attention. It was Demetri returning, he knew. Demetri had, at his instruction, convened a meeting of his peers, his partners, his competition. He got up and went into his bedroom, anxious to hear what he had learned.

The bedroom was huge, the bed massive. It stood on a dais. A bed fit for a king, the fag interior designer had said—and Papa had liked the sound of that phrase. A bed fit for a king.

Actually, it was a bed fit for a king and queen. It was far too large for one small old man. But back then he still had his dream. He still had visions of turning the house and his whole empire over to Nicky, who would bring his bride to that bed and beget there the grandsons the old man desired. That's why he had bought it—for his grandsons. He knew now it would never happen, but, in his Old Country heart, he still hoped. Nicky was still a young man. He could change. That is, if he were free to change. Prison, even a short sentence, would surround him only with men eager for his boyish body. It would ruin him for all time. Of that he felt certain.

There was a knock at the bedroom door and Papa Pappas, sinking into a huge, high-backed chair, called out, "Come in."

The expression on Demetri's face never seemed to change. It was always matter-of-fact, always impossible to read there good news or bad.

"Well?" Papa asked.

"They sympathize. They send their regrets. They will keep you informed of everything that happens about Nicky."

Papa nodded. He had expected that. Even his enemies respected him and would help him in a family matter. "What have they heard?"

Demetri stood in front of him and recited his report emo-

105

tionlessly. "There is a lieutenant named Tate. He is anxious for promotion. He has been promised it if he can bring you down. He thinks he can do that by proving Nicky killed Zakos."

He's right, Papa thought. If Nicky were executed or even sent to prison, he'd have nothing left to live for.

"Is this lieutenant dangerous?" he asked.

"No, he is a fool. He has his detectives running everywhere at once and finding nothing."

"What else?"

"A detective named Baroni."

That name again, Papa thought. Italian. The one who had gone to see the restaurant owner, Bacopolous. The one who was the Negro's friend.

Demetri went on. "He is dangerous."

"The Negro," Papa said, "this Wally Blue. Has he talked?"

"No. It is felt he won't."

"He owes Baroni his life," Papa reminded Demetri.

"To him, he may possibly talk, but it is not considered likely."

"What else?"

"Baroni has been asking questions in the right places. The other detectives can be ignored. Baroni, however, thinks."

"How old is Baroni?" Papa asked.

"He will be retired soon—one or two years."

Papa nodded. Baroni was an old-time policeman, a real policeman. That explained why he was dangerous.

"What was the feeling of the meeting," he asked. "How should this Baroni be handled?"

"Shahinian"—Demetri named Papa's chief competitor— "offered to arrange an 'accident' for Baroni."

It was a compliment, a tribute, that Shahinian, an Armenian, would make such an offer. It was a gift to a king. But Papa shook his head.

"No. Thank Shahinian, but say no. I am tired of killings."

106

"There may be no other way."

Papa sighed. "There must be." If Nicky had been a real man, his attitude might have been different. But to take the life of a real man to save Nicky—it galled.

"It is my opinion there is no other way."

Papa rose and moved wearily toward his bed. As he removed his dressing gown, he said, "It is too soon for such opinions."

Demetri said nothing.

"That time may come when he will have to be killed, but first we will wait." He sat on the edge of the bed and removed his slippers. "We will wait and let him make the next move."

Demetri helped the old man under the covers and then left. Hours later, when Papa Pappas finally fell asleep, his mind still mulled over the problem of disposing of Lou Baroni. What, he wondered, would be the best way of killing him?

When Lou reached the police station the following day he could see at once that something had been going on. The corridor was busier than usual, not with felons or citizens making complaints, but with reporters and photographers.

Whatever it was, it was over—and it didn't have a good feel about it. The men walking down the hall were plainly dissatisfied about something, and since they all came from Lieutenant Tate's office, Lou wasn't too surprised.

He was about to turn into the squad room when he realized that trailing the scratch pads and camera was Wally Blue himself, bony wrists cuffed, escorted by two uniformed officers.

Wally, his shoulders stooped, his frame trembling the way a hype's sometimes does when he's deprived of the stuff, saw Lou, and broke into a happy grin. Even before he reached him he raised his cuffed hands in a greeting and called out, "Lou, baby! Hiya, man! How's it going with you now?"

107

Lou shook his head. "Slower and slower, Wally. How about you?"

Wally paused to talk. One of the officers started to push him along, but Lou gestured for him to leave it.

"Lou," Wally said, "it ain't going so good with me. I need a fix real bad." His expression became grim. "I'm freakin' out without it," he said and then added, confidentially, "Everything looks real and it scares me."

"It scares everybody, Wally," Lou told him. "Why should you be different?"

Wally took a step closer. "Look, Lou," he said softly, earnestly. "I'm real shook 'bout the other day. Y'know I'd open up to you if I could, don't you?"

"Sure, Wally. Sure, I know."

"I'll snitch on anything else I hear—that's a promise—but this time—" He didn't finish. He just shook his head.

Lou patted his arm. "Forget it. I got the picture."

"No hard feelings, eh? I don't want no hard feelings."

It seemed important to Wally. Lou said, "No hard feelings, none at all."

Wally's face broke into its usual grin. "Thanks, baby—I won't forget—I owe you—and I know it—and I'll do something about it—that's a fact, man."

The officers moved Wally on down the corridor, and Lou stood a moment watching them go. It was funny about Wally. He was a hype, and a pimp when he could con a hooker, and a thief, and a snitch, and maybe even queer and a dozen other things, yet Lou knew he never lied—at least not to him. In his own way he was honorable. He turned and went into the squad room.

Miller was working at his desk. He looked up when Lou came in and sat down at his own desk nearby.

"Tate was looking for you."

Lou nodded. "What's been going on?"

"He pulled Nicky Pappas in for questioning."

"You're joking."

108

Miller laughed and shook his head.

"I bet it took his lawyers five minutes to spring him."

"You're wrong," Miller replied. "It took them about seven minutes. Six and a half at least."

Lou leaned back in his chair. "What in Christ," he said with wonder in his voice, "did Tate hope to gain?"

"It was a long shot. That's what he called it. He confronted him with Wally Blue. Nothing happened."

Lou nodded. "Nothing would. Wally's too bright." Then he said, "Did you get your contacts to double-check Hawley's bank account?"

"Yeah." Miller was obviously pleased with himself. "I've been waiting for you to ask."

"Well, I'm asking."

"Hawley hasn't got a bank account worth talking about."

"That's what Perry said. You gotta have more than that."

"Hawley hasn't got an account worth talking about," Miller repeated, "but Mrs. Hawley had."

Lou sat up straight. "Keep talking."

"It's an old joint-account," Miller continued. "They both opened it more than twenty years ago. But he never used it. He probably doesn't even remember it. She made all the deposits."

"All right," Lou said. "All right, you've saved it to the last. Now tell me—how much is in it?"

"Fifty-eight hundred."

Lou was disappointed. "Fifty-eight hundred?"

"Lots have been killed for less."

The door opened and Tate strode in, stopped, and surveyed the room. He held a sheet of paper in his hand. All the men present looked up from their work.

Tate saw Lou and walked quickly over to him. He began speaking loudly, at once, even before he reached him. "Baroni—weren't you told I wanted to see you?"

"I was just coming," Lou answered, leaning back in his chair.

109

Tate exploded. His recent fiasco with Nicky Pappas and Wally Blue had hurt and he was looking for a whipping boy. He threw the paper he carried on Lou's desk.

"What the hell do you mean by handing in a report like that?"

Lou, with deliberate slowness, pulled the paper to him so he could glance at it.

"What's wrong with it?" he asked.

"You were told to locate pushers and question them. You were ordered to!"

Lou shrugged. "They couldn't be found. They're all underground. I explained that in the report." He shoved the paper back across the desk toward Tate.

"I don't want explanations," Tate exclaimed. "I want results! Do you think I can go to the chief and give him explanations? No! I've got to have something concrete to give him. And when I tell you to get it, I expect you to do just that!"

Everyone in the room was listening, their expressions deliberately noncommittal. Tate suddenly became aware of the fact he had lost his temper in front of them and began striding back toward the door. However, before he left, he had to score a point. He stopped at the door to say, "Baroni, you're too close to your pension to lose it now. So be careful!"

Nobody said or did anything for a long moment after Tate left. Then, one by one, they went back to work.

"Come on, Lou," Miller offered. "I'll buy you a cup of coffee."

In the corridor Lou asked, "When did Hawley's wife make the last deposit?"

Miller looked at him surprised. "A couple of weeks ago. Lou, Tate's after blood. If he finds out you're still on the Hawley thing. . . . Maybe you'd better cool it."

"I can't."

"It could mean your pension."

110

"A policeman's pension!" Lou snorted. "I'm going for broke—a sergeant's."

Miller nodded. "You'll never make it. If Hawley ever sees you following him, if he complains to Tate—"

Lou cut him off. "Hawley is going to see me. He's going to see me everywhere he goes. In every doorway, around every corner. And when he can't stand it anymore, he'll break—and I'll be there to see him make the mistake I need!"

It wasn't a tactic he'd planned. Yet it seemed like a good one now that he said it. And he wasn't too worried about Hawley issuing a complaint. Murderers rarely complain to the police.

It was well after seven when Lou parked his car a few doors away from Hawley's place. Dusk had come, and though the sky beyond the buildings was still tinged red by the setting sun, the streetlights were already on, and so were the lights in many of the houses and apartments.

He sat finishing a cigarette. The day had been spent trying to chase down a lead—any lead—in the Zakos affair, without any success. Everybody connected with it was too afraid of Papa Pappas to even breathe a wrong word. He was glad he had chosen Hawley. Nicky Pappas would have been a more spectacular bust, but Hawley was a more certain one.

Lou got out of his car and walked slowly along the street. There was a streetlight exactly opposite Hawley's apartment. Lou leaned against it, knowing it would illuminate his face, making it possible for anybody to see him clearly.

Hawley's living-room window was lit, the curtains open. Hawley would just have to walk by that window and glance out to see him. It wouldn't take too much luck.

The street door to Hawley's apartment building opened and two couples came out—two men, two women. Friends, going out for the evening, Lou surmised. He watched them

111

move down the street, talking animatedly. He took out another cigarette and struck a match harder than necessary. For some reason the idea of others being together, enjoying one another's company, annoyed him. He stood alone against the lamp post and sucked heavily on the smoke.

A few minutes later an old, garishly colored Volkswagen van pulled to the curb directly in front of him, blocking him from Hawley's view.

The driver was a young man with long hair, faded jeans, and T-shirt—but clean. The kind Lou always categorized as a good kid just trying to make the scene. He was getting out of the van when Lou walked up to him.

"Mind moving it a few feet?" Lou asked.

The young man was surprised. "Why?"

Lou flashed his badge.

The young man looked at it and Lou could almost see his back stiffen. "Look," he said to Lou, "the sign says no parking before six. It's after that."

Lou nodded. "That's right. I'm just asking a favor. It'll make my job easier."

The young man seemed perplexed. Lou understood his quandary. Ordinarily he'd be pleased to cooperate, but helping "pigs" wasn't "in." He wasn't sure how he should act.

"I'll only be a few minutes," he said. "I'm just picking up a girl."

"It'll only take one minute to move your van a few feet."

The young man's dilemma was solved when the door to the apartment building directly behind them opened and Laurie Knight came out. The way his face lit up it was obvious she was his date.

"Hi," she said to both of them. "What's happening?"

"He wants me to move the van," the boy said.

Laurie turned to Lou. "You don't have to stand down here," she said. "You can use my balcony."

Lou shook his head. "Not tonight, thanks."

Laurie was puzzled. "I don't mind—"

112

The young man spoke up. "Laurie, he's a cop."

"I know," Laurie told him. Then she said to Lou, indicating the streetlight, "He'll see you down here."

"That's the idea."

She studied him for a moment, understanding his purpose. "You're so certain he did it."

"Uh-huh."

"I think you're wrong."

"I'll let you know," Lou said.

"That's a promise," she said. "Don't forget."

She got in the van then, and so did the young man. A moment later they drove off.

Lou leaned against the lamp post again, letting the light illuminate his face—for it was getting quite dark now—and looked up at Hawley's living-room window. It wasn't empty anymore. He could make out the figure of a man standing there. Hawley. He was obviously looking down at Lou. Lou looked back, until, a moment later, Hawley stepped away from the window and drew the curtain.

Lou smiled. Hawley had seen him.

He stayed there until eleven. During that time Hawley parted the drapes and looked out three times. When Lou drove home, he was quite satisfied with his night's work.

Because the traffic on the city's thoroughfares is particularly heavy during the evening rush hour, and the freeways bumper-to-bumper, many motorists choose the surface streets, congesting them as well.

Lou, driving toward Barstow the following day, found himself in a stop-go situation. Ordinarily he would have avoided the main streets, but today there was just no way he could. Today he wanted to be waiting at Hawley's bus stop when his bus arrived. He glanced at his watch. He still had twenty minutes. In spite of the snail's pace, he should make it, he told himself. Yet, like other motorists, his patience was worn thin.

Finally, he pulled off the main street and sped along a

number of side streets, until at last he was able to park a block away from his destination. His watch told him he had less than three minutes before Hawley's bus arrived, so he walked quickly back toward the thoroughfare. He reached it with only a few moments to spare. He saw the bus a block away, waiting for a traffic signal to turn. He took up a position in front of an expensive fish and poultry shop, directly across the street from the bus stop.

When the bus arrived, Lou feared for a moment that Hawley might not be on it, for he couldn't see him among those making their way down its aisle toward the exit. But then, when the bus pulled away, Hawley was there, standing on the curb. The others who had left the bus were hurrying on their way, but Hawley seemed in no hurry to go anywhere. Watching him, Lou could sympathize. He rarely had anywhere to go, in a hurry, after work.

Hawley walked slowly along the street, toward the corner of Barstow, but instead of turning to go to his apartment building, he crossed the intersection and stood in front of a store window, looking in. Lou moved along the opposite side of the street and saw with a touch of satisfaction that the store was a travel agency.

Hawley, oblivious to the people rushing by him, stared in the window unmoving for a long time. Then he turned and went inside.

Dodging traffic, Lou hurried across the street and went up to the window. The display pictured the sparkling beaches and towering palms of Pacific islands, girls playing in the surf, handsome men maneuvering sailboats, couples relaxing outside luxury hotels. A large sign proclaimed, LOW PRICES TO THE SOUTH PACIFIC.

Lou glanced into the store. Hawley was standing at a rack of travel folders which occupied most of one wall, carefully selecting several.

Lou grinned. He had wondered how long it would be before Hawley felt safe enough to make his move. Maybe, he thought, he was beginning to feel safe enough now. Either

114

that or he had been hurried by Lou's tactics. Either way, Lou was satisfied.

He stood there waiting for Hawley to turn. Minutes passed before he did, and then, of course, he saw Lou.

His expression changed. There was no fear as Lou had expected, nor annoyance. It was simply a look of recognition. It was as if Hawley had expected to see him.

They looked at each other for only a moment, then Hawley turned away and moved toward the door. Lou stayed where he was. When Hawley came out onto the street, he acknowledged Lou's presence with just a slightly perceptible nod of the head. Then he walked on in no more of a hurry than before.

Later, at home, when Lou sprawled in his easy chair, drinking a beer, he wondered for a moment if he might be wrong about Hawley. But only for a moment. Hawley was his only route to a sergeant's pension. He had to be guilty.

7

SWEENEY was a snitch—a short, fat, bulbous-nosed, reliable snitch. At least he was reliable when he was squealing to Lou Baroni.

They had known each other a long time. Once, when Sweeney had been hospitalized with a really bad case of the DT's, Lou had taken him boxes of chocolates. Once, when he was stomped on by some of his friends, Lou had carried him home and held him together with bandages. And Sweeney, like most street people, never forgot real kindness. That's why he agreed to meet Lou in a deserted parking lot at four A.M.

"Lou, the word's out all over town. You're looking for heavy pushers, right?"

"Right," Lou answered. And then, because Sweeney kept glancing nervously at Perry, who waited in the car, he added, "Relax—he's only interested in Nicky Pappas."

"That's what they're saying on the street," Sweeney said, "You want the pushers because of the Zakos hit."

"That's the idea," Lou replied. "But they've gone underground. Know where any of them are?"

"Uh-huh," Sweeney said. "One of 'em, anyway. A mean one. That's why I phoned. I thought you'd want to know."

"Who is it?"

"Harry Brazil. He's holed up with a broad."

The sign hanging outside the Apex Arms Hotel had to be a gag. A hole in the wall like the Arms couldn't possibly

116

have ever deserved so much neon, even when it had been new—about a thousand years ago, judging by the layers of grime that covered the walls of the one-sofa lobby.

The narrow hallways were even worse. Here a thousand years had left an odor unlike anything else in the world. But neither Lou nor Perry paid much attention to it. Their eyes were on the door at the end of the dark corridor.

They paused before the door in the dim light of a forty-watt bulb and drew their guns. Sweeney hadn't exaggerated when he described Harry Brazil as mean. He was more than that. Some street people considered him psycho.

"Ready?" Lou whispered to Perry. Perry nodded. Lou raised his foot and smashed it against the door. The wood holding the latch splintered and the door slammed open. Then Lou, followed by Perry, dashed into the room.

"What the hell!" Harry Brazil, a user himself, with every rib showing, sat up in bed.

"Police!" Perry yelled, his gun held before him in both hands, academy-style, aimed at Harry's head. "Freeze!"

Lou walked around to the other side of the bed where a girl was lying, wide-eyed.

"What the Christ do you want?" Harry demanded. "I ain't done nothing."

"Tell us about it."

"About what?"

"Zakos—Pappas."

"You're out of your skull!" Harry exclaimed. "What have I got to do with weirdos like that?"

"Maybe you sold them some snow?"

"That's a lie, a goddamn lie. Papa woulda wasted me good if I ever done that. And you know it!"

Lou's eyes had grown accustomed to the dim light. He took in every detail, including the woman lying in the bed beside Brazil. She was pale as a slug, skinny, with bleached hair, and like him, nude. Except now she lay under a sheet she had pulled up to her chin. That sheet bothered Lou. It didn't seem right. Hookers like her showed everything.

117

"Get up," Perry was saying to Brazil. "Get dressed."
"You can't take me in. You haven't got anything on me."
"We can book you on a dozen charges right now!"
"Want us to search the room?" Lou added.

Harry got out of bed on spindly legs.

Perry moved to inspect Harry's clothes, lying on a chair, before he allowed Harry to touch them. He found no gun—and that didn't seem right either.

"You guys broke in here without sufficient probable cause," Harry was saying as he pulled on his pants. It.saddened Lou a little, the way punks always knew the laws they could hide behind.

"You gotta have sufficient probable cause," Harry went on. "My lawyer's gonna tell you that."

"You won't need a lawyer," Perry told him, "not if you tell us what we want to know."

"For Chrissake, I already told you. I don't know nothing about Zakos!"

"You've been hiding out, haven't you?"

"You're goddamn right—'cause I knew this was gonna happen—'cause I knew you were gonna bust me any way you could. That's why everybody's hiding out. Nobody wants to get squeezed for nothing."

Lou stepped back into the shadows, but still near the bed. Perry was doing all the talking, holding the gun, and both Harry and the girl were watching him.

"Maybe you'll remember something to tell us when we get you in a cell," Perry was saying, "when you want a fix—"

It was then the girl made her move. She flung the sheet aside and brought her hands up with a gun in them—Harry's, which he probably kept under his pillow at night.

But Lou was ready. He moved forward, yanked the girl's head back by the hair with one hand, and with the other shoved the gun down hard onto her crotch. When it went off, the slug buried itself in the mattress between her knees.

It all happened so fast Perry had trouble assimilating it at first, but then, when he realized just how close he had come

118

to being killed, he was thankful—God, how thankful!—that Lou had been there. But one thought followed another and his gratitude vanished as he found himself resenting the fact that he owed Lou his life. It was a burden, an intolerable burden. Damn him, he thought, why in hell did it have to be an old crud like him? Why?

For the first time he really understood how Tate felt about Baroni. For the first time he was glad Tate had ordered him to screw the old bastard.

They booked Harry Brazil and the girl and spent most of the day questioning them. By noon Lou felt sure neither knew anything about the Zakos killing, but Perry wouldn't give up, not until almost four P.M. Then even he had to admit they had reached another dead end.

"I'm going to call it a day," he told Lou. "What about you?"

Lou stretched. "I was ready to quit hours ago."

"I think I'll go straight home and go right to bed."

Lou nodded. "That's what I'm going to do."

A few minutes later Lou watched Perry drive out of the station's parking lot and then walked over toward his own car. Miller was leaving too.

"Lou, the wife still wants you over for dinner."

Lou shook his head. "No more widows."

Miller laughed. "Then come on, and we'll go over to the Roll-Call"—it was a police bar not far away—"and have a few cold ones. Maybe shoot some pool."

"No thanks," Lou replied, "not today."

Miller was surprised and showed it. "That's a switch," he said. "Usually you're the one who suggests it."

"Got something else in mind for tonight," Lou told him.

Sergeant Perry didn't go home as he said he would. He drove over to Edward Hawley's apartment. It was after six when he knocked on Hawley's door, but he wasn't home yet. Perry decided to wait. He wanted Hawley to sign a complaint of harassment against Baroni.

He sat in his car until almost nine. Then he felt he'd bet-

119

ter go home. If he didn't, he knew his wife would accuse him of playing around again and he just didn't feel up to that, not today.

When he drove away, he wasn't aware that the attractive redhead he had admired the day Evelyn Hawley died had been watching him from her balcony. If he had been, he might have paid her a visit. As it was, Laurie Knight, who remembered seeing him, was left wondering why he'd been there.

Lou had lied, too, when he told Perry he planned to go straight home.

Shortly after five he parked his car in a no-parking zone opposite Hawley's office building. The tall building was already spewing forth hundreds of people, but Lou didn't think he had missed Hawley. Hawley, he was sure, would be one of the last to leave.

He was right. Twenty minutes later, when most of the crowd had rushed away, Hawley appeared, walking slowly.

Lou's intention was simple. He just wanted Hawley to see him there, waiting and watching as usual. He was sure he would, for he was parked next to Hawley's northbound bus stop. But, to his surprise, Hawley didn't cross the street at all. Instead, he turned as he left the building and walked toward the southbound bus stop.

Lou's pulse quickened. Here was a break in the pattern. Here, maybe, was what he was looking for. ,

He watched intently as Hawley reached the bus stop and stood there with the others waiting for the same bus. He looked them over. Maybe one was the meet. They were men, mostly, but there were also several attractive women.

But if Hawley was interested in any one of them, he gave no sign.

A few minutes later the bus arrived and Hawley got on. Lou tried to see with whom he sat, but from where he was, he couldn't even tell whether it was a man or woman.

He gave the bus a chance to move halfway down the block, then pulled away from the curb and followed.

The bus made a great many stops as it made its way south, but Hawley didn't get off at any of them. And the farther the bus went, the more Lou wondered where Hawley could be going.

Then finally Hawley did get off, but only to transfer to another bus, one moving west this time—one marked HARBOR.

But that fact only puzzled Lou more. He was sure Hawley wasn't running. He knew him too well to assume that. When Hawley decided to make his break, he'd prepare. He'd sell his furniture, close his apartment, pack. He didn't even have a suitcase with him now.

When the bus stopped near the waterfront, Hawley got off, and Lou, in his car about a block away, saw him hurry away from it like a man who was running out of time.

Lou quickly parked his car and began to follow on foot, matching his pace with Hawley's, staying a block behind.

After downtown, it seemed strangely quiet here, for there was little traffic, either vehicular or pedestrian. Most of the people who worked in the warehouses that made up the neighborhood had already gone home.

The air, here, was different, too. Fog replaced the smog. The tang of the ocean, still several blocks away, could almost be tasted and the definite smell of the sea was everywhere. It was an odor Lou liked but rarely got a chance to experience.

Hawley left the main street and turned down a deserted side street, one that led in the direction of the water. The street was narrow and the tall warehouses on either side shut out what little sunlight was left in the sky. It seemed suddenly as if it were midnight.

Hawley walked quickly and purposefully for a change. Several times he seemed to disappear into a shadow and momentarily Lou feared he might have lost him, but each time he reappeared, moving as before, toward the ocean, which Lou could see now ahead, sparkling with reflected lights.

Abruptly another figure appeared, a large man walking

121

toward Hawley, carrying a duffle bag, wearing a pea coat.

Quickly Lou stepped into a shadow and waited to see if the stranger and Hawley would stop, but they passed without even a nod.

Lou began walking again, hurrying now, to catch up with Hawley. When the seaman passed by, he didn't give him a second glance.

He was less than a block behind Hawley when the side street ended in a cross street that ran along the waterfront. He stepped into the shadows again to see which way Hawley would turn. But Hawley didn't turn, at first. At the junction of the streets, only a few yards from the ocean he looked about, possibly, Lou thought, for somebody he was scheduled to meet.

Hawley, however, was obviously not waiting for anybody, for, when the silence was suddenly shattered by the sound of a ship's whistle, he began to move along the waterfront in the direction from which it came. Lou left the shadows and followed. Soon it became apparent he was headed for a dock from which tugs were edging a cargo vessel out into the channel. Her lights were bright in the early evening.

The ship's name, the *Island Star*, was plainly visible on her bow.

The entrance to the dock itself was closed, a gate barring the way. But Hawley didn't seem to mind. He stood as close to it as he could, looking after the receding ship.

Lou, standing in the darkness of a doorway, was more puzzled than ever. Hawley wasn't acting like a man who had missed making a meet. He seemed quite content to watch the ship sail. For a long moment Lou wondered if that might be his only purpose in coming.

But then, he reasoned, maybe he was early. Maybe he was just killing time. Maybe he was still waiting for somebody to show.

Abruptly, Hawley wasn't alone. Somebody had stepped out of the shadows and joined him. Lou cursed under his breath when he saw it was a uniformed officer. A hell of a time for a cop to show up!

From where he stood, Lou could only watch the conversation, but the officer undoubtedly asked Hawley what he was doing there. Hawley apparently gave satisfactory answers, for the officer went on his way, leaving Hawley alone again. But the harm had been done, as far as Lou was concerned. If Hawley had been planning something, he'd undoubtedly change those plans now.

But he seemed loath to leave. He stood for a long time, watching the *Island Star* move out into the channel and then toward the harbor's mouth.

Finally he did turn to go. Lou didn't need to wonder where. He made that clear almost at once. Moving casually, he began to retrace his steps, returning the way he had come, obviously going back to the bus stop. Lou had no intention of stopping him. It wouldn't accomplish anything. But there was still one thing he could do.

He stood motionless in the dark doorway until Hawley approached. Then, just as he was about to pass, he struck a match and lit a cigarette, allowing the flame to clearly illuminate his face.

Hawley, startled by the sudden light, turned, recognized Lou, but his face showed neither fear nor surprise. He said nothing. He just kept walking, neither faster nor slower.

Lou stepped out of the doorway and watched him go, two men alone, but separate, on the dark deserted waterfront.

The next few days passed quickly. Most of the time Lou was involved with the Zakos-Pappas case—and the rest he devoted to Edward Hawley.

On his day off, he went to his daughter's for dinner. He didn't want to go. He kept wondering what Hawley might be doing, but he had put her off more than once lately, and he knew if he begged off again, she'd never forgive him. She was like her mother that way. She was a great unforgiver.

123

As usual he had no idea of what to expect when he reached her home. That's why he wasn't very surprised when she answered the door wearing an improvised kimono and an oriental hairdo.

"Honorable father," she said when she saw him, bowing demurely from the waist, "please to enter humble abode."

"Oh, God," Lou said, entering. He didn't get a chance to say anything else as there was the sound of a pot boiling over in the kitchen.

"Hoy ploy!" Toni exclaimed, running from the room. "Make honorable self at home."

Lou walked into the living-room area. A tablecloth, set with dishes, centered by a flower arrangement, sat on the floor, surrounded by cushions. Lou stared at it, a twinge in the small of his back.

"Toni," he called to the kitchen, "what happened to the table?"

Toni called back the obvious. "It's gone for today."

"I know that," Lou yelled back at her. "What I want to know is why."

Toni entered carrying a large bowl of steaming rice. "Because we're having sweet and sour chicken, pork chow mein, and moo goo guy pan."

Lou, looking about for a chair but finding none, said, "I knew if I asked you'd have a good reason." Then, "I don't suppose I could eat at a table if I asked?"

The smile left Toni's face. "No," she said, shaking her head. "That would set you apart. I want you to get used to being one of us."

Lou knew what she was thinking about. "Forget it. I'm not going to live here—ever."

Toni was kneeling on the floor now, placing the bowl of rice on the tablecloth.

"You are going to live here," she said, without looking up. "You have to."

Lou stuck his hands in his pockets. He wanted to smoke, but he didn't want to give his daughter reason to nag. "I don't have to live here at all. I'll find a job."

124

There were two candles standing on the tablecloth, on either side of the flower arrangement. Toni, lighting them, said, "There's more unemployment every day."

"I've still got a couple years—"

"No," Toni said. "Fourteen months—less a week."

"You're keeping track?"

"Of course."

Lou grunted. For some reason he didn't like his daughter keeping score. "I'll find something," he insisted.

Toni rose and walked toward the kitchen. "You shouldn't have to find something. You've got rheumatism, your feet hurt, your blood pressure's too high, you're overweight—"

Lou interrupted. "For God's sake, stop it. You'll have me dead in a minute."

Toni ignored the interruption. Returning from the kitchen with casseroles on a tray, she went right on, "You shouldn't live alone anyway. It's not right."

"It's the way I like it," Lou grunted.

"No, it's not," Toni replied, kneeling once again at the tablecloth. "You're lonely."

"I am not!"

"You are so. You wouldn't be persecuting that poor Mr. Hawley if you weren't."

Lou's mouth fell open. Toni had always had a habit of pulling remarks out of left field, but he had never gotten used to it.

"I'm not persecuting anybody—and what's that got to do with me being lonely, anyway?"

Toni turned and looked up at him. "It gives you something to do with your spare time, doesn't it?"

Lou blew up. "That's not why I'm doing it!"

Dave came down the stairs and joined them. He was wearing a dark-blue silk dressing gown and a fake Oriental mustache. Toni clapped her hands with pleasure when she saw him. Lou grimaced as he bowed toward him.

"Greetings, oh, venerable father-in-law."

"Dave," Toni exclaimed, "you look scrumptious!"

Dave acknowledged the compliment with another bow.

125

"Humble self is forced to contradict honorable wife, but dinner is indeed scrumptious."

"Well, it's ready," Toni replied. "If honorable husband will sit, we'll eat."

Dave turned to Lou and bowed once again. "Please honor humble home by seating self on sumptuous pillow."

Lou raised his eyes to heaven. "My God!" It was both an oath and a supplication.

The pillow was much too close to the floor. Lou had to lower himself toward it in stages, first by kneeling on one knee, then both, and then using his arms to lower himself the rest of the way.

Toni and Dave began passing the steaming casseroles around. They both had chopsticks beside their plates, but Lou was grateful that Toni had placed a fork beside his.

After a moment Lou asked, "Why can't you two be satisfied to be what you are?"

Dave grinned at him, his Fu Manchu mustache slipping a little as he ate. "Ancient ancestral proverb say, 'Why drink beer when imagination makes it sake?'"

Lou grunted. "I wish I had a beer right now." There was only a pot of green tea on the tablecloth. Toni moved it toward him as he gritted his teeth.

Dave turned to his wife. "Venerable father obviously had unfortunate day at honorable Fuzz House."

Toni, a bowl of rice near her mouth, plying chopsticks like a pro, said, "Tell us what's going on at work."

Lou shook his head. "Nothing. Talk about something else."

The sweet and sour pork was excellent. So was the moo goo guy pan. But he knew he'd enjoy it much more if he had a chair.

"All right," Dave said. "Something else. How's your friend Hawley?"

Lou stared at him. "Friend?"

"Well," Dave replied, "you two do see an awful lot of each other."

126

Toni nodded her head empathetically. "Dad, you should think about what you're going to do without him."

"What the hell does that mean?" Lou demanded.

"You're going to miss him when he's in the big house."

"Yeah," Dave agreed. "You won't have anything to do with your nights then."

Lou sighed and shook his head. "You two must be high on something. You must be."

Toni ignored the remark and went on eating. "I guess since you've made your mind up about him, I shouldn't wait too long to invite him to dinner."

"Toni," Lou exclaimed, "no!" He didn't doubt for a minute that she would. "I forbid it—absolutely!"

"But, Dad," Toni protested, "the poor guy's wife has gone. He's alone for the first time in years."

"Toni—I said no and I meant no!"

Dave spoke now, straightening his mustache. "That's too bad. I was looking forward to meeting him. I wanted to ask him what it feels like to be a down payment on a pension."

Lou threw his fork down with a clatter, "I am not using him to boost my pension!"

Dave looked at him challengingly. "Not consciously, maybe."

"He's guilty," Lou stated, "and I'm going to prove it."

"But, Dad," Toni said, "you haven't got any proof yet."

"I have so," Lou retorted. "A motive at least."

Dave was immediately interested. "What kind of motive?"

Lou picked up his fork, wiped the sweet and sour sauce off the handle, and resumed eating. "His wife held out on him—fifty-eight hundred dollars' worth."

Dave said nothing for a moment, thinking. "That's a lot of money to some people."

Toni was silent for a moment too. Then she said, "It doesn't really prove he did it."

It was Dave who answered her. "No, of course not. But it does indicate a possibility—a probability."

127

They argued again before he left. For some reason all his visits ended in an argument. When he reached his own place and sprawled in his easy chair with a beer in his hand, he thought about it. He regretted it—but accepted it. Their worlds were just too far apart. The trouble was, she wouldn't accept it. She wouldn't even consider it. He was her father, her family. She believed he had to fit in. And if not, changes would be made so he would. He winced. The changes, he knew, would be in him.

He got up and went to the refrigerator for a second beer. Well, he thought, there wouldn't be any changes in him. Not if he could help it. He'd make Hawley, get a sergeant's pension, and go on as he was.

That night, before he fell asleep, he made a decision. His plan to unnerve Hawley wasn't working. He didn't seem to mind being watched. So, he'd try something else. The opposite, perhaps. Yes, he decided, that was it. From now on, he wouldn't let Hawley see him. He'd follow him secretly, so he'd think he had given up. That, Lou reasoned, should give him a false sense of security—and that, in turn, might lead him to make his move, his mistake.

8

WHILE Lou was having an uncomfortable dinner with his daughter, Steve Perry was having an uncomfortable one with his wife. She had phoned out for fried chicken and salad and had served it with wine—and silence. She had hardly spoken to Steve for days. She had grown tired of his talk of imminent promotion that never seemed to happen. She wanted results. The only speech she had directed at her husband during the entire meal was a brief report of a girlfriend's husband who had just been made a vice-president.

Perry had left the meal unfinished and driven directly over to Hawley's apartment. During the drive he had, with effort, put his rage aside and had asked himself how best to handle the coming interview. He decided, after considering a cold authoritarian approach and even a strong-arm tactic, that casual good fellowship would be the best way. That's why a short time later, when Edward Hawley answered his door, Perry was standing there, smiling warmly.

"Mr. Hawley, I hope I'm not disturbing you." His voice dripped sincerity.

Hawley was plainly confused. "No, no, you're not." He was also puzzled. He stood at the open door, waiting, forcing Perry to go on.

"You remember me, don't you? I'm Sergeant Steve Perry. I was in charge of the investigation of your wife's accident."

Hawley nodded. He did remember Perry but still he stood there. He wasn't used to callers.

"I wonder if I might talk to you for a minute."

"Of course," Hawley replied, backing away from the door, allowing Perry to enter.

"Is something wrong?" Hawley asked once the door was closed.

"No, no," Perry answered effusively. "Nothing's wrong at all, and"—he broadened his smile—"I'm here to make sure everything stays that way."

"What do you mean, stays that way?"

Perry found it awkward standing. He pointed to a chair. "May I?"

Hawley remembered his manners. "Yes—please. I should have suggested it. I'm sorry."

Perry waved away his concern. "Forget it." He chuckled a little. "It's one of the drawbacks of being a policeman. People are never sure how to act when we're around."

Hawley nodded and sat down on the edge of the sofa. They made a strange picture—Hawley, more than middleaged, hair thinning, his face marked by years of acceptance, and Perry, tall, athletic, sharply dressed, self-confidence portrayed in every feature.

"First of all," Perry began, "I want to extend my condolences. That's really why I'm here." His voice was heavy with sympathy. "I had so many things on my mind at the time of the investigation—well, you can understand how I could neglect saying what I felt."

Hawley nodded. "It's all right." Then he waited for Perry to say more. Perry allowed himself a slight frown. It wasn't going the way he had hoped it would. He had expected Hawley to be annoyed, angry, about Baroni's unauthorized investigation. He tried a different tack.

"How are you getting along?"

"All right."

"No problems?"

Hawley seemed to think it over. "No—I guess not."

It still wasn't the answer Perry wanted. "Nobody's bothering you?"

130

"No," Hawley answered, puzzled. If he understood what Perry was getting at, he didn't show it.

"You know," Perry said, "that your case—the investigation of your wife's death—is closed?"

Hawley nodded.

Perry waited for him to say more. When he didn't, Perry decided he had to be more direct.

"Sometimes, you know, a policeman can become—well—overzealous. When that happens he can harass, unduly, an innocent person."

"Yes," Hawley replied gravely, "I can see how that could happen."

Perry waited for him to elaborate but he didn't. Perry lost patience.

"It's one of the reasons I'm here. To be honest, we suspect such a detective is harassing you."

Hawley seemed to study Perry for a moment. "You're talking about Detective Baroni, aren't you?"

"That's right," Perry replied.

"You want to know if he's harassing me?"

"Exactly," Perry said, smiling again. "And if he is, I'll see to it that he's stopped."

Hawley now seemed troubled. He got up before he spoke, moved away, then returned to face Perry. "I don't understand. Baroni's your partner, isn't he?"

The question caught Perry off base. He didn't want to seem disloyal to a partner, yet he knew he was being just that. "Yes," he said, trying to ease out. "As a matter of fact, he is. That's why I'm investigating him myself—"

Hawley interrupted. "You mean, you're really investigating your own partner?"

Perry's confusion was total. This wasn't the attitude he had expected from Hawley. "If he's harassing you," he said lamely, "it's my duty to do something about it."

"Then you don't have to worry," Hawley said. "He's not harassing me at all."

Perry was left speechless. "He's not?"

131

"That's right. He's not."

"Are you saying he hasn't been here—or following you?"

"He hasn't harassed me."

Perry lost his temper. "I don't believe it. You're lying!" He was standing now, face to face with Hawley.

"If you want to think that, all right—"

"I'll tell you what I want," Perry exclaimed. "I want you to sign a complaint against Baroni—something I can take to my lieutenant!"

"No."

"For God's sake, why?"

Hawley answered calmly. "I told you. He's not harassing me."

"I don't believe you. Tell me why!"

Hawley shrugged. "I don't want to get him into any trouble," he said finally, turning away. "I don't want to get anybody into trouble."

When Perry left, his mood was as foul as it had ever been. He didn't have anything for Tate. He didn't have anything for his wife. He still had both of them on his back—and why? Because that puky little bastard upstairs didn't want to get Baroni into trouble! It was nauseating.

He stood outside Hawley's building for a few minutes wondering what he could do next. Since Hawley wouldn't sign a complaint, he'd have to think of some other way of nailing Baroni. Maybe if he drove over to Baroni's place and looked around. . . . It was worth a try. Anything was. He didn't want to go home yet. He couldn't take any more of his wife's bitching tonight.

He was getting into his car when his eye caught the movement of attractive thighs across the street. It was a redhead in a short skirt, walking toward the entrance of the apartment building opposite—the girl he had seen the day Evelyn Hawley had died. Maybe, he thought, she's seen Baroni hanging around and maybe if he could charm her enough, she'd be willing to testify to it.

Anyway, he concluded, it wouldn't hurt to talk to her. In

fact, he expected it could be quite pleasant. He hurried across the road and entered the lobby of the apartment building where she was waiting for the elevator.

Laurie Knight liked the looks of the tall, youngish sergeant of detectives. She liked his smile and the way he wore his clothes. She didn't like his manner at all. Most of it didn't ring true. But, of course, she had expected that. She had known who he was even before he introduced himself. Lou Baroni had mentioned him more than once—never flatteringly. As they rode the elevator up to her floor, she found herself wondering how she should react to such a man if she were ever called on to play such a part. Perhaps, she thought, she should be coy.

Once in her apartment, he sat on the sofa and she stood looking down at him. "How about a drink?" she asked. It seemed the required gambit.

His smile broadened. "Whatever you've got. I've had a long, hard day."

All she had was vodka. She kept it in a cupboard above the sink in her kitchen alcove. And she knew when she reached for it that he was looking at her legs, the swell of her breasts. She was satisfied. He was reacting according to cliché.

Perry's thoughts weren't nearly so analytical. She was turning him on. The surge of virility made him feel good—as it always did. He felt more sure of himself, more confident. The hell with his wife. The hell with Tate.

Laurie poured vodka and orange juice into two glasses. He watched her walk toward him. He liked the way she moved. He wondered what she'd be like nude, thrashing around under him.

"You said you wanted to ask me some questions," Laurie reminded him. The trend of his thoughts was only too obvious. She often wondered if men really thought women were always pleased by their hardly hidden leers.

Perry decided he should appear businesslike, at least for

133

a little while. "Miss Knight—Laurie—you remember the 'tragedy'"—he used the word deliberately, wanting her to feel he was moved by it—"that happened across the street? The woman who fell to her death?"

Laurie nodded. She sat down on her ottoman facing Perry, her knees pressed together.

"Our investigation revealed the death was the result of an accident."

"That's what I heard," Laurie said. "That's why I'm wondering why you're here." She was pleased with the remark. If she were playing a role, it would establish the perception and intelligence of the character she portrayed.

"To tell the truth," Perry explained, "I'm here because one of our detectives won't accept that fact."

Laurie raised her eyebrows.

"He believes it was premeditated. Murder."

Laurie decided to appear shocked. "But if the case is closed, if he keeps on, isn't that against the law?"

Perry nodded, pleased. She was reacting according to plan. "Yes, it is most definitely against the law. It's harassment, malicious persecution. And that's exactly why I'm here." He went on, making an effort to appear very sympathetic. "I believe poor Mr. Hawley has suffered enough."

Laurie nodded, her expression one of concern. "Oh, I agree. But if you know who this man is—this detective who's persecuting Mr. Hawley—why don't you stop him?",

Perry leaned toward her and spoke earnestly. "We need proof. We need someone who can point him out and say, 'He's the one I saw watching Mr. Hawley's apartment.'"

"Oh," Laurie said sadly, nothing in her manner betraying the fact that she knew perfectly well he was talking about Baroni, "but I haven't seen anything like that at all."

Her answer brought Perry to a full stop. Damn, he thought, she must have seen *something*. He got up and went to her balcony. "You could have seen him easily from here. Maybe you just don't remember." He turned back to her.

"No," she said, still sitting, "I'm sure I'd remember." She

was enjoying her role. She decided to embellish it. "Maybe if you described him—"

"Heavy—thinning hair—some gray—five eleven—looks fifty, but he's probably more—sloppy—"

"No," Laurie said, her expression revealing how hard she was trying to remember, "no, I've never seen anybody like that."

Perry moved back to her and looked down into her up-turned face. "Think again. Try. Sometimes it comes back."

Laurie shook her head prettily. "No. I'm sorry. I wish I could help—but I really haven't seen him."

The blouse she wore was open at the throat. She knew he could see her cleavage. She let him look.

"What about Mr. Hawley? Maybe you should ask him."

"I have," Perry replied. "He hasn't seen anything either." The hell with it, he thought. He wasn't interested anymore anyway. He was interested in her. He reached down, took her hands and pulled her to her feet.

"Maybe it'll come to you later," he said softly.

"Maybe it will," she replied.

Looking deeply into her eyes, he said, "Right now, let's just think about us. Right now, we're all that really matters."

It was such a corny line, she had to fight to keep from smiling. "All right," she said, demurely.

She allowed him to kiss her. Afterward, while he was still holding her, she asked, "What will you do now—I mean—to prove this detective is harassing Mr. Hawley?"

"Follow him," Perry replied, his voice husky. "Follow him until I make him."

Laurie was silent for a moment, then she asked, "What will happen to him—when you get your proof, I mean?"

"He'll be kicked out of the department without a cent." Then he added, venomously, "He's too old anyway. He's in the way."

Laurie sighed deeply. "That seems so cruel."

Perry decided he'd better appear more sympathetic. "It

135

is. But it can't be helped. He's been warned, again and again." Then he added, to impress her, as his hands moved over her body, "Anyway, we can't allow policemen to molest members of the public, can we?"

"No," she said, still leaning against him. "No, we can't."

She got rid of him a few minutes later by telling him she had just begun her period.

After he left, she curled up on the sofa and dialed Baroni's number. It wasn't really late, but Lou was already in bed. The phone rang ten times before she heard his sleepy hello.

"I thought you'd like to know I just had a visitor," she told him. "A detective named Perry."

His response was immediate and she was pleased by the way his voice was suddenly wide-awake.

"What did he want?"

"Besides me, he's trying to prove you're harassing Hawley. He was over there—and then he came here."

"Did he get anything?" Lou's voice asked.

"Not from me," Laurie answered, "and not from Hawley either. He said so."

There was silence. Laurie knew what Lou was wondering. Why hadn't Hawley told Perry that Lou had followed him?

Finally, Laurie said, "He said he's going to follow you from now on."

"Follow me?"

"'Make you' was the way he put it."

Lou cursed loud and long. Laurie had never heard him curse before. He probably wouldn't have, in her presence, she thought. He was old-fashioned.

"I just thought you'd like to know."

"I do. Thanks. You're a big help."

When she hung up she was quite pleased with herself. She didn't know why she was siding with Baroni, but it "felt" right. Certainly a whole lot more right than helping Perry. But what about Hawley? She walked out onto her balcony. The lights in Hawley's living room were still on. Probably watching the late show. She still couldn't believe he was a murderer. She found it even more difficult now. If he were, he would have jumped at the chance to get Baroni off his back—wouldn't he?

Lying in bed, Lou pondered the same problem. Why hadn't Hawley told Perry he had followed him?

He didn't go back to sleep until he decided Hawley had simply chosen what he considered the lesser of two evils: He considered Lou less of a threat to his freedom than he did an involvement with the department in the form of a signed complaint against an officer. It wasn't very flattering, but it made sense . . . in a way.

The next morning Lou got up early and before going to work drove over to the east side and rousted a bookie from bed.

"Lou, for Christ's sake—it's only six thirty. You outa your gawdamn mind?"

Clayton Hoyle was a small, wizened player who made a buck now and then running one of the least-successful handbooks in town. Lou, and most of the other cops who knew him, left him alone because he didn't do much harm, and the other bookies tolerated him because he never took anything bigger than a two-dollar bet.

He lived in a building that had been condemned long before but never torn down. The fact that he might be ousted anytime didn't bother him because he only owned a cot and a candle anyway. The street was his real home, and that's where he spent all his time, taking bets or blowing his capital on fat hookers.

"I want you to do something for me," Lou told him. "I want you to make a phone call."

The reason Lou had selected him was his reliability. He could be counted on. Everybody knew it. Pimps and prostitutes and pushers and all the other street people had a habit

137

of believing the word when it came from him. "According to Hoyle" was authentication enough.

"Lou—you know I'm no snitch," Hoyle said, sitting on the edge of the cot. He slept in his underwear.

"I'm not asking for a squeal," Lou told him.

"What then?" He was a suspicious little man, weighing the odds in everything.

"You know Steve Perry?"

"A sergeant—smartass—college type?"

"That's him."

"He's never been square with anybody."

Lou nodded. "I want you to phone him around four or five. I want you to tell him you're a snitch. I want you to make it sound like you got something on the Zakos killing, and you got it for him alone."

"You're kidding!"

"Like hell I am."

"He won't believe me."

"He's so hungry, he'll believe anything."

"He'll want to know my name."

"Fake one."

"He'll work me over when we meet."

"You won't be there."

Hoyle studied Lou for a moment with his shrewd little eyes. "You just want him out of the way for a while?"

"That's it."

"Where do I set up the meet?"

"There's a gas station at the foot of the freeway off-ramp that leads to Hellenic-West Village—"

"Jesus—Papa Pappas' place!"

"It'll make the squeal sound real."

"But Pappas . . . Lou, don't do this to me!"

"You'll be miles away."

Hoyle thought about it for a while. "It won't give you much time. He won't hang around once he gets there."

"He will. You're going to tell him you'll have to wait for a

138

break to get to him. Make it a strong maybe—sometime between six and midnight. Maybe tonight. Maybe tomorrow night. Maybe the night after."

"He'll never buy it."

"He will. He's starving. And if you come on big—talk about papers, records, ledgers—he'll buy."

Hoyle considered it. "What's my reason?"

Lou had it worked out. "Zakos was wasted. You're afraid you're next. You want to buy police protection."

"He'll really go for it?"

"All the way."

Hoyle was silent, thinking, hesitating. Lou wondered if he need remind him of the many times he had looked the other way so the little man could make the price of an overweight prostitute. He didn't need to.

"Okay, Lou. Around five. You got my word."

Both Lou and Perry were in the squad room when the call came in at four forty-five. Lou continued to peck away at his typewriter but he glanced at Perry as often as he dared. He couldn't hear what he was saying, but from the look that gradually came to his face, it was obvious that Perry had taken the bait.

When Perry put the phone down, his mind was racing. He had planned on following Baroni, but the hell with that now. And the hell with Hawley and Tate, too. This was the break he'd always been waiting for. The big payoff. The elevator to the top. He didn't know who his informant was—he had never heard of the man—but if he really did have the documents he said he had, then he, Perry, had it made! He could already see himself walking into the chief's office, not Tate's. He could hear himself explaining how he had, single-handed and at great personal risk, gathered all the evidence necessary to bring down the whole Pappas empire. And he could feel the chief's pat on the back, hear the words that would make him a lieutenant.

139

At five he called his wife and told her he'd be working late and, for once, he didn't care when she began to bitch about other women. He simply hung up on her.

At eight Lou was standing in the shadows across the street from Hawley's apartment building, looking up at his lighted living-room window, hoping he would make his move soon. With Perry on Lou's back, time was running out.

The traffic was light, but a number of people walked by. None stopped, however, at Hawley's building.

Abruptly the light in Hawley's window went out. He's either going to bed or going out, Lou thought. He opted for the latter. Hawley never went to bed so early. Besides, a lot of time had passed since Evelyn Hawley's funeral. If Hawley did have a mistress who was staying out of sight, he must want her real bad by now.

A few minutes passed and then the door of the apartment building opened and Hawley came out. He didn't seem in a hurry, but he did seem more dressed up than usual.

Lou watched him start walking south toward the thoroughfare. Then he followed, staying in the shadows as much as possible. This time he didn't want Hawley to know he was being tailed.

A number of young couples walking along the street passed Hawley—he was the only one alone. Even when he reached the main street and turned east along it, he was still the only single pedestrian. If he intended to meet somebody, that person, presumably by herself, was nowhere in sight. It didn't occur to Lou that Hawley really wasn't the only person who was alone. He was alone, too.

The neighborhood changed as Hawley walked. The stores and offices gave way to a number of small bars and several dance halls. He hesitated in front of these and then stopped. Lou couldn't tell if he had planned to do so or if it had just been an impulse.

Lou stayed where he was. He had crossed the street and

140

now stood on the south side. For a moment he felt Hawley had reached his rendezvous. His meet, he figured, was probably scheduled right there, outside the dance hall. But Hawley surprised him. He turned and entered the place.

Lou crossed the street quickly and followed Hawley inside, where he lost sight of him completely. The place was so crowded, the flashing psychedelic lights so harsh, he couldn't make out anything at first. In a moment he was wedged into a corner by the crowd just inside the entrance and deafened by the hard rock that blared from the loudspeakers.

It was the type of place Lou disliked intensely. It was too noisy, too smoke-filled, too dark. As his eyes became accustomed to the gloom and flashing lights, he saw what he had seen in so many other places like it: tiny tables around which people were packed; drinks being sold at exorbitant prices by rude waiters; a small, overcrowded dance floor filled with the squirming bodies of young girls who delighted not so much in the movement of their bodies but in their display. But what really disgusted him were the older men who sat watching the vibrating bottoms under their tiny skirts or tight pants.

For a moment he wondered if Ed Hawley could be that kind of man, if that's why he had come to this place—but then he spotted him. He had been put at one of the tiny tables already occupied by three young girls who had obviously faked their ID cards. But instead of being pleased by the miniskirts and tight sweaters, he seemed acutely uncomfortable, having trouble finding a place where his eyes could look that wouldn't embarrass him. The girls were talking among themselves, ignoring him. To them, Lou saw, he was just another old creep.

Lou stayed where he was, watching. This place was a likely place for a meet. Not one of the underaged girls, of course, but one of the older women.

But it wasn't a woman who approached the table. It was two young men—boys with unkempt hair and dirty sweat-

141

shirts. They appeared abruptly and began arguing angrily with the girls. Hawley looked more uncomfortable than ever.

One of the girls snarled at one of the boys, who raised his hand as if to strike her. The girl—instinctively, Lou presumed—moved closer to Hawley, resting her hand on his arm. The boy glared at Hawley and shouted a challenge at him.

Without thinking, Lou immediately began to force his way forward to Hawley's side, but was blocked by a dozen tables and the dense crowd.

Hawley, by this time, had risen to his feet and was trying to reason with the boy, but it wasn't working. The boy clenched his fist, and Lou, still trying to shove his way to Hawley's side, felt it was about all over. It was—but not as he expected. Instead of seeing Hawley pummeled, he saw a big man, obviously the bouncer, appear, wrap a beefy arm around the boy's neck, and drag him away.

Relieved, Lou relaxed and allowed the crowd to edge him back against the wall.

Hawley, he saw, sat down again, still disturbed. The girls, however, began talking and laughing among themselves again as if nothing had happened. Then, a few minutes later, three more boys came over and the girls got up to dance with them, leaving Hawley alone at the table. If they stopped to thank him in any way, Lou didn't see it.

Standing there, watching Hawley squirm uncomfortably, Lou found himself feeling sorry for the man. It must be hell, he thought, to be so lonely you'd come to a place like this. But then he reminded himself that Hawley was there for another reason. He had to be.

But if Hawley was there to meet the woman for whom he had killed his wife, she didn't show up—and he didn't wait for her very long. Impulsively, without even waiting for the drink he had ordered, he got up and fought his way through the crowd. He passed within a few feet of Lou but didn't see him in his eagerness to get outside into the relatively fresh night air.

142

Lou waited for a moment and then left too. The air outside was smog-laden, but it was infinitely quieter than it had been inside. Lou was grateful to Hawley for leaving.

He looked around for him and saw him moving slowly along as before, his shoulders stooped a little more now, perhaps, apparently still without any planned destination. But Lou wouldn't let himself accept that. He had to have a destination.

Lou followed at a safe distance. People passed, in pairs or groups, talking, laughing. Only Hawley and Lou walked silently, alone.

Hawley finally paused in front of a neon-bright cocktail lounge. Lou stopped a few doors away and stood in a shadow. This was more like it, he thought. A man would meet a mistress in a place like that. But Hawley didn't enter right away. For a time he seemed to be indecisive. Then the doors of the lounge opened and a man and woman came out. The man was Hawley's age, not much more impressive. The woman was a young swinger, dressed to sell, and Hawley's eyes followed her hungrily as she and her companion crossed to a parked car. After that Hawley's mind seemed made up. He turned and entered the lounge.

Lou gave him a few minutes and then followed. The light inside was dim but restful. No flashing psychedelics here, and the recorded music was soft, not ear-splitting. And there were plenty of empty tables.

But Lou, standing near the door, saw that Hawley hadn't chosen a table. He had gone to the bar, where he now sat beside two unescorted young ladies. Selecting a table in a corner, Lou sat down and watched.

He wondered for a moment if the woman next to Hawley—a blonde with impossibly long eyelashes—could be the reason he had murdered his wife. But if she was, she was playing it very cool, ignoring Hawley completely.

The bartender paused before Hawley and he ordered a drink. When the bartender brought it, Lou saw it was a single. He hadn't ordered anything for the girl.

The girls continued to talk to each other, obviously

143

bored. Lou had just about decided they were a false alarm when one of them, the girl who sat farthest from Hawley, slid off her stool and walked toward the ladies' room. Lou sat up, wondering what would happen now that Hawley and the other girl were alone.

At first nothing happened, except a waitress came over to Lou, and Lou ordered a drink. Even so, he never took his eyes off Hawley, who was staring down at the bar in front of him, only occasionally casting a furtive glance at the girl beside him. If it was an act, Lou thought, it was a damn good one. He really did look like a middle-aged man trying to work up enough nerve to pick up a girl.

The girl took out a cigarette and then began to look through her purse for a light. Hawley seized the opportunity and picked up a book of matches from the bar and turned to the girl with them. Lou saw the girl turn her head, waiting for him to light her cigarette—which he did, eagerly.

When the cigarette was lit, Hawley pressed his advantage. Smiling broadly, he said something to the girl who, a bored expression still on her face, nodded. Lou, interested, thought that perhaps this was the one he had come to meet after all. But nothing much happened. Hawley simply signaled the bartender and ordered another drink for the girl.

What followed, Lou thought, was sad. Hawley tried hard to be charming, but he smiled too much, gesticulated too much, talked too much. If the girl was interested at all, she hardly showed it. At one point he raised his glass to her in a toast, but when she raised hers, it was only to knock back effortlessly all it contained.

Lou slouched in his chair. He knew what was coming and for some reason he didn't want to examine, he found himself feeling sorry for Hawley.

The other girl came back and the one sitting beside Hawley slid off her stool and walked away with her, leaving him alone at the bar.

The bartender came over and placed a check before Hawley. He took his wallet out and paid for the girl's drink.

144

Lou shook his head. Hawley was so green it was pitiful. Yet, he reminded himself, he had come in here. Why? Just because he was lonely? No. He wouldn't accept that possibility. There had to be another reason. Maybe, if he hadn't come to make a meet, he had come to look for somebody. Yes, he decided, that was always possible—somebody who might frequent a hard-rock dance hall or a cocktail lounge.

Yet, when Hawley left the bar and returned to his apartment without talking to anybody, Lou felt a sense of relief mixed with a disappointment he wouldn't acknowledge.

9

"BARONI! His name is Lou Baroni!"

It was Papa Pappas speaking. Actually, he was shouting. Even so, his son, who had been summoned peremptorily, wasn't listening.

They were on the patio of Papa's palatial home in Hellenic-West Village the following day, having lunch. Nicky was having lunch. Papa wasn't interested in food just then.

It was a beautiful day. The downtown smog didn't reach that far west yet and so the sun shone in a perfectly clear blue sky that revealed the surrounding mountains.

Nicky, dressed in yellow, his skin a golden tan, suited the weather, but his father did not. There wasn't anything about the old man's mood that could be said to be sunny.

Leisurely sipping coffee, Nicky observed, "Papa, you're upset about nothing."

"Nothing? Weeks have gone by since you killed that Zakos boy and still the case is number one with the police!"

Nicky smirked. "That's why I'm not worried. If they were going to get anything, they would have by now."

Papa, standing now, his hands on the table, leaned forward to yell at his son. "You keep ignoring Baroni! You keep forgetting the Negro!"

Nicky shrugged elegantly, nibbling at a slice of cinnamon toast. "I've told you what I think should be done."

"Tell me again."

Nicky spoke slowly as though to a child. "There's only one man who knows I killed Spiro—Wally Blue. There's

146

only one man Wally would tell—Baroni. Therefore, we should have them both killed."

"No," Papa exclaimed. "Stop talking like a Sicilian! The days of killing are over!"

"Papa," Nicky said, smiling, "you asked me."

Later, after he had watched his son drive away in his powder-blue sports car, Papa returned to his patio and sat there in a grim mood. Demetri, silent as usual, stood nearby.

"Demetri," Papa said after a long time, "must we really put out more contracts?"

"Nicky is your only son. He must be protected."

Papa sighed and let his eyes roam over the sparkling water of his swimming pool, the marble patio, the lawns and hedges, and the lake beyond. It was all so beautiful, so peaceful, so much the way he wanted it now that he was old that he put off, once again, what he felt to be inevitable.

"We will wait," he said. "We will watch and wait. And if they come closer"—he meant the police, he meant Baroni—"we will do what must be done."

Nicky Pappas wasn't quite so patient. When he returned to his all-white apartment, he made a long-distance call to a professional assassin with a fine reputation, a man who, he had determined, wouldn't be concerned with his father's edicts. Unfortunately the man had a prior commitment, but once it was done, he would be pleased to entrain to California. He wouldn't fly. He was afraid of airplanes.

Something else almost as significant also occurred that evening. Demetri, driving home from an errand, noticed Steve Perry sitting in his parked car near the entrance of Hellenic-West Village.

The sun failed to shine at all the following morning, and the clouds grew more ominous as the day progressed—a fairly unusual event in Southern California.

By noon the rain began. A slight drizzle at first, it seemed to gather strength steadily. By the time Lou Baroni pulled

147

his car to the curb near Ed Hawley's bus stop it was coming down heavily and relentlessly.

The bus was late, but Lou wasn't surprised. Traffic was barely crawling along. With so little rain, California motorists weren't skilled in coping with it. And what made matters worse, the storm sewers on many streets weren't designed to handle so much water. All over the city intersections were flooded; underpasses were impassable. When Hawley's bus did arrive, it was almost a half hour late.

Sitting dry and comfortable inside his car, Lou watched Hawley run from the bus and attempt to seek shelter under the eaves of a building. But, of course, there was no real shelter there. Gusts of wind blew the falling rain in all directions. Within moments Hawley was soaked. Lou guessed what he would do. Wet already, he might as well accept it and go home. He turned up his collar and began to walk along the street, hurrying but not running. Lou pulled out into the slow-moving flow of traffic and followed.

When Hawley turned the corner onto Barstow, he went into one of the small shops that occupied the intersection—a butcher shop. Lou pulled over to the curb again and watched him inside the store, standing at the counter, dripping wet, waiting his turn. When it came he indicated something inside a showcase and a few moments later he was paying for his purchase.

The rain refused to abate. It grew heavier. Lou, grateful to be dry, drove slowly along behind Hawley, watching him slosh through the puddles that formed on the sidewalk.

A gust of wind came up and blew a sheet of water against him, forcing him to turn his back to it for a moment before walking on. Lou shook his head. Hawley still had several long blocks to go.

Without thinking, acting on impulse, Lou pressed on the gas, moved ahead, and pulled to the curb beside Hawley. Hawley turned his head and saw Lou. He wasn't surprised.

Lou rolled down the window and shouted out to him, "Come on, get in—we're both going the same way."

148

Hawley didn't hesitate. He got in the car and a moment later Lou was driving along Barstow again.

Hawley, wiping his face with a Kleenex said, "Thanks."

Lou shrugged. "Forget it."

The traffic was backed up. The cars were barely creeping along.

"Hell of a day," Hawley said.

"Yeah," Lou replied.

"You ought to be glad you're not on a motorcycle."

They were silent for a moment, the rain on the car's roof the loudest sound. Then Hawley said, "I went for a walk last night. I didn't see you."

Lou grunted. "I had to work last night."

"Oh," Hawley answered. "I thought it had to be something like that."

A few minutes later Lou parked in front of Hawley's apartment building. "Here you are."

"Looks like this rain is going to last all night."

Lou nodded. "Looks that way."

"Well, thanks for the ride."

"Sure," Lou said.

Hawley paused as he opened the door, as if to say something, but didn't. Then he dashed for the shelter of the building's entrance.

Lou turned his eyes to the rearview mirror, looking for a break in the traffic. None was in sight. He glanced back to the entrance of the apartment. Hawley was still standing there, his butcher's package in his hand, watching him. Suddenly he ran back to the car and opened the door.

"Look," he said, "if you're going to stay out here watching my windows all night, you might as well come in—I bought a couple of steaks."

Lou shrugged. It seemed like a sincere invitation. What the hell, he thought. A moment later, he too ran through the rain to the shelter of Hawley's apartment building.

Hawley hadn't changed the apartment much at all. It

149

looked just about as Lou remembered it, except, of course, the last time he'd been there, a vacuum cleaner had sat on the floor, its hose near the window.

Hawley hung his dripping coat over the bathtub and took Lou's jacket and hung it in the closet. Then he went into the kitchen and placed the steaks in the stove's broiler.

"How do you like your meat?" he asked.

Lou, standing in the kitchen doorway replied, "Medium rare." Then, as Hawley returned to the living room, "Want me to do anything?"

"You can set the table," Hawley said, "while I get out of these wet clothes." His pants were so wet they clung to his legs.

"Where are the dishes?" Lou asked.

"Over the sink," Hawley replied, going to the bedroom.

Lou went into the kitchen and opened the cupboards. He took plates and placed them on the table of the breakfast nook. Then he dropped a handful of silverware onto the middle of the table. He took two beers from the refrigerator and placed them beside the plates. The table was set.

He was about to go back into the living room when he wondered about something. He returned to the refrigerator and opened the freezer section. As he had expected, it didn't contain a single frozen TV dinner.

In the living room he could hear Hawley sneezing and coughing. Then the bedroom door opened and Hawley called out, "There's bourbon on the bureau if you want any."

"Thanks," Lou called back gratefully. "You sound like you need some."

"I guess so," Hawley called back. "Two fingers."

There were glasses beside the bottle, the label of which Lou looked at with approval, and he poured them each three fingers. Then, just as he was about to drink his, he noticed something else on the bureau—a scrapbook with one word written on the cover: "Talua."

150

"What's a Talua?" he called out

Hawley started to reply, but began coughing. When he could, he called back, "It's an island in the South Pacific."

Lou opened the scrapbook. Inside were a number of newspaper clippings about the island, photographs cut from magazines, a section copied from an encyclopedia. He took it and his drink to the sofa where he intended to get comfortable and read it, but as he sat down his eye caught some travel folders on the end table. Glancing at them, he saw they were entitled "South Pacific Hideaways"— "Escape to Paradise"—"Little Known Islands of the South Pacific." There were also several sailing schedules.

Hawley, wearing dry pants, shirt, and slippers came back into the living room and crossed to the bureau for his drink. He sneezed twice before he got there.

"I think I've caught a cold."

Lou indicated the travel folders. "Planning a trip?"

Hawley nodded solemnly. "Been planning it for years."

Lou grinned wryly. "You mean you want to sail off into the sunset to some South Sea paradise?"

"That's the idea."

Lou looked up at him. "You serious?"

Hawley drained his glass and poured himself another. He seemed to shiver, as though still chilled by the rain. "It sounds corny, but it's possible. I know, I've checked."

Lou thought of the money Evelyn Hawley had put in their joint account—the only motive for murder he had been able to uncover. "You'd need a lot of money to make such a trip, wouldn't you?"

"A whole lot," Hawley replied, staring into his glass, swirling the amber liquid around. "Ever since Evelyn died, I've been trying to think of a way to save it." Then he added, "Maybe if I give this place up, live in a cheap room somewhere—"

Lou interrupted him impulsively. "No. You can't live like that. A man needs more than a bed and a closet." It

151

was a subject Lou thought about a lot. Hawley nodded. "You're right," he said. "A man does need more—at our age, anyway."

Then he coughed again. "There's a flu going around. Maybe I've caught it."

They were silent for a moment, Hawley standing, leaning against the bureau, Lou sprawling on the sofa, their drinks in their hands.

Lou, thinking about apartments, looked around Hawley's. He saw now there really had been some changes made since Evelyn Hawley had died. The bric-a-brac was gone. So were the doilies and the old towel on the floor by the front door on which you were supposed to wipe your feet. And now there were magazines scattered here and there and a newspaper or two. It wasn't as neat as it had been, but it looked more lived-in, more comfortable.

"It's a nice place here," Lou said finally.

Hawley nodded. "Evelyn took good care of it." Then, looking directly at Lou he asked, "What makes you think I killed her?"

Lou shrugged. "Just a feeling I've got."

Hawley seemed to nod a little, as if confirming a conclusion of his own. "Feelings don't count in court. Your Sergeant Perry told me that."

"He's right," Lou said. "They don't count—to anybody but me."

"I could report you for following me."

Lou nodded. "Why haven't you?"

This time it was Hawley who shrugged—a gesture very similar to Lou's. "I don't like making trouble for people." Then, finishing his drink, he turned toward the kitchen. "I'd better turn those steaks."

Lou followed him into the kitchen and leaned against the doorjamb while Hawley opened the oven. Smoke billowed out.

"Evelyn never broiled steaks. Said it smoked up the apartment too much."

152

"Guess she wasn't much interested in South Sea islands."

Hawley turned to look at Lou before answering. "She was the one who found Talua. That was twenty-five years ago. Before we were married. It wasn't on any of the maps then. It still isn't on many, for that matter. She found a reference to it in a book somewhere and followed it up." He moved the steaks about a bit under the broiler, then closed the oven.

"It was her dream to begin with, but she gave it up. In the end she hated it."

He went to the table and opened his beer. "She gave up many things I used to admire."

The way he said it prompted Lou to say, "You sound like you miss her."

Hawley nodded, and without looking at Lou, replied, "You're right. I do. A lot. I've been missing her a lot for at least the last fifteen years."

As Papa Pappas had told his son, interest in the Zakos murder refused to wane. The heir of an oil magnate, his death intrigued millions. His way of life, his homosexuality, added spice to the newspaper stories. And each edition increased the pressure on the police department to find his killer.

Of course, that pressure descended through the chain of command until it reached Lieutenant Tate, who was rapidly running out of excuses to explain his failure.

He, naturally, increased the pressure on his men. When Lou Baroni arrived at work the following morning, he found the place a flurry of activity. Tate had ordered every man to follow up every crank phone call, every rumor, every possibility, no matter how unlikely they seemed.

When he walked into the squad room, he found Segel, the young detective who had attempted to talk back to Tate, going through a filing cabinet near the door.

"Lou," he said, "would you believe it? I've got to reinter-

153

view, for the third time, everybody who lives in a four-block radius of Zakos."

"Tate's idea?"

"You got it."

Lou shook his head. Tate had been grasping at straws for days.

He found a note on his own desk. *Report to Lt. Tate at once.* Lou crumpled it up into a ball and dropped it into his wastebasket, wondering what asinine assignment Tate had for him today.

When he went back to the door Segel looked up from his work. "Did you see the note on your desk?"

Lou nodded.

"Five gets you ten he's going to tell you to reinterview the people he told me to reinterview."

"No bet," Lou said. "I'd probably lose." Then he went out into the corridor—and almost bumped into Wally Blue, in handcuffs, being escorted along the hall by Miller.

"Lou, baby! How's it going, man?"

"Just like Epsom salts, Wally," Lou answered, then he turned to Miller. "What's going down?"

Miller shrugged and sighed. "Tate wants to talk to him again—the same old questions."

Wally laughed. "Let him ask. I ain't gonna tell that ass-hole nuthin' 'cept where he can shove it!"

They walked along the corridor toward Tate's office together. "How are they treating you?" Lou asked Wally.

Wally grinned. "Man, I like it here. The cells ain't as big as the ones in jail, but the food's better. And sumpthin's always going on." Then he grew serious. "But I sure could use a fix. I'm freakin' out without it."

"You ought to be over the worst by now."

"Sure. I don't shake no more, but I still hurt like hell."

Lou pulled out a package of cigarettes and slid them into Wally's pocket. "It's the best I can do."

Wally nodded. "Yeah, man, I know. Thanks anyway."

They had reached Tate's door, where all three paused. Miller turned to Lou. "He called you too?"

154

Lou nodded. "The note said 'at once.'"

Miller knocked and a moment later Tate opened the door. He was wearing a fawn-colored suit and a checkered vest, and looked much more like an insurance salesman than a detective. But his manner was no longer smooth, charismatic. It was tense and harried.

Wally greeted him first. "Hi, Loot! Getting any?"

Tate ignored Wally completely, speaking to Miller. "Keep him out of here for a minute. Lou, you come in first."

Tate closed the door behind him. "We're not making any progress on the Zakos killing at all." The way he said it made it sound as if it were Lou's fault. "Nick Pappas is still the most logical suspect, but we haven't any proof yet."

Lou didn't say anything, but he thought a lot. Tate was repeating himself. He'd been saying the same thing for days.

Tate stood by his desk and stared at Lou. "Unless you've come up with something concrete, we're going to have to try a new approach."

Lou, standing there, thought, He's been saying that for days, too.

"For example," Tate said, "consider your friend Wally Blue. If he were released, he could lead us to some hard evidence."

It was presented as a statement, but Lou knew it was really a question. Tate wanted his opinion. He gave it.

"Not a chance."

Tate's temper flared. "Don't be so quick to be so damn negative!"

"I'm telling it as it is."

"I'd have one of our best men tailing him—somebody young, aggressive, and what's more, somebody his own kind—black."

Lou snorted. "All that means is, Wally's friends won't even call him mister when they kill him."

Tate turned away, obviously in an effort to control his temper. Lou took advantage of the pause.

"Something else—if Wally does know something, and

155

you turn him loose, you won't have to follow him. He'll turn up himself—dead." Tate still didn't say anything. "They're not going to let a witness just go wandering around until he makes up his mind to finger somebody."

Tate glared at Lou. He didn't like his juniors to talk to him like that, but he forced himself to ignore it. "I'm aware of the danger," he said. "I haven't made a firm decision yet. But what I want to know from you—all I want to know—is, if my tail should lose him, would you be able to find him again?"

"Only if he wants me to," Lou answered.

Tate lost control. "Damn it, Baroni, can't you ever say anything helpful?"

"Not if you want me to tell the truth," Lou retorted. "This town's full of holes. Wally could drop into any one of them, and he could stay there till hell freezes over."

Tate started to reply angrily, but controlled himself. "All right. But just in case I should decide to release Blue, I'll want you to keep your ears open."

"I always do," Lou replied, "and if I hear anything, I'll pass it on—in triplicate."

Tate glared at him again. "Baroni, it's remarks like that which indicate your flagrant disregard for authority."

Lou raised his eyebrows.

"You don't challenge your superiors—and you don't go on with an investigation after the case is closed."

"You're talking about the Hawley case?"

"That's right," Tate replied. He hadn't meant to mention it yet, not until he had something concrete, but Baroni's irritating manner always made him say things he hadn't planned.

Lou walked to the door. Opening it, he said, "What I do with my free time is my business."

Tate exploded. "That's not true!" Lou, at the partially opened door, turned back to him as he went on. "You have no free time. You're supposed to be concentrating on the Zakos killing, not on Edward Hawley."

"Hawley's guilty."

"No. That case is closed!"

"Reopen it."

"No!" Tate moved closer to Lou. "I'm warning you, Baroni, I'm seriously entertaining the idea of an official reprimand. And you know what that will do to your pension."

Lou didn't reply. But Tate wasn't going to let him leave so easily.

"If you're smart, you'll forget Hawley—or else retire early." Early retirement was something else Tate hadn't meant to mention, but it wasn't such a bad idea. Not as satisfying as a disgraceful discharge, but still not bad. "All it takes is a recommendation from me and a request from you."

Lou shook his head. If he retired now, he'd just have his detective's pension. He had to make sergeant first. That was a must. "I'll see my time out."

Tate smiled grimly. "Think about it. Don't be so quick to answer. You could lose your pension completely."

Lou ignored the threat. "I said I'll see the rest of my time out." Then he opened the door the rest of the way and went out. Wally Blue and Miller were still there, and it was obvious they had heard most of what had been said behind Tate's partly opened door. Wally looked disturbed.

"Lou—you gonna get heaved?"

Lou shook his head. "Don't make book on it."

But Wally still looked deeply troubled. "It's my fault, ain't it, Lou? If I opened up to you, told you what that shit in there wants to know, it'd be all right, wouldn't it?"

Lou started to say yes, but Wally went right on, shaking his head from side to side vigorously. "But I can't tell you, Lou, honest, even to help you. I'd be cutting my own throat if I did. Ya know that, don't ya?"

"Sure, Wally, sure." Lou patted Wally's arm. "I know. Don't worry about it."

Lou started walking down the corridor toward the squad room. Wally called after him. "Man, I'm sorry, real sorry, y'know?"

Lou, down the hall, just waved back without turning. Miller, who had been standing beside Wally all this

157

time, now indicated Tate's door. "Inside," he said.

Wally turned to Miller. "You hear him say something 'bout some guy named Hawley?"

"Forget it."

"Who is he? Why's Lou want to bust him?"

Miller sighed and shoved Wally toward Tate's door. "The lieutenant's waiting. Go."

Tate's interview with Wally was as unsatisfactory as all the previous ones. Perhaps even more so, because his mind was on Baroni. He didn't admit it to himself, but Lou Baroni had come to represent all the frustrations, all the reprimands, all the problems he encountered in the police department. He never actually formulated the thought, but he was convinced his career would never make any further progress as long as Baroni was around. That's why, as soon as he had dismissed Wally Blue, he summoned Steve Perry.

Perry came in smiling and enthusiastic as always, the proper attitude for an underling, but it failed to placate Tate. He stood behind his desk and glared at the sergeant. "Baroni—what have you got?"

Perry, startled, searched his mind frantically for an excuse. "I've been concentrating on Zakos."

"You mean you haven't got anything yet?"

"No, sir."

"I gave you explicit orders!"

"Yes, sir. But—"

"I'm tired of excuses!"

And Perry was tired of being Tate's whipping boy. Besides, he was still hoping, desperately, he wouldn't need Tate much longer. For once he spoke back.

"I talked to Hawley—he won't sign a complaint."

"Won't—"

"He doesn't want to get Baroni into any trouble."

"For Christ's sake!"

"And I talked to one of the neighbors. She couldn't remember seeing Baroni hanging around at all."

"I won't accept that," Tate said. "I won't. He just admitted to me, practically, that he's going on with the case."

158

Perry wasn't really listening. He was thinking about Spiro Zakos and Nicky Pappas and the informant who had phoned. He hadn't shown up yet, but when he did, when he turned over those ledgers, Perry wouldn't have to go on standing there, sucking up to Tate any longer. God, how he longed for that!

Tate was still speaking. "Keep after Hawley. Stay on Baroni's tail. Get me proof."

"Yes, sir."

Tate's manner softened, warmed. He walked around the desk to put his hand on Perry's shoulder.

"Do this for me," he said, "and I promise you, you'll benefit by it."

"Yes, sir," Perry replied. "I'll do my best."

"Good, good." Tate smiled warmly. "I know I can count on you—and I am. I want you to know that. I am."

Perry smiled back at his superior, warmly, but under his breath he murmured, "Fuck you, Tate."

When Perry returned to his desk, his mood was bleak. In spite of his hopes, he was beginning to doubt his informant. He had spent hour after hour, day after day, near Papa's Hellenic-West Village, waiting for him, but so far he hadn't put in an appearance. Of course, he had been warned he'd have to wait for the right moment, the safe time, but still, he had to admit to himself it could have been just a crank call.

But he wouldn't let himself think of that. He couldn't. Without the hope it offered, he had nothing, just Tate's empty promises, and his wife, who was bitching more and more now that he was away every evening. She just wouldn't believe he was working. She was certain he was spending all that time with some broad, like the redhead who lived near Hawley. Well, he'd show her, and Tate, and all of them—if he ever got his hands on those ledgers. If.

It was then the phone on his desk rang. He picked it up, expecting a routine call, but it was far from routine. He even recognized the voice. His informant.

"Perry?"

159

"Speaking."

"I'm being watched. Every minute. I couldn't get away. I'm taking a chance now just calling you."

"Tell me your name. I'll find a way to get to you."

"No—too dangerous. Just do as I say."

"I have been. I've been waiting right where you said."

"I know. I saw you. I almost reached you once. I even had the evidence in my car."

"Tell me something now. Give me something to go on— Nick Pappas' connection with the Zakos killing."

"Forget that. What I've got is much more important."

"What is it?"

"I told you—everything—complete records—drugs, girls, extortion—names, dates, places."

Perry felt his pulse quicken. "I need it now."

"I know. And I'll get it to you—soon."

"When? When will you get it to me?"

"This week—sometime this week, for sure. Maybe to-night. Just be there from six on as before."

"All right."

"One more thing—you've got to promise me something."

"What?"

"Not just protection. A place to hide."

"All right."

"A good place—a safe place—I don't want to die."

"You won't," Perry replied, sincerely. "I promise you. You won't have to worry about anything—not if you turn those ledgers over to me."

"I will—within a week. And you'll have a safe place ready?"

"Right. I'll have a safe place ready."

The caller hung up and Perry leaned back in his chair and smiled. It was still all right. It was going to go down just the way he wanted it to. And a safe place for his informant? He grinned. To hell with him. Once he turned over those ledgers he didn't matter. In fact, if Pappas had him killed, it would make it even better.

160

Clayton Hoyle was smiling too when he put down his phone. The hunger in Perry's voice pleased him. So did the bit about wanting a safe place to hide. That was a nice touch, he thought, a note of reality. That really ought to make Perry believe he was on the level. And that bastard had been only too quick to promise. Lou Baroni would never have done that. Lou would have said he'd do what he could, but he wouldn't go further than that. That's why he liked Lou. Lou was always square. That's why he didn't mind making these phone calls for him. Besides, he found he enjoyed screwing Perry. Perry was extremely screwable.

The room in which Clayton Hoyle now sat, dressed only in his shorts, was a remarkable clutter of worn furniture and a hodgepodge of cheap, sentimental knickknacks—mementos from a girlhood long gone. There were faded photographs, picture postcards, ashtrays with place-names on them, pillows from Oregon, and Syracuse, and Alabama, and even some broken dolls. It wasn't Hoyle's place, of course. It belonged to his present girlfriend, Beebee.

She lay in the bed that occupied most of the room, a huge mound of flesh that seemed to rise from the mattress like a mountain, for Clayton Hoyle, small, almost tubercular in build, liked his women really fat. The fatter the better. And Beebee was almost unbelievably fat. He actually couldn't wrap his arms all the way around her, and that fact alone turned him on like nothing else did.

Beebee was a night worker, a dishwasher in an all-night coffee shop where she ate almost everything left on the plates before she rinsed them. And she slept most of the day—that is, when Hoyle wasn't around. The little man, puny as he was, usually kept her busy all the time he was there. That's why she was awake now, her tiny eyes squinting at him past the folds of fat that were her cheeks.

"You really called a cop?" she asked, her voice surprisingly girlish.

Hoyle, usually more cautious, was feeling cocky. "Sure. You bet I did."

161

"And you lied to him—you made up all those things?"

"That's right."

"And he's going to be waiting and nobody will come?"

"That's the idea."

"Oh, you're awful!" It was her favorite expression. "You'll get into trouble, won't you?"

"No way. He doesn't know who I am," he said, climbing back into bed with her, "and he never will—not if you keep that big fat mouth of yours closed." Then he pinched her in a rosy place and she exclaimed, "Oh, you're awful!"

But, of course, she didn't keep her mouth closed. She couldn't. Too little happened in her life that she could talk about. But everybody she told about it did promise to keep it a secret.

Lou received a phone call that day, shortly after lunch. He recognized the voice even though it was hoarse. "Hawley?"

"I'm sorry to call you at work, but I didn't know who else to call."

"You sound like hell. What's the matter?"

"I think I've got some sort of cold."

"It sounds worse than a cold."

Hawley began to cough. It was a few moments before the conversation could continue.

"I didn't go to work today," Hawley said when he could. "And I don't want to go out. I'm sweating a lot. So I was wondering, if you're going to come over and watch me tonight, could you pick up something at a drugstore?"

"Sure," Lou replied. "What do you want?"

"Ask the druggist. Anything he suggests."

He began to cough again.

"You sound like you need a doctor."

"No," Hawley answered. "It's not that bad, but I'd appreciate the medicine."

Lou looked at the pile of work on his desk. "I won't be able to get there until six, maybe seven."

162

"That's all right."

"You sure?"

"Yes—just so I know it's coming."

After he hung up, Lou sat staring at the phone. Hawley could have called a drugstore—most of them still delivered—but he knew why he hadn't. He was sick and he wanted company. Lou had been in the same situation himself. He had even called his daughter once, though he had known she would end up criticizing him for living alone.

He went back to work, pecking out his reports with two fingers. But his thoughts stayed with Hawley. He had sounded terrible, and it was still a long time till six. Finally, he picked up the phone and dialed Laurie Knight's number.

It was almost seven when Lou knocked on Hawley's door. Laurie answered.

"How is he?"

"I put him to bed," she reported, "and I had a doctor here. It's some kind of flu."

Lou started for the bedroom. Laurie went with him.

"You won't get much out of him," she said. "The doctor gave him a shot and then something to make him sleep."

Hawley looked small, alone in the double bed. His face was flushed and his eyes were glazed. He had to look at Lou for a long moment before he recognized him.

"Thanks," he said.

"What for?"

"Her." His voice was little more than a whisper.

"Forget it."

"She called a doctor."

"You can afford it."

"I've been trying to save my money," he said sleepily, "for Talua."

"Sure."

He fell asleep. Lou and Laurie went back into the living room.

"Thanks for coming," Lou told her, dropping into Haw-

163

ley's easy chair. He was beat. Laurie went to the bureau and without asking poured him a long shot of bourbon and brought it to him. Then she sat on the sofa opposite, tucking her legs up under her. She was wearing a knee-length skirt and a man's shirt with the tail out.

"You know," she said, "your phone call really shook me."

Lou looked at her questioningly.

"After telling me to stay away from him, after warning me he's a killer, you call and ask me to look after him."

Lou shrugged.

"I don't get it," Laurie said, asking for an answer, wanting to understand.

"He's sick."

Laurie shook her head. "That's not enough. I still don't get it—none of it." Then she added, "And you know something? I don't think you do either."

She got up and started for the kitchen. "I was just going to make something to eat. Have you had supper?"

"No."

Lou poured himself another shot of whiskey and followed her into the kitchen, where she started making an omelet.

After a moment she said, "You could have called a doctor yourself and sent him here."

"He needed somebody to stay with him."

Laurie glanced over her shoulder at him. "You're always that concerned about your suspects?"

Lou just shrugged.

While they were eating, Laurie said, "He kept talking about Talua."

"It's an island in the South Pacific."

"I know. I read his scrapbook. Is it for real?"

"The island is."

"And he really wants to go there?"

"Uh-huh."

Laurie shook her head in wonder. "It's just like an old movie. You know—with Dorothy Lamour. *The Road to*

Talua." Then she added, "You never know what's going on in real life, do you?"

She had put the coffee on. It was perking now, so she got up and poured them each a cup. "I hope he makes it," she said after a moment.

"What?"

"Talua," she replied. "Don't you?"

Lou answered more slowly than he realized. "I can't. I'm going to prove he killed his wife."

"Why?" Laurie asked.

"I've got my reasons."

"I still don't get it." She was trying valiantly to understand. "You like him, yet you're trying to convict him?"

"Who says I like him?"

"I do."

"He killed his wife."

"No, I won't accept that. You're not interested in the law just for the law's sake. You're not one of those."

"He killed his wife. I've got to prove it."

"He's your friend."

"No," Lou said. "No, he isn't!" He said it too vehemently. It even sounded that way to him.

Laurie left at ten. Lou stayed. Around midnight Hawley awoke and Lou fed him some consommé.

In the morning when Laurie came back to look after Hawley, she found him sleeping peacefully and Lou fast asleep in a chair beside the bed. Looking at them both, she thought, What a strange world it is.

She didn't wake Lou until she had breakfast ready.

The approach to Hellenic-West Village was impressive. Parklike lawns dotted with pepper trees, weeping birches, and eucalyptus bordered the road, and fieldstone pillars, slightly reminiscent of the marble pillars of ancient Greece, marked the boundary.

Just outside the pillars Sergeant Steve Perry sat in his car smoking cigarette after cigarette. Two more evenings had passed since he had received the second phone call and

165

hope had given way again to doubt. Not only that, but unless the informant appeared with those ledgers tonight, this was going to be the end of it. It had to be. As much as he hated giving up the possibility of a real coup, he couldn't go on spending his evenings there. Tate was expecting him to come up with something that would nail Baroni, and Shirley was becoming unbearable.

It was going to be his last evening waiting there, for a reason he wasn't aware of as yet. Shirley had gone to Tate to check up on him.

When he finally went home that evening, he found Tate sitting cozily with Shirley, in his living room, waiting for him.

Another man might have been jealous—his wife was wearing her most revealing lounging pajamas, and both she and Tate were drinking—but all he felt was dismay, for he knew he'd have to explain where he'd been and why.

It didn't take him long to do so, and although he tried to make excuses, it soon became painfully clear Tate realized perfectly well why he had kept the information to himself.

"He called twice?" Tate asked, when Perry had finished his monologue.

"That's right."

"The second call came just as you were getting tired of waiting for him to show up?"

"Yes," Perry replied, wondering what he was getting at. He was having trouble concentrating. Shirley was looking at him smugly, almost smirking.

Tate went on. "And so, after the second call you spent two more evenings out there, wasting time—"

"Not 'wasting,' sir. I felt I—"

Tate interrupted. "Yes, wasting. That's what the calls were all about. You were meant to waste time."

Perry tried hard to justify his behavior. "No, you don't understand—"

Shirley interrupted. "For God's sake, don't you see? You've been made a fool of!"

166

"Very effectively," Tate added. "You were wanted out of the way, so you were sent out there."

Perry made a further attempt at saving face. "I thought of that," he lied. "But the payoff was so big, I decided it was worth the gamble. That's why I didn't tell you about it, sir. I didn't want to waste anybody else's time with such a long shot."

"Bull," Shirley said.

Perry glared at her, then turned back to Tate, speaking quickly. "Besides, sir, I couldn't see why anybody would want me out of the way during the evenings only. This was my free time—"

Tate held up his hand. "Incorrect. You had an assignment during those hours. I gave it to you myself."

"You did?" Perry asked. Then it came to him. "Baroni?"

"Exactly."

"But, sir, I figured the Pappas thing, even as a long shot, was so much more important—"

"That's just what you were supposed to think."

"What? But why—who?"

"Baroni!" Shirley exclaimed in disgust. "Anybody can see that!" She crossed to the bar and mixed herself another drink.

"No—" was all Perry could say.

"Somehow he found out you were told to watch him," Tate said, "so he arranged those phone calls."

Perry's face went white. "Baroni! That old bastard!"

Tate could have been angry, authoritative, dictatorial. Instead he decided to be friendly, fatherly. He got up and placed a hand on Perry's shoulder. "Steve," he said magnanimously, shaking his head sadly. "I'm afraid you've really been had." He enjoyed being magnanimous when it didn't cost him anything. Besides, he was impressing Perry's wife. And the way she was dressed, she was worth impressing.

Perry was almost shaking with rage. "I'll get that bastard. I promise you, I'll get him good!"

167

10

FOUR days later Hawley was well enough to return to work. To mark the occasion, Lou and Hawley decided to eat out.

Lou picked the restaurant. It was Giovanni's Italian Palace, a small, storefront affair not far from Hawley's apartment. Lou drove there directly from the station.

He wasn't alone. Steve Perry followed. Lou, since he wasn't following Hawley anymore, no longer worried about Perry. That's why when he entered the restaurant he didn't see Perry parking across the street.

The restaurant was far from crowded and Lou walked directly to one of the tables covered with a checkered tablecloth. Giovanni, a youngish man with prematurely gray hair, was busy at the cash register, but as soon as he was free he came over.

"Lou, baby—good to see you. How's the police department?"

Lou shrugged. "Like always—lots of customers."

Giovanni laughed. "Not like me, eh? Sometimes I feel like I should close up during the week."

"Why don't you?"

"I'd lose my help. Where do you find cooks, dishwashers, and waitresses who only want to work on weekends?" He handed Lou a menu. "Know what you want or do you want to read for a while?"

"I want to wait for a while. I'm expecting a friend."

Giovanni made curving motions with his hands. "It's

168

about time. You should have a chick warming your bed."

"It's not a chick. It's a man—business. And he should be here in a few minutes. Why don't you bring a coupla beers?"

Giovanni nodded and left. A moment later a waitress, the youngest and prettiest in the place, brought two beers to the table. Lou knew Giovanni had sent her deliberately.

"You're new here?"

"Yes, sir," the girl replied. The bodices on the uniforms Giovanni bought were low-cut. Usually it didn't make much difference. This time it did. Lou was aware of a lot of cleavage.

"Like it here?"

"Yes, sir," the girl answered. It seemed all she was capable of saying.

Lou knew Giovanni was listening. "If that gray-haired bastard who runs this place gives you a hard time, you let me know, understand?"

Confused, the girl said, "Yes, sir," again and went away. Lou glanced over at the cash register. Giovanni was there, grinning.

Lou nursed his beer for five minutes before Ed Hawley came in.

"You're late," Lou said matter-of-factly.

Wearily, Hawley sat down opposite Lou. "The office manager called me in to see him just as I was leaving."

"What did he say?"

"They're considering a thirty-percent cut in personnel."

"You mean you might get fired?"

Hawley shook his head. "It's just his way of saying I shouldn't get sick too often."

"The bastard!" Lou said, angry.

"How was your day?"

Lou grimaced. "Quiet. They've got me file searching."

"What does that mean?"

"I'm going through old arrest reports, looking for anything that has a tie-in with Zakos or Pappas."

"But can't a clerk do that, or a computer?"

"Sure," Lou answered. "A clerk's supposed to do it—but Tate's got me doing it."

Hawley's face became angry now too. "What's he trying to do—make sure you don't become a sergeant before you retire?"

Lou saw the anger on Hawley's face and realized it was on his behalf. "Forget it. It's my problem. Drink your beer."

Hawley took a drink. "What'll you do—if you don't get a promotion, I mean—move in with your daughter?"

Lou sighed. "Only if I have to."

Hawley leaned across the table. "Look—I've been thinking. And, mind you, this is just a suggestion. You could move in with me, you know—or me with you—we could split the rent, everything else, too."

Lou nodded, not looking at Hawley. "I've thought of that myself."

"Your regular pension would be enough, then, to pay half the rent. And I'd be able to save twice as much toward the fare as I'm saving now."

"What fare?"

"To Talua."

Lou shook his head. "It won't work."

"Why not?"

"You're a killer. I've still got to prove it."

Hawley leaned back in his chair. "I forgot about that."

"Want to order now?" Lou asked.

"Yeah. I'm starved."

Lou beckoned to Giovanni at the cash register. Giovanni sent a waitress over—the young one with the cleavage.

Perry was waiting in Tate's office when he arrived the next morning. His feelings were mixed. He felt he was going to enjoy the coming interview. He knew it might result in a postponement of his promotion, but even so he was looking forward to Tate's reaction to his news.

"Morning, Steve," Tate said when he saw him. "What

can I do for you?" He had just about written Perry off as a comer, so he could afford to be magnanimous.

"I've something to tell you," Perry started.

"All right, if it won't take long." He went over to his desk and began going through a number of reports.

"It's about Baroni."

Tate looked up expectantly. "You've finally got something?"

Perry nodded. "You could say that."

"Well, tell me."

Perry was pleased to see he was eager, anxious. "I followed him when he left here yesterday."

"And he followed Hawley or harassed him some other way?"

"Not exactly," Perry replied.

Tate became impatient. "Well, what, exactly?"

Perry told him about the Italian restaurant, the dinner they had shared, and the evening they spent together afterward.

Tate's mouth fell open. "What the hell's going on?"

"Nothing," Perry replied. "They're just a couple of buddies."

Tate began pacing angrily. "They can't be. We'll never get Baroni on harassment, or invasion of privacy, or a breach of regulation if they're friends."

"I know," Perry said, hiding his feeling of satisfaction. "That's why I came in early. I knew you'd want to know right away."

Tate continued to pace, thinking hard. "He must be working some sort of scam on Hawley. He must have some sort of angle."

"I thought of that," Perry said. He had. For once he wasn't lying. "But as long as they're buddy-buddy, there's not much we can do."

Tate wheeled to confront him. "Oh, yes there is. We can be ready when he makes his move. We can find out his ploy."

Perry was beginning to suspect that Tate was a little off

171

balance where Baroni was concerned. He had thought his news would make him forget about getting Baroni because of Hawley. He had really thought that.

"But how?" Perry asked. "Who—I mean, if he *is* working a scam how are we going to find out?"

Tate stared at Perry hard. "I made you a sergeant," he said coldly, "because I felt you had ability. Well, it's time you used it. Don't ask me questions. Just get me answers!"

When Perry left Tate's office, he didn't have any idea of where to begin. He didn't think of Laurie Knight until later.

Papa Pappas was doing a great deal of thinking that day, too. As a boy in the Old Country he used to sit on the stone jetty that formed the pulsing heart of his village and watch the fishermen unloading their catches and dream of far places and great riches. Now that he had achieved those dreams, he often sat on the tiny redwood pier on the edge of his island to watch the pleasure boats on his manmade lake and wonder why the dreams of that small boy now seemed so empty. If he had had a son—a real son—his achievements might have some meaning.

He shuddered. Thoughts of Nicky always depressed him. He heard steps on the wood planking behind him and turned to see Demetri approaching. He knew that because he carried a newspaper, he had come to discuss something unpleasant.

"Well?"

Demetri unfolded the paper and showed him the headline. It berated the police for failing to find the Zakos killer.

"They won't leave it alone," Demetri observed. "The public is too interested."

Papa shrugged. He thought very little of the public. "Don't worry about it. As soon as something else happens— another scandal in Washington, a war, an election, they'll lose interest."

Demetri nodded, but added, "Until then the public pushes the police."

172

Papa sighed. Why must there always be trouble? Sometimes it was best to ignore it. "The police are doing nothing. Not even this Baroni."

Demetri, standing stolidly before the old man, said, "A detective named Perry has been sitting in his car every evening lately at the entrance to the Village."

"Sitting—" Papa tried to grasp the significance of it. "But why? What for?"

Demetri told him of an informant who had overheard a certain stout dishwasher telling her friends a secret about a phone call, a promise of evidence to be delivered.

"The question," Demetri went on, "is why was this done. What is the reason?"

"Who is this man—the one who made the phone call?"

"A bookmaker named Hoyle. A small independent. One of those you allowed to go on making a living." It was a reproach. Demetri had wanted Papa to put them all out of business. Papa had said they weren't of any consequence.

He turned back to the water. It was so calm, not at all like the angry sea he had watched as a boy. But back then, though the water had been turbulent, his life had been peaceful.

"Maybe," he mused aloud, "there is a connection between this and Nicky."

"It is possible," Demetri agreed.

"Maybe Nicky has not told us everything there is to tell."

"Maybe," Demetri repeated.

Papa made up his mind. He had to know. "Send somebody to bring this bookmaker, Hoyle, here."

The next day was Saturday, Lou's day off, and he had agreed to visit Evelyn Hawley's grave. Hawley hadn't been there since the funeral and he admitted to a vague feeling that he should go. Lou knew the feeling. He had had it once.

The morning haze had dispersed when they reached the cemetery. The sky was blue and the sun was bright and

173

pleasantly warm. A soft breeze blew through the trees and across the wide expanses of lawn. Whenever Lou went there he couldn't help feeling it was all designed simply to sell plots, to please the prospective buyer more than the bereaved—in short, just another rip-off. The lack of jutting tombstones made it seem even more that way. It was an outing, a walk in the country. But, of course, he didn't say these things as he accompanied Hawley, who said very little, but carried a bouquet of flowers stiffly before him.

Looking at them, Lou said, "You shoulda bought those downtown. They charge double for 'em out here."

Ed nodded. "I'm still new at this."

"There are angles to everything," Lou said.

They walked on in silence. Finally Hawley asked, "How often do you think I should come out here?"

"To pay your respects?" Lou asked.

"Uh huh. Does anybody ever come here for any other reason?"

"You paid for 'eternal care,' didn't you?" Lou asked. "You gotta come out here once in a while and check the grave to make sure you get it."

They reached Evelyn Hawley's grave a few minutes later. The grass had been newly cut, the weeds removed, and the small marker, lying flat on the ground, had been brushed clear of debris.

"Funny how fast grass grows back," Hawley said.

"It never died," Lou said. "They just remove the sod, then replace it. It goes on living."

"Evelyn never cared much for grass," Hawley confided.

"It don't make any difference to her now," Lou replied.

"You know," Hawley said, "I can't really believe she's down there. I mean that anything that matters is down there." He turned to Lou. "You know what I mean?"

Lou nodded. "I feel the same about mine."

Hawley turned to Lou, "Where's yours—the grave, I mean?"

"A bit further on, in one of the older sections."

174

"You got a headstone?"

"No, just a plaque like this."

Hawley bent over and placed the flowers on the grass. He seemed embarrassed. Straightening up, he said, "I feel a little foolish."

"I always did, too. That's why I don't bring flowers anymore. Somebody just steals 'em anyway."

Hawley took another long look at the grave. "In the movies they always say something—you know, about how much they miss them and all that."

"Do you miss her?"

"Sometimes."

"Well, that's all you have to say and you just said it."

They moved on to Lou's wife's grave. The trees here were bigger, older, the path dirt, not concrete, and even though the hedges were trimmed and the grass was mowed, it still seemed something that belonged to the past.

Lou led Hawley across a few graves, stopping in front of a marker near an old, dying oak. Some of the leaves had fallen and cluttered up the marker. Hawley bent down to brush them aside.

"Marie Rose Baroni." Hawley read the inscription aloud. "Beloved wife of Louis Chalmers Baroni. Chalmers?"

"My mother's maiden name—forget it."

"My middle name is Carol," Hawley said. *

"It's in your records."

"My mother wanted a girl."

"That's all we ever had," Lou said, "a girl—Toni. Looks a lot like her mother when she was that young." He smiled. "She was really something when I met her. My wife, I mean. She was still a good looker even after Toni was born. We had a few good years, Marie and me."

Hawley read the rest of the inscription. "Born 1926—died 1968."

"Seems a long time ago," Lou said.

Hawley asked, "Miss her?"

Lou nodded slowly. "Couldn't stand her most of the

175

time, but after she was gone . . . . There are nights, sometimes, when I'd give anything to hear her voice—especially like it was when we first got married. There was something in it then, a— Well, anyway, it changed."

Hawley nodded. "I know what you mean."

"The last six or seven years she was alive she bitched about everything. Nothing was ever right." He paused. "There ought to be a law to stop women from changing after they marry."

"You're right," Hawley agreed. "But we change, too. We disappoint them as well—"

Lou went on. "It's the last six or seven years I remember most when I think about her. There were times then when I had to shove my fists in my ears to keep from hearing her, 'cause I knew if I had to go on listening to that whining voice of hers, I'd kill her."

Hawley didn't say anything for a long moment. Then, looking directly at Lou, he asked, "Is that why you're so certain I killed my wife—because you wanted to kill yours?"

Lou raised his head slowly. He stared back for a moment, then turned and walked away. Hawley followed.

If Wesley Price ever wrote his autobiography, it would obviously contain an explanation of why he decided to become a professional killer. The choice was quite deliberate, the decision reached only after a great deal of thought. And he had inherited a suitable background.

He had been brought up with death. His father, a thin, round-shouldered man, had been an undertaker in a small Midwestern town. As far as he could remember there had always been a body resting in the parlor of their home or one being embalmed in the basement, for the elder Price hadn't been a very successful mortician. Separate quarters were quite impossible. He, his wife, and their only son, Wesley, shared an old two-story frame house with death quite frequently.

176

It wasn't until Wesley was old enough to understand the cruel jibes of his schoolmates that he realized that, to most people, death was an alien, ugly, dirty thing. Of course he resented their teasing and drew apart and learned to live within himself. Thus it was he acquired, at an early age, two traits that enabled him in later years to reach the top of his profession: his nonchalant acceptance of death and a preference for being alone.

From his mother he also acquired a trait that influenced his future. She had come from a wealthy family and had been trained to appreciate all the finer things that her husband couldn't afford. Nevertheless, she talked about them, and from her, young Wesley learned that life could be gracious, that good manners, fine clothes, and a familiarity with all the arts should be one's rightful inheritance.

He didn't turn killer all at once. He had held another job previously. His parents hadn't been able to buy him a college education, so he had had to satisfy himself with only a high school diploma. He hadn't really minded the deprivation. At that time he was a tall, slender, intense young man, and he had already reached the conclusion that formal education really had very little value in the practical, dollars-and-cents world where the good things always went to the rich, and the rich got that way, not by understanding Aristotle, but by understanding the needs of the influential people around them.

His father had firmly refused to allow him to enter his undertaking business. A bitterly disappointed man who never managed to collect the money owed him, he wanted something better for his only son and found him a job as an apprentice manager in a local department store.

At first Wesley had been pleased, but then he realized that every male employee was called "apprentice manager," and in reality the title meant nothing.

He wasn't too disturbed by the discovery. What did disturb him was the loss of so much of his own life. The hours were long. He rarely saw much of the sun, and when he did

177

have a day off, his pay was hardly sufficient for the fine restaurants, the concerts, the good life he desired.

However, even that would have been acceptable if he had had something to look forward to. But, as he discovered, there wasn't anything in the future. The most he could hope for was an eventual promotion to a managerial position. But the manager put in even longer hours than the apprentices did.

This fact depressed him like nothing else ever had. He began to feel trapped, imprisoned in a life he didn't like and refused to accept.

But how, he had posed the question, could he free himself? Money was the obvious answer. The owner of the store spent most of his days on a golf course.

Wesley began to study, systematically, all the methods by which he could gain a great deal of money with the smallest expenditure of his life.

He was forced to discard one after another. Successful doctors need practice only a small part of each day, but it took irretrievable years of study to become a doctor, and even then there was no guarantee of success.

Teachers did have the summer months to themselves, but the remuneration was hardly what he had in mind.

Some actors made a great deal of money for the time they actually spent at their craft, but they were exceptions. Most worked hard all their lives and achieved nothing.

He considered, and eliminated, for obvious reasons, politics, law, art, even the priesthood. Then he turned his mind to the dangerous occupations—those that included high hazard pay—for he had decided that even a short, full life was better than a long one spent in drudgery.

The hard work such jobs entailed did not disturb him. He knew, if he worked at it, he could become strong and muscular. However, he discovered such occcupations weren't really the answer either. They required too many hours of work, and besides, such fields were already too crowded.

One day he sat alone in his bedroom and listed, firmly,

his requirements. The job, whatever it was, would have to pay a great deal, require a minimum of his time, and—lastly—the work would have to be something that was in great demand and short supply.

He pondered the problem for several years. During this time, still an apprentice manager at the department store, he considered and discarded robbery, embezzlement, forgery, and espionage. It was only when his mind turned to murder that he felt he had come upon the one vocation that met all his requirements—high pay, short hours, and something in demand.

He was too practical to embark on that profession without any preparation, so he conceived and began a training program. Already familiar with death, thanks to his upbringing, he had no fear of it. He went to the local YMCA every night after work and developed his muscles. He played badminton and volleyball and Ping-Pong to develop his timing. He joined a shooting club and a karate club and he taught himself to throw knives. On Sundays he went to the woods and developed his skill with the bow and arrow and even the bola.

He also haunted the libraries for chemistry texts, becoming a fair toxicologist. He even took a drama course at the local little theater where he specialized in makeup.

Eighteen months after he began he was ready. He selected his first victim himself. The owner of the department store was a portly gentleman in his fifties who had a well-known affinity for young girls. Unfortunately he also had a wife who refused to give him a divorce.

One Sunday, after a long discussion with the owner, Wesley strangled, robbed, and raped the wife. The rape, he felt, was a touch of genius, added not for pleasure, but for effect. The semen found by the medical examiner convinced the police—as Wesley had known it would—that the crime was genuine.

The cold-blooded brutality of it also paid another dividend. The store owner, who had never really thought Wesley would do it, and who had not intended to pay him anyway, was absolutely terrified of him afterward. He couldn't hand over the money fast enough.

Wesley spent most of the following year in France learning to appreciate fine wines.

When Nick Pappas had phoned him in Chicago, he had been practicing his new profession for ten years, and during that time he had perfected his skills, refined his talents, until he had become the undisputed leader in the field. His fees were high, but since he always guaranteed satisfaction or money back, they were never disputed.

He knew Southern California, so he rented a Volkswagen and left the city, driving to a marina in a town about an hour away, where he booked a luxury suite overlooking the ocean.

While driving through the city, he had left the freeway only once—to visit a suburban post office where, with a key mailed to him by Nick Pappas, he had removed an envelope from a post office box rented for just that purpose.

Now, as he sat on the balcony of his suite, overlooking the yachts moored in the marina below, listening to the surf, he opened the envelope and withdrew two newspaper clippings. Each contained a photograph—one of Wally Blue and the other of Lou Baroni.

There was also a note which told him Wally Blue was still in jail, and suggesting he deal with Baroni first.

No one has ever quite understood the mysterious manner by which certain types of news can spread so rapidly. Few have attempted to determine the means or motivation. Certainly not Clayton Hoyle. But he was the recipient of such a mouth-to-mouth communiqué.

He was plying his bookmaker's trade on east side streets when the word reached him: Papa Pappas had ordered his muscle to pick up Clayton Hoyle.

The pimps and prostitutes, the junkies and drunks, who relayed the message couldn't believe it. Clayton Hoyle, a two-dollar bookie, was less than nothing. Why would Papa want him? And for what? To bruise him a bit? To waste him completely? It didn't make sense. What connection, they kept asking, did Hoyle have with Pappas?

Clayton Hoyle could have told them. While they speculated, he began to sweat. Those phone calls he had made for Lou Baroni—he had told that cop, Perry, he had Papa's records! He had talked of a ledger and other disclosures! Somehow, somebody had let it be known he had been the caller. Somebody had opened her big fat mouth once too often.

There was only one thing he could think to do. He had to split, fast!

He left the streets, taking to the back alleys, working his way west toward the bus station where he could get a ride to Vegas or Reno, or even farther.

He hesitated a few moments in his flight to make a phone call. He had to tell that bastard Baroni the kind of trouble his harmless little phone calls had caused.

Lou was at his desk when Hoyle's call came through. He ignored his bitter recriminations and insults. Then he hung up the phone slowly, completely puzzled. What in hell was going on? he wondered. Then another thought struck him. If Pappas did pick up Hoyle, the little man would run off at the mouth. He'd be only too eager to explain why he had made those calls. And that raised an interesting question: What would Papa make of it all? And, more important, what would he do?

Lou leaned back in his chair. The whole Pappas thing was much too big, too involved, too dangerous. He hadn't wanted any part of it and he still didn't. If he were smart, he'd move fast and get out of it entirely. Insulate himself some way from it. Behind a desk, maybe. Yes, if he could put up with a desk job until he retired he wouldn't have to worry about whether or not he'd live to retire. But desk jobs like that weren't easy to come by. He could put in a request for one, but he knew he wouldn't get it—not without sergeant's stripes. He shook his head. It always came back to that: a sergeant's rating.

He thought of Hawley. He still seemed the answer to everything. It had to be Hawley.

And he is a killer, he reminded himself. He did murder his wife. So he'd better get on with it, build his case, prove Hawley's guilt, and get it over with.

Yet, even though he had made that decision, for some reason he refused to examine he wasn't anxious to succeed.

At five o'clock he put away the pile of arrest reports he'd been checking and left the station to keep his date.

11

LOU felt like going to Hawley's place, putting his feet up, and having a few beers, but his daughter had invited him to dinner, and since he had begged off last week, he didn't dare make another excuse.

When he knocked on Toni's door he was wondering what it would be like this time. Indian? Hawaiian? Japanese? There was no way of telling. He got his first hint when Toni opened the door.

"Hi, Dad," she said, smiling, stepping back to let him in. She wore a neat, housewifely dress—the kind worn by thousands of American homemakers.

But even so, he didn't anticipate what was to come. Once inside, he had to stop and stare.

"You're late," Toni said. "I was beginning to think you had to work late again."

The room Lou saw was very ordinary—no oddball posters, no weird, uncomfortable furniture. Instead, a multicolor shag carpet on the floor, a dinette set with a plastic top and chrome legs, an ordinary sofa and ordinary end tables with ordinary plaster-based lamps and pleated shades. And the table itself was set with plastic plates, stainless steel cutlery, and gilt-edged water glasses—the kind customers used to get at gas stations.

"My God," Lou exclaimed. "What happened?"

Toni's smile widened. She was pleased with his reaction. "We just wanted you to feel at home, that's all." She kissed him on the cheek. "Dave! Dad's here."

183

Moving toward the kitchen, she said over her shoulder, "Make yourself at home. Dinner's almost ready."

Lou stood in the middle of the room. If it had been done in early Genghis Khan, or even late Hottentot, he wouldn't have been so surprised.

Dave came in, still wearing his working clothes—a suit, white shirt, and tie. But what was even more startling, he carried a bottle of liquor.

"Hi," he said. "I bought some bourbon."

"Bourbon?" Lou echoed. "What happened to your antipollution policy?"

"Gone with yesterday's rose." Dave crossed to a sideboard where he poured whiskey into two glasses.

Lou shook his head, as if to clear it. "I'm in the wrong house."

"We're even thinking of joining the PTA," Dave said smiling, handing Lou his glass. His smile, however, wasn't very convincing.

With a sweep of his hand, Lou indicated the room. "The rest of the place like this, too?"

Dave nodded. "There's even a plastic flower on the toilet."

Lou took a long swallow. He needed it. "What's the big idea, anyway?"

Dave sat down on the sofa. Rather stiffly, Lou thought. "Toni and I had a long talk after you left last time, and we decided it was time we grew up. We've been living like this ever since."

Toni came back into the room, carrying a platter. Smiling proudly, she said, "Here it is. Sit down, please. Dad, you at the head of the table."

The smell of the dish caught Lou's attention as he sat. In the past he never could recognize anything his daughter cooked, but this smelled familiar.

"What is it?" he asked.

"Your favorite." Toni was obviously pleased with herself.

"It's meatloaf," Dave said.

184

Lou stared at his daughter. She confirmed his fear.

"And I made it just like Mom used to make it for you!"

Lou couldn't help himself. "You're kidding?"

Dave turned to Toni, who was slicing and serving the meatloaf. "See. I told you he didn't like it."

For a moment Toni looked stricken. It was a look Lou had never learned to bear. "You do like it, don't you? You ate it all the time at home."

"Yeah, I ate it all the time at home. You're right." He looked down at his plate. It even looked exactly like the meatloaf his wife used to make.

Toni turned to Dave. "You're not so smart after all, are you?"

But Dave had certain views nothing would change. "Well then, even if he does like it, *I* still don't."

"Then don't eat it," Toni replied angrily.

Lou took a small bite of the meatloaf and fought to hide a grimace. "You're right. It is just like your mother used to make."

But Dave wasn't fooled. He passed Lou the bourbon bottle. "Take another shot."

"Thanks." Lou reached for it.

"But, Dad," Toni interrupted, "shouldn't you wait till after dinner?"

Lou took the bottle and started to unscrew the cap.

Toni went on. "I went to a lot of trouble to flavor the hamburger just the way Mother did. Now, if you drink that whiskey, you won't even be able to taste it."

Lou sighed and screwed the cap back on.

Dave shook his head. "Well, since I'm not eating the stuff anyway, it won't spoil my taste buds." He drained the bourbon still in his glass and reached for the bottle.

Toni glared at him, but since he ignored the look, she turned back to her father. "And just wait till after dinner. I've got a really big surprise for you."

"What is it?"

"You'll find out."

"I don't like surprises. You know that."

Dave interpreted. "She's talking about your room."

Toni was shocked. "Dave!"

"Wait'll he sees it. That'll be surprise enough for any man." Dave turned to Lou. "She really went to a lot of trouble to fix it up. It looks exactly like a room in a motel."

"Don't listen to him," Toni said. "He complains about everything lately."

"I just think," Dave went on, "you should have consulted your father first."

Toni glared at him. "You know he'd say don't bother!"

"Yeah," Lou said, "and I'd mean it."

Toni looked hurt. "You both act as if I've done something terrible. It's not wrong for a girl to want to look after her father."

"It is if he doesn't want to be looked after."

"He hasn't got any choice—remember!"

"And you're making him eat that junk," Dave said, pointing to the meatloaf on Lou's plate.

"Oh!" Toni exclaimed. She turned to her father. "I'm not making you eat it, am I? You're eating it because you like it, aren't you? Tell him so. Please."

Lou looked from her to Dave. Dave was watching him, waiting to see if he'd tell the truth. Lou said, "Honey, I appreciate all the work you've done—and the thought was real nice."

"Tell him you like it!" Toni exclaimed, almost in tears.

"I can't, baby," Lou said. "I hate it. I've always hated it. Your mother made it because she liked it and thought everybody else should."

Toni, in tears, threw her fork down on the table and ran from the room. Both Dave and Lou turned in their chairs to watch her go. Then Dave handed Lou the bottle again.

"Thanks." Lou poured himself a stiff one. "I don't think I've ever heard you two fight before."

"We never did before."

"How long has it been going on?"

Dave sighed. "It started, precisely, when we bought these plastic plates."

Lou looked down at them. They were, literally, square.

"Remember," Dave said, "how we used to eat off grape leaves sometimes, or out of rice bowls, or coconut shells?"

He paused, trying to sum it all up in his mind.

"I guess we really need our make-believe, our games. We haven't got anything but monotony without them."

Lou found himself feeling sorry for his son-in-law.

Leaning closer, Dave asked, "How do other people get along without them?"

"They don't," Lou answered. "They fight."

Dave shook his head. "I couldn't live like that—like this—bickering all the time—for long."

Lou was making up his mind. "Neither could I—not again."

Dave sensed Lou's resolution. "What're you going to do?"

Lou got up from the table and started toward the door. "I'm going to play that long shot for all it's worth. I've got to. I've got no choice."

Dave nodded. "I feel sorry for Hawley. But just the same, good luck."

Lou made one stop on the way, at a liquor store where he bought a quart of bourbon. A few minutes later he was knocking on Hawley's door.

When Hawley opened it and saw him, his surprise and pleasure showed. Letting him in, he asked, "I thought you were spending the evening at your daughter's?"

Lou went directly to the bureau for two glasses. "The evening ended early." Taking the bourbon from the brown paper bag, he held it up for Hawley to see. "And when we've finished this, we'll find a bar somewhere."

Hawley looked at him, troubled. "What's happened?"

"Nothing." Lou handed Hawley a tumblerful of whiskey. "Drink. You've got some catching up to do."

Hawley took the glass. "Something's wrong, isn't it?"

"Nothing at all." Lou raised his glass. It was only a third full.

"Then what brought all this on?"

187

Lou, sinking into the sofa, answered, "Just something my son-in-law said."

"What?"

"Toni's fixed up a room for me. It looks like a motel."

"Oh," Hawley responded, understanding. He sat down opposite Lou and took a long swallow.

Watching him, Lou said, "That's it. I'm half a fifth ahead of you and I don't like getting drunk alone."

"I've never been really drunk in twenty-five years."

"Do you good."

"We should drink to something "

Lou nodded, raising his glass. "Here's to the next twenty years. They're gonna be good ones, no matter what."

Hawley nodded. "I'll drink to that—and to Talua."

Lou frowned. "You're always drinking to Talua."

Hawley stared at him. "And you never do. I've noticed that. Why?"

Lou got up, went to the bureau, brought the bottle back, and filled Hawley's glass again even though it was still half full. "Why? I'll tell you. White sand, surf, tropical vegetation on the slopes of an ancient volcano—just too good to be true, that's why!"

"But it *is* true."

"No," Lou argued. "It can't be. It's too corny—a South Sea Island Paradise—all you have to do is 'sail off into the sunset'!"

Hawley nodded solemnly. "That *is* all you do have to do."

Lou sprawled on the sofa again. He wasn't drinking nearly as much as Hawley was.

"What's so wonderful about Talua besides the scenery?"

"I've told you that many times," Hawley said patiently.

"I forget. Tell me again." His intention was to keep him talking so he wouldn't notice how much he was drinking.

"Well," Hawley began, "it's one of the few true tropical paradises left. Contentment's really possible there. Nobody's in a hurry. Nobody has any appointments, nobody has to go anywhere.

Lou snorted. "A rich man's paradise!"

"No!" Hawley exclaimed. "You don't remember anything I've told you. You don't need money on Talua—not for the important things. The lagoons are full of fish. There's wildfowl all over the island. Nobody has cut down the trees, so there's still plenty of fruit. And there's no smog, no pollution—"

Lou poured himself three fingers and then refilled Hawley's glass. "How come nobody's built hotels yet?"

"I told you. It's too far off the trade routes. It doesn't pay most ships to go that far out of their way, and there isn't enough level land for an airport long enough for the big jets." Hawley took a long swallow and looked down at the floor sadly. "That's why I'm still here. You've got to pay those ships a hell of a lot of money to go that far out of their way."

Very casually, Lou observed, "They should be willing to take you there for fifty-eight hundred dollars."

Hawley looked up. "Hell, they'll do it for that, but where am I going to get it? I've only been able to save seven hundred so far."

Lou hadn't really expected to trap Hawley that easily, but he had expected some kind of a reaction when he mentioned the exact amount of money his wife had deposited in their joint account. But there hadn't been any reaction at all.

They finished Lou's bottle of bourbon around eleven. By twelve, they killed what little Hawley had and then went out to a bar. Around three thirty, when the last bar they visited was closing, Lou used his badge to cajole the bartender into selling him a bottle.

They hadn't taken Lou's car, so they walked slowly along the almost deserted thoroughfare back toward Barstow Street and Hawley's apartment.

The night was warm, a balmy Southern California night when the air is still, the smog gone, the stars bright. The streetlights were on and so were a number of neon signs, but they failed to spoil the beauty.

As the two men retraced their steps, they came to the bar

189

in which Lou had watched Hawley try to pick up a whore.

Hawley stopped and pointed to the place, weaving slightly.

"You know something, Lou?" he said. "I tried to pick up a girl in there once."

Lou nodded grimly. "Yeah, I know. I was tailing you."

Hawley turned to Lou, regarding him seriously. "She was a real good-looker, wasn't she? A real nice girl."

Lou snorted derisively. "Hell, she was a tramp!"

"No!" Ed exclaimed. "She wasn't!"

"She was a hustler, a hooker, a prostie!"

Hawley became defiant. "I bought her a drink!"

Lou shook his fist in Hawley's face. "She made a goddamn fool outa ya!"

Hawley was taken aback by his vehemence. "What're you getting so mad for?"

"I told you," Lou replied.

"So what? Who cares? I enjoyed buying her a drink."

"I coulda slugged her," Lou shouted. "I shoulda!" He was trembling with rage.

Hawley put his hand on Lou's arm. "Forget it, Lou. Take it easy."

Lou calmed a bit. "I don't like people who make fools outa other people!"

Hawley deliberately changed the subject. He stopped under a streetlight, took the bottle of bourbon from Lou's hand, opened it, and raised it to make a toast.

"I've got a great idea," he said. "Let's drink to the *Mary J.*"

"What in hell is the *Mary J*?" Lou asked.

"A ship! She's a ship that goes near Talua!"

Lou's mind, in spite of the alcoholic haze, came together. "How do you know she goes near Talua?"

"I know all about her. I know about all of them—I've checked up on every ship that goes near Talua."

Lou regarded him soberly for a moment, then asked casually, "You mean, since your wife died?"

Hawley shook his head. "No, not since my wife died. For

years I've been doing it. I can tell you the class, the tonnage, and the cargoes of every one of 'em."

"Yeah?"

"Take the *Island Star*. She carries six passengers and a cargo of fertilizer. She's the cheapest, but she's already gone and won't be back till next year. The *Mary J* costs more, but she's a better ship."

He raised the bottle again. "So here's a toast to the *Mary J*. May she have a good voyage when she sails."

Lou watched him drink. "When does she sail, the *Mary J*?"

"On the twenty-seventh."

Lou did some quick mental arithmetic. "Today's the twenty-fifth. That's only two days away."

Hawley grabbed Lou's arm. "You gotta come down to the docks with me, Lou," he said earnestly. "You gotta help me wave her good-bye."

Lou remembered the night he had followed Hawley to the waterfront, sure he was about to make a meet. He remembered watching him stand at the water's edge staring at a ship edging out into the harbor.

Hawley didn't see the emotions that flickered across his companion's face.

"I've seen 'em all leave. I've waved good-bye to the *Island Star*, the *Ocean Queen*, the *South Sea Princess*—"

He broke off abruptly, startled, as Lou suddenly grabbed his lapels and began shaking him hard, his face livid.

"You're lying to me!" Lou screamed. "You goddamn stinking drunk, you're lying to me!"

Lou's sudden rage had a sobering effect on Hawley. His face went white. For a moment he looked terrified.

"I'm not lying," he tried to say, but Lou went on shouting.

"You've been lying to me all along! You've been making a goddamn fool outa me!"

A man and woman walking along the opposite side of the street turned to look at them and then hurried on, not wishing to be involved in a fight between two drunks.

"Lou," Hawley finally managed to say, "I don't know what you're talking about. I don't know what you mean."

"That ship, you bastard—the *Mary J*!" He still held Hawley's lapels. "You're not going to wave good-bye to her! You're going to be on her!"

Hawley managed to break loose. He took a step back and then stood, confronting Lou. He was angry too.

"You're drunk," he exclaimed. "You're drunk, Lou. And you're a goddamn fool when you're drunk. How can I sail on the *Mary J*? How am I gonna pay the fare?"

Lou moved closer to Hawley. "You got fifty-eight hundred dollars!"

"Me?"

"Yes, you!"

"You're crazy!"

"Your wife had it in the bank!"

Hawley stared at Lou. There was something in the way he said it—he was serious.

"Evelyn had it?" Hawley asked dumbly.

"That's what I said!"

"Fifty-eight hundred dollars?"

He was utterly bewildered, but Lou wouldn't let himself recognize it. He couldn't. "Knock it off!" he shouted. "You knew about it all the time."

Hawley seemed stunned. He backed away, leaned against the window of a poultry shop. Lou kept close to him.

"I didn't know," Hawley said. "I didn't know."

"You did. You've known all the time. You wanted it from the beginning—for your South Sea island."

But Hawley wasn't listening. He just stood numbly, his face reflecting the effort his mind was making to grasp it. "You mean, it's mine?" he asked. "All of it?"

"All you have to do is sign for it," Lou said. "It's in an old joint account. You might have to pay some tax—I don't know—but most of it is yours. Just as you planned it from the beginning."

192

Lou's words slowly penetrated the confusion in Hawley's mind. "Planned?" he repeated. "What do you mean, planned?"

Lou looked at him hard, the way he had with so many criminals. "You killed her for the money, didn't you?"

"Killed her for the money?" Hawley echoed. "Is that what you think?"

Lou nodded, and Hawley suddenly, abruptly, lost his temper, shaking a fist at his companion.

"You goddamn fool," he exclaimed. "I didn't know a damn thing about the money. How could I kill her for it? I killed her because I couldn't stand the nagging bitch a minute more!"

They stood in the almost empty street for a long time after that, looking at each other. The words, Hawley's confession, lay there between them.

Then they turned and walked on, side by side, in silence. When they reached the corner of Barstow they turned toward Hawley's apartment building.

"She must have been saving it for years," Hawley decided. A black-and-white patrol car came down the street and cruised by them. "No wonder we never had enough money for a vacation." Hawley's anger was growing. "I wore the same suit for five years. I gave up bowling because it cost too much. I gave up smoking for the same reason." But his anger vanished with his next thoughts. "Fifty-eight hundred dollars. All those dead, dreary, dismal years, just so she could have fifty-eight hundred dollars for her old age."

Their minds occupied with their own thoughts, they walked on in silence.

Then Hawley asked, "How come I didn't find a bankbook in her things?"

Lou shrugged. "Maybe she didn't keep one—just so you wouldn't find it. The bank always has records."

When they finally reached the entrance to Hawley's apartment building, Lou shoved his fists into his pocket and said, "You should have killed her sooner."

Hawley nodded his agreement.

When Lou awakened the next morning on Ed Hawley's couch his mouth tasted foul and his head throbbed. The curtains were open and bright sunlight poured in, but it wasn't that which had awakened him. It had been the sound of something breaking in the kitchen.

"What the hell's going on?" he demanded.

Hawley, wearing wrinkled pajamas, appeared in the kitchen doorway. "I dropped one of Evelyn's china cups. Sorry." Then he disappeared back into the kitchen and a moment later returned with two cups of steaming black coffee.

"Here. You'd better drink this."

Lou sat up painfully. "Thanks."

"How do you feel?"

"As bad as you look," Lou replied, sipping the coffee. "What time is it?"

"Six. You've got to go home, shave, change your clothes, and go to work."

"Christ," was all Lou was able to say.

Hawley sat down in the chair opposite and drank his coffee. "Want some breakfast?"

"God, no!" Lou answered.

Then, after a moment, Hawley said, looking into his coffee cup, "I thought I'd go back to bed after you left. You can come and get me whenever you want."

Lou looked up. "Huh?"

"Or do you want me to go with you now?"

Lou shook his head to clear it. Hawley wasn't making sense. "What are you talking about?"

"My confession—last night. You remember, don't you?"

Slowly Lou nodded. "I just did."

Hawley got up and took a sheet of paper from the bureau and placed it on the coffee table in front of Lou. "I wrote it all out while I was waiting for the coffee to perk. I wanted to make sure everybody understood it wasn't premeditated. I mean, I meant what I said last night. I couldn't stand her

194

nagging a minute more, but it still wasn't premeditated. I just lost my temper and slapped her. She stepped back and tripped. I couldn't believe my eyes when she fell through the window."

Lou picked up the paper and read it slowly, then let it drop back onto the table. "Forget it. I'm not going to take you in."

Hawley stared at him incredulously.

"I don't believe it. After all the trouble you went to?"

"I made a mistake."

"The hell you did!" Hawley was angry. Lou looked at him, surprised.

"What are you getting sore about?"

"Why shouldn't I get sore? You're trying something!"

"You're crazy!"

"Hah!" Hawley got up. The cord on his pajamas was loose. The pants drooped.

Lou started after him, his eyes still bleary. "I don't get it. You're sore. You got no reason to be."

Hawley turned to face him. "I have so!"

"What?"

Hawley came to stand near him. "All right, I'll tell you. To begin with, last night you said you don't like being made a fool of. Well, neither do I!"

"Who made a fool of you?" Lou asked.

"You did. Every time you walked through that door"—he pointed to the hall door—"as my friend."

"That's not so—" Lou started to say, but Hawley interrupted.

"When did you first find out about the money?"

Lou tried to avoid answering that one. "That's got nothing to do with anything."

"It has. Tell me! I want to know how long I've been a sucker."

Lou banged the coffee cup down on the table. "For God's sake, don't you listen? I just told you I'm not going to take you in. Do you think I'd say that if I was trying to make a fool out of you?"

195

Hawley paused for a moment. "But you were making a fool of me, in the beginning, weren't you? Playing me along?"

"Sure," Lou admitted. "Sure—in the beginning." He picked up his jacket from the couch where he had used it as a pillow. "Forget about that now. I'm going to forget all about your confession."

Hawley watched him put on the jacket and search through his pockets for his car keys. Finally, he wanted to know, "You won't make sergeant if you don't arrest me, will you? You won't get that bigger pension?"

Lou shrugged and walked toward the door. "They probably wouldn't have given it to me anyway. It was a crazy idea. You'd better get yourself straightened out, too, or you'll be late for work."

Hawley shook his head. "I've still got sick days coming. I'm going to take one of them." Then, as Lou opened the door, he added, "Maybe you'd better arrest me. If you found out about the money, somebody else can, too."

Lou waved the thought away. "Forget it. By itself it's not enough. Anyway, Tate's closed the case."

Lou started to go, but Hawley thought of something.

"Lou, if you're not going to arrest me anymore, that means we can talk about sharing an apartment now?"

The thought seemed to clear Lou's head a little. "Yeah. I forgot about that. We can."

"Your regular pension would be enough to pay half the rent, wouldn't it?"

"Maybe," Lou said thoughtfully. "I'll have to figure it out. Look—I'll come back here after work. We'll talk about it then. Okay?"

"Okay," Hawley replied, shuffling into the bedroom.

12

THE day before, after Clayton Hoyle had finished giving Lou Baroni hell on the phone, he had only one thought in mind—to get out of town fast. The morning's markers were still in his pockets—he hadn't even placed the bets yet—but that didn't matter. Nothing did but the fact that Papa Pappas had put out a pickup order on him.

The day was sunny and warm, but Hoyle felt cold. Usually the busy streets, the crowds and constant traffic, invigorated him. Now they oppressed him. He felt watched, hemmed in.

He still had only one destination in mind—the bus station. If he could get on a bus, he felt he'd be all right. But the station was miles away.

He saw a large, black Chrysler coming down the street. It seemed out of place in the rundown neighborhood. He didn't wait to see if it was after him or not. He ran down an alley and didn't stop running until he was a dozen blocks away. Then he had to pause for breath. He wasn't naturally athletic and he was in terrible shape.

Standing there, wheezing, he thought of the obvious. A taxi. He had the morning's take in his pocket, plus his own roll. Why not a taxi? He was about to hail one when he saw a dark-blue panel truck slowly cruising toward him. Did any of Papa's men use a panel truck? In the back of his mind he seemed to remember hearing that they had, once. He started to run again, using back alleys and driveways whenever he could.

About two hours later he could run no more. His heart pounded, so did his head, and he had trouble catching his breath. But there, only a half a block away, was the bus station.

He forced himself to walk normally toward it. When its doors swung closed behind him he felt a tremendous sense of relief.

The waiting room was fairly busy, as it always was, but he was in luck. There was one ticket-window free. He hurried to it and bought a ticket on the first bus scheduled to leave—a nonstop to San Diego.

But he had fifteen mintues to kill, and that made him nervous. He looked around the waiting room, wondering if any of the people there were working for Pappas, but none seemed interested in him and he continued to hope.

He began to cough. His chest felt funny. He was still having trouble breathing and his face felt hot. Maybe, he thought if he washed it with cold water he'd feel better.

He stayed in the rest room for ten minutes. When he came out he did indeed feel better, mainly because it was now time to board his bus.

He had almost reached the double doors marked DEPARTURES when he saw the two men standing near them. He tried to turn, to duck behind the other people walking to the gate, but he was too slow. The men recognized him. His mind went numb, but fortunately instinct took over. Before the two men could react he had wheeled and raced for the street.

He never was sure what happened, exactly, in the following hours, but he did recall moments when he dodged in and out of heavy suppertime traffic, when he ran into one entrance of a department store and out another, or raced along sidewalks, turning corner after corner endlessly.

The following morning Lou Baroni and Ed Hawley weren't the only ones who felt lousy, but in Clayton Hoyle's case, it wasn't because of booze. It was mainly be-

198

cause he had spent a sleepless night shivering in an abandoned junkyard.

Now, chilled and feverish at the same time, stiff and sore and still exhausted, he faced the new day with a desperate need as old as Man himself: a warm, dry, safe place in which to hide. He didn't dare go to his own room—it would be watched. And he didn't dare go to Big Beebee's or to any of his other girlfriends—they were all known—and besides, those fat broads all talked too much.

When he finally forced himself to his feet, he swayed, dizzy as well as weak.

He made his way to the street and began to walk along it, through the bright morning sunlight, past the endless row of small grocery stores, fruit stands, bottle shops, bars—all closed because it was still so early.

A few cars passed—but very few—and there were hardly any pedestrians around at all, so he wasn't too worried about being picked up by one of Pappas' men. But he was having trouble putting one foot in front of another. And his eyes wouldn't focus properly. Everything had a tendency to swim before them.

He forced himself to stagger on for half an hour, completely unaware of where he was going. Then, in front of a closed massage parlor, he collapsed.

When he awoke, hours later, he realized he was in a hospital and smiled. Nobody, he thought, would look for him here. Then he went back to sleep.

When Lou went to work that morning he could feel something had gone down the minute he entered the building. In the squad room Miller looked up from his desk to grin at him.

"You gonna tell me what it is?" Lou asked, "or am I supposed to guess?"

Miller leaned back in his chair and stretched with pleasure. "The chief, the whole commission, had Tate on the carpet last night."

199

"For the count?" Lou asked.

"Just about," Miller replied. "Produce or out—that was the gist of it."

"The Zakos case." Lou's expression, unlike Miller's, was troubled.

"Right," Miller replied. Then, seeing Lou's worried look, he added, "Don't tell me you feel bad about it?"

"Not about Tate. I'm just wondering what it'll make him do."

Miller shrugged. "He's got us working around the clock as it is. Not much else he can do."

Lou shook his head. "He'll think of something."

Lou was right. After lunch Tate ordered Wally Blue's release. When Lou heard about it, he blew up. Miller tried to talk to him, to calm him, but he pushed past him and stormed into Tate's office without knocking.

Steve Perry was there, talking to Tate. Both turned at Lou's entrance.

"Do you know what you've just done?" Lou demanded of Tate without preamble. "Do you have any goddamn idea at all?"

"Now hold it—" Perry started to say.

"Stay out of this!" Lou barked at him.

"You've put a slug through Wally Blue's head, a shiv in his back—"

Tate said nothing, waiting for Lou to run down. But his facial muscles were taut, his eyes cold.

"Why didn't you just ask me to waste him?" Lou asked. "It would have been cleaner. He won't last twenty-four hours on the street!"

"You're exaggerating," Perry said.

"Goddamn it," Lou exclaimed, "I'm not! If he knows anything at all about the Zakos killing, he's a dead man!"

Tate spoke for the first time. "He's being tailed by two of our best men. They'll look after him."

Lou snorted. "He'll dump them before dark."

"I don't think so," Tate spoke evenly, but his fists were clenched.

"What do you hope to get out of it?" Lou demanded. "He's not going to lead you to Zakos' killer. He's going to stay miles away from him."

"I'm aware of that," Tate said.

"Then what's the angle?" Lou asked. "Where's the percentage?"

Tate didn't answer, but Perry grinned.

"Well?" Lou demanded, looking from one to the other. "What's the pitch? If he gets killed, you've got nothing. You've lost your only possible informer—"

He broke off then as it finally struck him. He had the answer—the reason for Wally's release. Wally had refused to talk. Somebody else, however, might.

"You're not having him tailed to protect him at all," Lou accused. "You're having him tailed so you can pick up his hit man and then try to make him talk!"

"It's not as cold-blooded as that," Tate began. "We'll do our best to protect Blue—"

"But you want his killer first, alive. That's what really matters, doesn't it?" Lou glared at Tate. "You don't give a damn whether Wally's wasted or not."

Tate held in his anger. "I've made an executive decision. I don't intend to discuss it with you—"

"The hell you don't!" Lou said, turning toward the door. "You will when I find Wally and bring him in before—"

"Baroni!" Tate barked, no traces of refinement in his voice now. "I'm warning you, I want no interference. That's a direct, unequivocal order, made in front of a witness. If you disregard it, I'll have your badge—that's a promise—and you'll have nothing!"

Lou didn't bother to hide the scorn he felt. Finally he turned and left the room.

Miller was waiting in the hall. He had heard just about everything. "Lou, listen," he said urgently. "He's got all the aces. Lay off. Think of your pension."

"The chief," Lou said. "I'll go to the chief."

"No," Miller said. "The chief approved of the idea. I just heard that. He doesn't like it, but he approved it."

Lou's voice was bitter. "What about Wally? Did he approve?"

"Lou," Miller said, shaking his head. "Back off. Wally's going to be all right. He's got two tails."

Lou snorted.

"Really," Miller added. "Two was the chief's idea. He even picked 'em. Good men, the best. One from Vice, the other a Narc—there's nobody better. They'll look after Wally. You can count on it."

Lou didn't reply. He walked down the corridor to the squad room where he went back to work on the pile of old arrest reports that covered his desk.

Hours later, when his watch was finally over, he drove downtown through the heavy suppertime traffic. He had no real destination in mind, but it was here, in the ghetto areas, where Wally would look for a fix. Wally was hurting, he knew. Worst than most.

Of course, he didn't find Wally. He wasn't really looking. But he thought it might make him feel better if he were nearby. It didn't.

It was after seven when Lou finally said the hell with it. Wally wasn't his responsibility, and Tate had ordered him off, anyway. Besides, he couldn't risk his pension just because some junkie had put his neck in a sling.

He drove over to Hawley's place, thinking about the pension. A plain detective's pension wasn't much, but it was something. And if he shared an apartment with Hawley, it might be enough.

Laurie was at Hawley's apartment. They were watching a television show in which she had a big part for a change—the "other woman" in a jet-set triangle that ended in murder. She played a greedy beautiful bitch with a malicious tongue and a taste for blackmail. Lou found it odd to see her on the screen dressed in high fashion while she sat on the floor cross-legged wearing jeans.

And she was surprisingly good. When it was over, both Lou and Hawley told her so. She laughed with pleasure, accepting the compliments gracefully.

202

Later they sat around the table eating salami sandwiches and discussing the idea of Lou and Hawley sharing an apartment. Lou was preoccupied, but he forced himself to take part. He didn't want to think of what might be happening to Wally Blue.

"It could be this place or yours," Hawley said. "Or somewhere else if you like. It doesn't matter to me."

"We'd need two bedrooms," Lou pointed out, "so we wouldn't get into each other's hair."

Hawley considered it for a moment. "You're right. But a two-bedroom apartment would cost a lot more."

Laurie spoke, reaching for another sandwich. "I think you should stay here. You'd only be together evenings. Ed would be away at work all day. And even after Lou does retire, he should be able to find a job of some kind. He wouldn't be here all the time, either."

"A two-bedroom apartment might work out better, even so," Hawley told her. "Lou's used to living alone."

"But what about your savings?" Laurie asked. "You should save as much as you can each month or you'll never get to Talua."

Hawley sighed. "I know. But, well, maybe someday— But if this thing works out with Lou—"

"No!" Laurie interrupted. "No, don't say that. No more 'maybe somedays'—you've got to go—it's been your dream for years!"

"That's it, exactly," Hawley replied. "My dream—not Lou's. I don't have the right to make him put up with a one-bedroom apartment just so I can save more for Talua."

Laurie turned to Lou. "You really wouldn't mind, would you? And besides, I think you should go to Talua with him."

Lou hadn't really been listening. "What did you say?"

Laurie studied him for a minute. "Something's wrong. I felt it the moment you walked in. Now I know it."

"It's nothing," Lou replied. "You said something about Talua?"

But they wouldn't let him off. They made him tell them

203

what was on his mind—about Wally Blue's danger, about Tate's order to lay off, about his threats.

"But, Lou," Hawley said, "if you're fired now, before you retire, you won't get any pension at all—will you?"

"No," Lou answered. "None."

"The men following Wally Blue," Laurie said, "they'll look after him . . ." It was half a statement, half a question.

"Their main job," Lou explained, "is to get the man who has Wally's contract."

"But they won't let him be killed," Laurie insisted.

"They'll do their best," Hawley added.

Lou poured himself another shot of bourbon. "Their best might not be good enough."

"But they'll try as hard as you would, won't they?" Laurie asked. "I mean, there's no reason for you to feel bad about it. They can do as much as you could, can't they?"

Lou didn't get a chance to answer. The phone rang. Hawley answered it.

"Hello?" He listened for a moment and then said, "Yes, he's here." He turned to Lou. "It's for you."

"Me? Nobody knows I'm here."

Hawley shrugged. "His name's Miller."

Lou took the phone. "How'd you know I was here? You guessed good. What's gone down?"

Laurie and Hawley watched Lou's face. Finally he said, "You figured right. I did want to know. Thanks." Then he hung up.

Laurie didn't like the look on his face at all. "What is it?" she asked. "What's happened?"

"Wally Blue shook both tails an hour after he was released. The damn fool's on his own."

For a moment they remained silent, unmoving. Then Lou started for the door.

"Lou, wait!" Laurie cried. "Remember what your lieutenant said about your pension and—"

But Lou didn't wait for her to finish. He was gone.

News of Wally Blue's release spread quickly. He hadn't been on the street for ten minutes before the phone in Nicky Pappas' white-wallpapered apartment rang. After he heard the news he made two phone calls himself. Seated at a small white and gold telephone table, he called one of his special friends and gave him brief instructions: Spread the word. Find out where Blue is and where he goes.

The second call was long distance—to a hotel at a marina.

Wesley Price hadn't been idle since his arrival. He knew the city fairly well from previous assignments, but even so, in the few days since his arrival, he had taken several long drives in his rented Volkswagen through the downtown areas in which both of his intended victims spent most of their time. He disliked every minute of it. He loathed the dirt and the smog, the noise and the people.

He had spent the rest of his time studying the material Nicky Pappas had given him. It didn't bother him that the Negro, Wally Blue, was in jail. His first hit, he felt, had to be the detective, anyway. Otherwise, the death of Blue would alert Baroni and make that particular hit more difficult.

He was seated on his balcony, watching a graceful schooner slide through the sunlit water of the harbor, mulling over the manner in which Lou Baroni was going to die, when his phone rang.

The sound annoyed him. Nobody was supposed to call him here.

"Hello." His voice was cold, angry.

"This is Nicky Pappas. I must see you right away."

"Impossible." His tone brooked no debate. "I never meet my clients." It was true. No one knew what he looked like.

"It's imperative. There's been a new development."

"Write me about it." He meant, write to the mail drop they had arranged.

"There isn't time. It must be now."

205

Wesley Price considered the matter for a moment. He had checked Nicky Pappas out. The man was a homosexual but still considered formidable. Also intelligent. If he wanted to talk, he must have a good reason.

"All right, we'll talk—but on a safe phone. I'll call you back in forty-five minutes. Where will you be?"

A few minutes later he left the hotel and drove to a phone booth six miles away. When he dialed Nicky's number he had to wait only a moment before it was answered.

"Hello?"

"You said there was a new development?"

"They released Wally Blue."

The news troubled Wesley Price immediately. Blue had been charged with possession. Because of so many priors, he had been refused bail. Now, suddenly, he had been freed.

"Why?"

"That's not important."

"It is. It could be a trap."

He heard the voice at the other end of the phone laugh. "Of course it's a trap. I know that. Why do you think I'm paying you so much money?"

Wesley Price didn't like Nicky Pappas' attitude. It wasn't professional. Pappas seemed to be enjoying a game.

"Take care of Blue tonight."

"Impossible."

"It has to be done. Blue talks in his sleep."

"No."

"Are you refusing the contract?" This last was asked in a menacing tone. Wesley Price knew Nicky would spread the word, tarnish his reputation.

"I haven't completed my workup on him or the detective."

"Work up the detective later. You won't need one for Blue."

Price knew instantly what Nicky had in mind. "I don't like setups."

"I'll make it foolproof."

206

"I prefer to do my own."

"There's no time."

"You wanted an accident. An accident can't be arranged in a hurry."

"Forget it. Give him an overdose if you can. If you can't, use a knife or a gun. He'll be in that kind of a neighborhood anyway."

It was becoming more and more distasteful. "You need a cowboy, not me."

"I've got you. You've got my money."

It was true. He had accepted the retainer. He sighed. Some days nothing went right. "When and where?"

"Later. I'll let you know later."

He hung up, a foul taste in his mouth. Amateur! He hated working for amateurs! But since it had to be, he'd make the best of it—the very best.

Once in his room he slowly underwent a physical change. Since he couldn't become a Negro, he became something almost as inconspicuous in the ghettos. He changed into a faded pair of torn Levis. His immaculate shirt was exchanged for a dirty one, over which he wore a greasy, fringed, and beaded jerkin. He also had a long-haired wig, a full mustache, and a heavy beard, but he didn't put these on until he was back in the Volkswagen driving toward the city.

After Lou left Hawley's apartment, Laurie commented, "He might not get fired. I mean, since those other detectives lost Wally Blue, they might want Lou to find him."

"Yes," Hawley replied. "That's possible."

"Besides," Laurie said, moving back to the table, "he might not be able to find him."

Part of her second sandwich lay unfinished on her plate, but she wasn't hungry anymore. She cleared the table, took the dishes to the sink, and began washing them. Hawley picked up a towel and began to dry.

"It's funny," she said after a moment, "how lives intertwine."

207

"What do you mean?" Hawley asked.

"A year ago I didn't know you or Lou even existed. Now, the idea that he might get fired or you might never get to your island makes my blood boil."

Hawley had to smile at her intensity. "You shouldn't get so wound up. Things always have a way of working out."

She stopped to look at him. It was just the kind of thing she would have expected him to say. She realized, then, that there was a much better way to learn the actor's art than just watching people through binoculars. And this was it—to become a part of their lives.

She left a short time later and returned to her apartment across the street to do some thinking. She did it sitting on her balcony in the dark.

Somehow it seemed right for a man like Edward Hawley to long for an island in the South Pacific. Once, if she had been called on to play such a part she would have objected. It would have seemed too unreal, too far-fetched. Now it didn't at all.

Next, there was Lou Baroni. He was "doing what he had to do." It was a cliché she had heard and scorned a thousand times, and yet, now, it seemed perfectly plausible and she could accept it without a qualm.

Lastly there was herself. She was surprising herself. Suddenly Hawley's dreams and Lou's ambitions were terribly important to her, almost as important as her own ambitions. She longed to help them, and the sudden realization that she was no longer thinking only of herself startled her. There was a knock at the door. Since she wasn't expecting anyone, she called out, "Who is it?"

"Police," came the reply. "Sergeant Steve Perry."

She smiled to herself. Maybe there was a way she could help Lou Baroni after all. She paused to bring deliberately to mind a girl she knew who lived the sex thing twenty-four hours a day. She decided to adopt her smile, her stance, her inflections. That done, she finally opened the door.

Perry leaned against the doorjamb, a bottle of whiskey in his hand.

208

"I've come to interrogate you," he said, grinning.

She grinned back, leaning against the doorjamb on her side of the door. "Before you ask, I confess to everything. I work for the KGB. I print my own money. And I sleep in the nude. Come on in and make yourself comfortable while I slip some ice into some glasses."

A few minutes later he was seated on the sofa and she on the floor at his feet. She was proud of the staging, having chosen her position to make him feel more dominant—and it very obviously did.

Looking up at him, seductively, she hoped, she asked, "Did you really come to interrogate me?"

He laughed. "Believe it or not, I did come for that too."

Laurie leaned back on both her hands. The position, she knew, thrust out her breasts. "Interrogate away."

"It's about Baroni—that detective I told you about—the one who was harassing that man across the street."

"Was?" Laurie wanted to know. "Isn't he anymore?"

Perry snorted. "No. They're buddies now. If I didn't know better, I'd say they're queers."

Laurie sipping her drink, almost choked.

"Is that what you wanted to ask me, whether they're queer?"

Perry shook his head and smiled. "I've got something much better in mind."

Laurie looked at him quizzically.

"Have you ever seen anything pass between them? Has Hawley, for instance, ever given Baroni an envelope?"

"You're kidding!" she exclaimed. "You expect me to see something like that from up here?"

Perry shrugged. "It was just a thought."

She looked up at him through lowered eyelids. "You didn't really come to interrogate me, did you?"

Perry's grin became a leer. "Yes, I did. For instance, do you really sleep in the nude?"

"Sometimes. What's supposed to be in the envelope?"

"What envelope?"

"The one you want me to see Hawley giving Baroni?"

He reached down, took her hands, drew her up on the sofa beside him. "Would you say you saw it if I asked you to?"

She leaned her body against his. "That depends."

"On what?"

"On what's in the envelope."

"Money," he said, kissing her.

She allowed the kiss to linger. She wanted him in a talkative mood.

"What money?" she asked when the kiss ended.

"You don't need to know. There's no way you could. You just have to say you saw the envelope change hands."

"Why?"

Perry's grin was mean and smug. "I've got my reasons."

"What? I'm curious."

"No."

She started to move away. He drew her back, but she resisted.

"Tell me."

"It's just an idea I've got."

"For what?"

"To get Baroni fired."

"How?"

She didn't find out until they were in bed together. She let him fondle her but nothing more until he told her everything.

Perry's plan was to charge Lou with accepting a bribe. He would claim Lou had found proof Hawley had killed his wife but had sold his silence for a large sum of money.

For a moment, after hearing Perry's scheme, Laurie felt like kneeing him in the groin, but she didn't. He was her only link to the "other side." And she might want to find out more from him in the future.

She allowed him to make love to her then. She really didn't mind. She told herself she really wasn't involved. It was just a part she was playing.

When Lou Baroni left Hawley's place, he had only one

210

thought in mind—to find Wally before his killer did. He had no facts to back up that belief, just the instinct of an old cop.

He went to each of Wally's favorite hangouts, talked to his friends. In almost every case, other detectives had been there before him, and nothing he could say managed to restore the confidence of his informers. If they had seen Wally, they wouldn't admit it.

But the other detectives didn't know Wally as well as Lou did. They didn't know all the places the tall, skinny hype might go.

The Soul Spot was a two-bit bar on the edge of the black ghetto, crowded in between a massage parlor and a porno house.

There were only two lights on inside when Lou entered. One illuminated the solitary pool table that occupied most of the room, and the other illuminated Myra, the nude who waited on the bar.

Although most of the Soul Spot's clientele were black, Myra was Caucasian. Mack, the dude who ran the place, figured a whitey would attract more customers. But Myra wore a huge Afro hair style anyway, her idea of a gesture of goodwill between races. It made her look top-heavy.

She grinned at Lou when he came in and called out, "Hi, lover!"

Lou waved back, sat down at the bar, and waited for her. She was a big broad. Once she had been well built, but now she was running to fat. Not that anybody cared. They'd seen it all before, anyway.

When she was free she came over and leaned on the bar. "What can I do for you, Lou baby?"

"Nothing, right now. Where's Mack?"

Myra shrugged her bare shoulders. "Where else? In the back room."

"I've got to see him."

Myra shook her head. "No way."

Lou looked at her hard. "This is important. Press the buzzer."

211

"Lou, I can't. You're a cop. Mack would ream me!"

"It's about Wally Blue."

"He hasn't been here." She said it much too quickly, but Lou let it pass.

"He's been set up. He'll be wasted for sure unless I get to him first."

Myra hesitated. "You sure?"

"I'm sure. Press the buzzer."

Myra sighed. "All right. But make it right with Mack, will ya?"

Lou nodded and walked to a door at the rear of the room. When his hand was on the knob, Myra pressed a button at the bar and the door unlocked. Lou opened it and went in.

There were six men inside playing poker, and judging by the amount of money on the table, the stakes were high. Several of the players jumped to their feet as soon as they saw Lou.

"Easy," Lou told them. "This isn't a bust."

The men settled back in their chairs uneasily—all but one. A big, powerful Negro at least a head taller than Lou came around the table, took Lou's arm, and led him to the far side of the room.

"Hell, man, you wanna give my place a bad reputation?"

Lou shook his elbow free. "Mack, I've got to find Wally Blue fast."

Mack backed off a step. "Christ, Lou, you don't think I'm dealing—"

"There's a contract out on him."

Mack whistled. "Jesus! That a fact?"

"A fact," Lou lied. "If I don't get to Wally first—" He let the rest of it hang.

Mack stopped to think for a moment. "I don't want to get mixed up in anything that heavy."

"Just tell me where he is."

Mack shook his head. "I can't. That's the truth. I don't know where he is."

"Mack, you listen, you big bastard—I've got to find Wally!"

212

Mack threw up his hands in dismay, a peculiar gesture for so big a man. "All right, all right—but you gotta keep me out of it, y'hear?"

"You're out."

"He was here 'bout an hour ago. He's real strung out, hurtin' real bad. He's been trying to feed that arm of his all day, but nobody would deal. Word got around he was being tailed by two of your brother pigs."

"Yeah—but he shook them."

"That's what he said. But I still didn't have anything for him. I don't deal, you know that. I'm no pusher."

"Okay, you're no pusher."

"That's the God's truth. All I could give him was a handful of dimes."

"Dimes?" Lou asked. "For the phone?"

Mack nodded. "I wouldn't let him use mine. He went outside. When he came back he had that big stupid grin on his face."

"He'd set up a meet?"

"That's what I figured."

"Who with?"

"I don't know. He didn't say."

"When?"

"I don't know that either. But I know the place. Second Street and Elmore. He was bitching about it when he left. Said he was gonna have to run all the way to get there in time."

The restaurant where Nicky Pappas sat was crowded, but he still remained alone in the vinyl-padded booth. People standing in the foyer, waiting for a table, scowled at him for taking up so much space. But that was just what he wanted. Let them scowl. They'd remember he was there.

Actually he was quite pleased with the world at that moment. As he sipped his coffee he was thoroughly bemused by his thoughts. Fate was remarkable. It was amazing the way it cooperated sometimes. The present instance was a perfect example of what he meant. He had his friends

213

searching for Wally Blue all day, without success—and then Blue, himself, had actually tracked him down and called him right there in the restaurant. The call couldn't have been more opportune—nor could his request. He had to have a fix right away, he had said. He was hurting. And he had begged for a meet, anywhere, anytime.

Of course, Nicky had been properly sympathetic and he had agreed to the meet. But naturally, he was going to stay right where he was, establishing an alibi. But that didn't mean Wally was going to be stood up. Not at all. Nicky had arranged to send Wesley Price in his place.

It was going to be easier than he had thought, Wesley Price concluded as he pulled the Volkswagen to the curb. He still didn't like to be rushed. He still didn't like an amateur arranging his setup. But so far everything was working. As he sat in his car across the street from the brightly lit Rock Heavy, a dilapidated dance hall covered with weird posters, he had to admit he was pleased with the arrangements. The neighborhood was foul, but that was ideal. Even better, it seemed to be crawling with long hair and beards. In his hippie outfit he'd never be noticed. He'd just be one among many.

Also, Wally Blue was coming alone, and he was eager. That meant he'd be far from cautious. Such factors always made a job go more smoothly.

Price left the Volkswagen parked among a number of other Beetles and buses and walked casually over to the entrance of the small dance hall. The doors were wide open— it was a warm night—and the blaring music was deafening. That was good, too. It would cover the sound of a gunshot if he were forced to use a gun. He didn't intend to. He preferred something more subtle. In this case he planned to use a knife, although even that didn't please him. If he had been allowed to prepare properly, he would have opted for a hotshot, something Wally would administer to himself when Price was miles away. But there wasn't enough time for that now. A knife would have to do.

A couple of teen-age girls hung around the Rock Heavy door, eyeing him as he passed, but he ignored their invitation, turning the corner to walk along Elmore Street.

The alley Nicky Pappas had chosen for the meet was between Rock Heavy and an old warehouse. It too seemed ideal. Dark, cluttered with cans and packing cases, it provided a number of places where he could wait unseen, and since the rear windows of the dance hall were open, the music here was even louder than it had been on the street—especially the drums.

Price glanced at his watch. It was almost time. He stepped behind a pile of boxes and drew his knife.

Lou drove as quickly as he could toward Elmore and Second, tires squealing as he skidded around corners. He didn't know exactly when the meet was scheduled, but once the skinny Negro got his heroin, he'd crawl into a hole and not surface again for days—that is, if he wasn't killed first.

As he drove, Lou wondered whom Wally had called, who his supplier could be. Not one of the street peddlers. They'd been scared off by Tate's men. And besides, they had a way of wanting their money up front and Wally didn't have any. No. It had to be someone who was a special friend—a girl maybe, or Nicky Pappas.

Suddenly, as he ran a stop sign, he caught the flash of a red light behind him. Damn, he thought, a black-and-white! Cursing, he pulled over to the curb, losing precious minutes as he showed his badge to the uniformed officers and explained his hurry.

Wesley Price didn't hear Wally Blue enter the alley because of the music. He first realized he was there when he saw him silhouetted by a streetlight.

Wally stopped on the sidewalk just inside the entrance to the alley, and called out, "Nicky?" When there was no answer, he called out again, louder this time, "Hey, man—you in there?"

Price remained where he was, silent. He wanted Wally to

come farther into the alley, away from the street. He was surprised to see that he was tall. He had mentally prepared himself for a shorter man. Now he'd have to revise his thinking. That was the trouble with poor preparation. Too much had to be improvised on the spot.

Wally started to walk up and down at the mouth of the alley. He wasn't going to come in. He was waiting where he was, thinking he'd been the first to arrive. Price realized he'd have to improvise again.

"Hey, Wally!" He had to shout to be heard over the music. "Come on in here!"

Wally, startled, wheeled to peer down the dark alley. "Nicky?" he called. "That you?"

Price didn't answer. But Wally didn't move.

Price shook his head. It wasn't going the way it should. "Wally, come on in here. You want everybody to watch?"

Wally took a few tentative steps into the alley, away from the streetlights, then stopped.

"You ain't Nicky. You don't sound like him!" He seemed ready to run.

"I never said I was Nicky," Price called out quickly. "He couldn't come. He sent me instead."

Wally was still troubled. "He said he'd come himself."

Price sighed. He was losing patience. "You want the stuff or not? I got better things to do."

"I want it," Wally yelled quickly. "I'm hurtin' real bad. Like, you know, something's inside eating out. Where the hell are you, man?"

"Right here. Come on. Out of the light before somebody sees you."

Wally seemed to sway back and forth, at a loss as to what to do.

"Why don't you come out a little?" he asked, pleading.

It was taking too long, Price felt. He stepped out from behind the packing cases, his knife in his belt where he could reach it quickly, his gun in a holster under his arm. He felt foolish standing there like some villain in a cheap Western.

216

"There," he called out. "You see me now. All right?"

Wally was still frightened. The man in front of him looked like a hippie. When did Nicky start hanging around with hippies? he wondered.

All right, Price said to himself with a sigh, I'll go to him. Holding out his left hand, extended as though he carried something, he walked slowly toward Wally.

It was the left hand that enticed Wally. The prospect of the heroin being that close was too much for him. Forgetting his caution, he rushed forward, seeing light glint off the blade at the last moment.

"Hey!"

But Wesley Price, for the first time since he had begun his specialized profession, had miscalculated. He was still thinking of a short man. The blade entered Wally's body too low. It missed the heart by more than an inch.

Wally screamed, jerked away, and ran, collapsing on the sidewalk at the entrance to the alley. But he had gone far enough, for Lou, speeding up to the intersection, had glimpsed a man fall. When Price ran forward to finish his work, Lou was out of his car, gun in hand.

Price drew his gun, but never had a chance to fire it. Lou got off one shot, all that was necessary.

Wally was conscious, lying on his back, his hand over his wound. He had heard Lou's single shot and seen his assailant fall to the concrete beside him. And he heard the black-and-white screech to a stop at the curb.

He looked up to see Lou Baroni's concerned face looking down at him. He managed a weak grin.

"Lou, baby. Hiya, man. Guess I owe you again, huh?"

Then he lapsed into unconsciousness.

13

THE patrolmen from the black-and-white went about the business of securing the area. There wasn't much to do. There were no eager spectators watching Wally bleed. The raucous music blaring from Rock Heavy had drowned out the shot, and the sight of speeding police cars in that neighborhood was too common to attract attention.

Lou knelt on the sidewalk beside Wally, trying unsuccessfully to stem the Negro's bleeding. He kept at it until the ambulance came. Then he followed it to the hospital. He meant to stay only long enough to find out if Wally would live. But while the tall, emaciated Negro was in the operating room, Lou fell asleep in a chair in the hospital's waiting room. It was almost three thirty A.M.

Clayton Hoyle, in another hospital miles away, woke around four A.M., and for the first time since he had collapsed the morning before, his mind was clear. He'd been fed, injections had reduced his fever, and—most important—he had slept.

But the small man knew he didn't dare rest much longer. Papa Pappas had put a pickup order on him. It wouldn't be neglected. Besides, hospitals had a way of prying. There were forms to fill out which demanded certain incriminating statistics.

He decided an hour later that it would be best if he left the hospital right away.

His clothes were in a closet. He had a few touchy moments sneaking past nurses and orderlies, but once on the street, breathing the cool night air, be began to think he had made it. He took a taxi to the airport. The taxi company belonged to one of Pappas' legitimate ventures, and the driver, once he recognized Hoyle, made a brief radio call.

A short time later the cab stopped at a downtown intersection and two men joined Hoyle in the back seat. Hoyle knew who they were at once—Papa's men.

When he was young, Papa Pappas rarely rose before nine, but now that he was old, he never slept that long, usually waking before dawn. He found this both a blessing and a curse—a blessing because he could stand on his balcony and watch the sunrise, a curse because of the long day stretching before him.

On this particular day, when he stepped out onto his balcony, the soft glow that bracketed the mountains was just beginning, but it did nothing to dispel the weariness that had accompanied him to bed the night before. The miracle of dawn, now, simply meant a renewal of yesterday's problems—and they all centered around Nicky.

He was seated on his patio, still in his dressing gown, when a taxi rolled to a stop in front of his home and three men got out. He wasn't aware of it, of course, but his friend and servant, Demetri, was. After serving Papa his coffee, Demetri had gone to the front door to await the taxi's arrival. Now he opened the door to admit one of the three men— the small, nervous one. The others returned to the taxi, which then drove back toward the city.

The sun had risen above the mountains, and Papa sat watching graceful swans glide effortlessly across the calm waters of his lake. He felt he should be enjoying the scene, but he wasn't. Even his coffee tasted bitter.

He looked up when he heard footsteps. It was Demetri, followed by a small, worried-looking man who was sweating profusely even though the morning was still cool.

"This is Clayton Hoyle," Demetri said matter-of-factly.

219

Ah, yes, Papa thought, the bookie who had made those phone calls to a police sergeant.

The little man kept closing and unclosing his fingers, trying desperately to appear at ease but unable to do so. Inwardly, Papa sighed. Fear. He had seen it so often. And he was so tired of it.

The little man managed to speak. "It's a great honor to meet you, sir. After all these years, hearing so much about you—good things, I mean—a great honor."

He's pale, Papa thought. Not only frightened, but sick, too. "Sit down," he said, pointing to a chair beside the patio table. The little man sat quickly on the edge of the chair, as if obeying an order.

"You don't look well," Papa said. "You should take care of yourself."

"Oh, I will," Hoyle promised. "I will."

"Coffee?" Papa asked. Then, without waiting for a reply, he turned to Demetri. "Another cup." Demetri turned and left.

Clyton Hoyle was puzzled, not sure what he had expected, but it certainly wasn't a soft-spoken old man who seemed genuinely concerned about his health.

"Do you sleep well, Mr. Hoyle?" Papa asked.

"Yes, sir," was all Hoyle managed to reply.

"When I was a boy in the Old Country," Papa said, "I could sleep in the fields, on the beach, anywhere. Now I sleep badly even in bed."

Demetri returned and placed a cup of coffee on the table before Hoyle, who jumped visibly.

"Sometimes," Papa said after a moment, "I think I would sleep better if I had less problems."

Here it comes, Hoyle thought. He's going to tell the big goon to start working me over.

"Do you know my son, Mr. Hoyle?" Papa asked.

"No," Hoyle answered. "I mean, I know of him—everybody does—but I've never met him."

220

Papa sighed. "He's one of my biggest problems. Beside him, you are only a small problem."

Hoyle put the coffee cup down. He couldn't force himself to drink any more.

Papa went on. "As Nicky's father, I must do everything I can to keep him out of trouble. You understand?"

Hoyle nodded to signify that he did.

Papa leaned back in his chair. "Tell me," he said, "why did you phone that detective—what's his name—"

"Perry."

"A friend of yours?"

"No—no friend at all—not him."

"Then why did you tell him you'd give him my records? Why did you have him sitting in his car near here for so many evenings?"

He knows all about it, Hoyle thought. Everything. What can I tell him?

Hoyle searched for words, failed to find them. Finally he blurted out the truth. "Honest, Papa—I mean, Mr. Pappas—I really don't know the reason for it. I was just asked to. On my mother's grave, I swear it!" He looked from Papa to Demetri, who was standing slightly to one side, a few steps behind him, to see if either believed him. He couldn't tell from their expressions.

Finally Papa said, "Well, Mr. Hoyle, since you don't know why you made the calls, maybe you know who asked you to make them?"

"Sure," Hoyle said with relief in his voice. Here was a question he could answer. "Sure—I thought I told you that. It was another detective—a guy who could bust me if he wanted to. A guy named Baroni. Lou Baroni."

Now Papa did something that Hoyle had expected all along. He lost his temper. "Baroni!" he exploded. "Always Baroni!" He banged his fist on the table, spilling the coffee. Hoyle held his breath.

"Why can't this Baroni investigate somebody else?"

221

Papa demanded, rising. "Why can't he leave me alone?"

"I don't know," Hoyle managed to say. "He didn't tell me—"

But Papa wasn't listening anymore. He turned and stormed into the house, his face contorted with anger.

After he was gone, Hoyle sat where he was, still facing the table, wondering what would happen to him now.

"Go," Demetri said bluntly, pointing to a path that led around the side of the house.

Hoyle went, scurrying across the patio and along the path like a frightened mouse.

In the house, Demetri found Papa in his study, about to light a forbidden cigar, his expression a mixture of anger and worry.

"Baroni," Papa repeated. "Always Baroni!"

"Nicky was right," Demetri said. "This Baroni must be killed."

Papa turned to face him. "No. No, not yet," Papa replied. "It could destroy all this." With a wave of his hand, he indicated his home, his island, all of Hellenic-West Village, everything that still meant anything to him.

"It may be necessary to risk it," Demetri pointed out.

"There must be another way," Papa said.

"There isn't."

"I will find one. I will have him killed only if there is no other way."

"When?" Demetri insisted.

"Soon," Papa promised. "But first I will talk to him."

They brought Wally Blue from the operating room an hour before dawn and placed him in Intensive Care. It was there Lou found him several hours later. Unconscious, Wally was a shallow mound, under a white sheet, surrounded by plasma bottles and the paraphernalia of a recovery room.

At first the nurse wouldn't let Lou in, but he showed her his badge, changing his request to a demand. She acquiesced, but only to the extent of calling Wally's doctor to

222

deal with the problem. He turned out to be an old man, too old for night work, and he was very tired. But he was the kind of man Lou could talk to.

"Friend of yours," the doctor asked, "or just somebody you want to send to jail?"

"Friend," Lou said. "It comes from sending him to jail so often."

The doctor nodded, rubbing his eyes. "Well, you might not get a chance to do that again."

"You mean it?" Lou asked.

"I mean it," the doctor replied. "He's got a chance, but I don't give you a nickel for it—even at today's prices."

"I didn't think the knife had gone that deep," Lou said.

They were standing in the open doorway of Wally's room, looking in at him. "It didn't," the doctor explained. "If he dies, that won't be the cause. It's the cancer that's killing him."

"Cancer?"

"You didn't know?"

Lou shook his head. "Son of a bitch!"

"I cut out as much as I could, maybe even all, but in his weakened condition he has no recuperative power left. He's been living on margin for years."

"No wonder he was mainlining," Lou said.

"Didn't he ever complain about the pain?"

"He complained. He always complained. Every junkie does when he's clean. They all say they're hurting, but I never figured he was hurting that much."

The doctor sighed. "He should have come here. We would have given him all the morphine he needed—legally."

Lou shook his head again. "The poor, stupid bastard," he said softly.

Wally woke an hour and a half later. Lou was sitting on a chair beside the bed, half dozing.

Wally had trouble turning his head, but when he recognized Lou, his face broke into its usual lopsided grin.

223

"Hiya, Lou," he said feebly. "How's it going, man?"

Lou stood up, then laid a hand on Wally's arm. "Still dragging, Wally—over broken glass—and it's getting heavier, too. How about you?"

"Don't feel so good—got shived."

"Yeah," Lou answered, "I know. You were set up. You shouldn't have shaken those tails."

Wally had closed his eyes again. For a moment, Lou thought he had fallen asleep.

"You saved me, didn't you, Lou?" he said, his eyes open. "I remember. You wasted the mother—"

"You better take it easy. Don't talk."

But Wally wanted to talk, even though the effort was painful. He felt he had something important to say. "I owe you, Lou. I want you to know I know I owe you. And I'll pay you back for sure. That's a fact, man."

"Sure."

"Soon as I get outa here, I'll find a way, Lou."

Lou's next words were bitter in his mouth, but it was his job. "Want to tell me who tried to ice you?"

"Don't know. Never got a good look at him."

"But you do know why, don't you? And who wrote the contract?"

Wally's expression was one of anguish. "Lou—don't ask that. I can't tell you. I would, if I could, but I can't. You know that, don't you?"

"Sure, Wally," Lou answered, patting Wally's arm. "Sure. Forget it."

"I know I owe you, Lou—and I'll pay you. But not that." Tears came to his eyes. "I can't tell you that."

Lou changed his tack. "Hell, Wally, look what they did to you! Don't you want to make the bastards pay?"

Wally tried to shake his head. "I ain't sure, Lou. Anyway, I can't snitch on this one. I just can't. He's been—" He broke off. It seemed as if he had used up the last of his strength.

Lou stood beside the bed, looking down on the emaciated

face, the heavy lines that marked it, the sunken eyes, the yellow, crooked teeth that showed a little between the cracked lips, and thought, he's not even thirty yet, but he looks like an old, old man. Christ, Lou said to himself, and he wasn't sure whether it was a curse or a prayer.

Wally's breathing was extremely shallow, so Lou wasn't sure whether he was really asleep or not. But in case he was, he tiptoed toward the door—just as it burst open and Lieutenant Tate, followed by Sergeant Perry, stormed in.

"Baroni! I knew I'd find you here!"

"Keep it quiet!" Lou said, indicating Wally in the bed.

"He still alive?" Perry asked. "We just talked to the doctor—"

"Shut up," Lou said. "He might be listening!"

Tate ignored Lou's anger. "Never mind that," he said. "Did he talk?"

"No," Lou said. "He can't."

"What do you mean, he can't?" Tate demanded, glaring at Lou. "The knife went in the chest, not the vocal cords."

"I mean, he doesn't know anything."

Tate looked at him incredulously. "You believe that?"

"Yes," Lou answered.

"Baroni"—Tate jabbed a finger at Lou's face—"let me tell you something. I've never liked your attitude and I like it even less now!"

"Too bad," Lou replied, turning toward the door.

"Come back here," Tate exclaimed. "That's an order!"

Lou turned at the door. "Do we have to talk in here?"

"Yes, we do. That addict's the key." Tate waved a hand in Wally's direction. "Now tell me everything he said, every word."

Lou sighed. "He didn't say anything. I told you that."

"He must know who tried to have him killed."

"He knows you set him up."

Again Tate waved a finger in Lou's face. "Baroni, be careful what you say. I've already had you suspended pending an investigation."

225

"Suspended?" Lou became aware of a sinking sensation in his stomach.

"Yes, suspended. I have the power to do that—or had you forgotten?"

"You got to have a reason," Lou protested.

"I've got a reason, a damn good one. You know you deliberately disobeyed my orders. You know I wanted Wally Blue's hit man captured alive so we could establish his connection with Nicky Pappas. But you killed him anyway."

"I had to," Lou said. "He was killing Wally. He drew a gun on me."

"Oh, no"—Tate's smile was grim—"oh, no. You don't get out of it that easily. The whole thing could have been prevented if you had followed proper procedure. You rushed to the area yourself—I've got two men in a traffic car who will swear to that—but you didn't call for backup. There were three cars in the area, but you didn't radio ahead. You could have had that alley staked out as soon as your snitch talked."

Lou felt like asking him what snitch, but he knew better. Tate was guessing. He was right, but he was still guessing. Lou wasn't going to confirm or deny anything. That way it couldn't be used against him later.

Tate was still grinning mirthlessly. "You've really done it this time, Baroni. You're out for good now. And that means no pension, no separation pay, nothing!"

"In that case," Lou said, "I don't have to stand here and listen to all this crap!" As he walked out he didn't see Wally raise his hand a few inches, trying to beckon him. Nor did Tate or Perry notice.

After the door had closed behind Lou, Perry asked Tate, "You really suspended him?"

"Pending an investigation, yes."

"Think it will stick?"

"It will if you can get me something to go with it. Some additional breach of regulations or even the possibility of

226

one. I told you I'm counting on you. You'd better come through."

For once Perry wasn't disturbed by Tate's threat. This time he merely smiled confidently. "How about the possibility of bribery?"

Tate looked at him with increased interest. "Bribery?"

"Suppose there's a reason why Baroni spends so much time with Hawley. Suppose the reason is a payoff?"

"You mean Baroni found evidence of murder and is using it to blackmail the suspect?"

Perry nodded smugly.

"Can you prove it?"

"I might have an eye-witness who'll say she saw Hawley handing Baroni a package the size of money. But even if she won't, the fact we pull her in for questioning will plant the possibility, the doubt—and that's all we need now, since Baroni disregarded a direct order, isn't it?"

Tate nodded, his expression indicating his pleasure. He placed a hand on Perry's shoulder.

Wally Blue had never really been asleep. It was difficult for him to keep his eyes open for long, or to speak, but there was nothing wrong with his hearing. He had heard Tate firing Lou and had cursed him silently for a long time. Damn, he had thought, if only he could tell Lou what he knew about the Zakos killing. That would really fix that motherfucking lieutenant. But he couldn't. Nicky had always been good to him. He couldn't, wouldn't, believe he had put the contract on him. Papa Pappas he'd buy, but not Nicky.

Yet he felt he ought to do something to help Lou get his ass out of hot water. He had to. He owed Lou.

He'd been thinking this when Perry mentioned Hawley's name. He wasn't sure what it was all about, or even who this guy Hawley was, but he did remember, in a hazy way, the conversation he had overheard outside Tate's office.

227

Lou had wanted to bust Hawley, but Tate had kept saying the case was closed. Yeah, Wally thought now, Lou had really wanted to bust that guy Hawley good.

It was Perry who noticed Wally's eyes open. "He's awake," he told Tate.

Tate pushed Perry aside, drew up a chair, and sat down. "Blue," he began earnestly, "Wally—do you know who I am? I'm your friend."

Wally's eyes closed for a moment. Tate took this to signify yes.

"They tried to kill you. You know that, don't you? Your other friends, I mean."

Again Wally's eyelids closed momentarily.

"You don't owe them anything now," Tate said. "You can tell me everything now, you know."

Again the eyelids closed and opened.

"Who killed Spiro Zakos? What's the name of his murderer?"

Wally lay motionless, his face a mask, his eyes open, staring at the ceiling.

"Then who did this to you?" Tate insisted. "Who had you hit?"

This time Wally's head moved slightly from side to side, signifying no.

Tate was becoming exasperated. "All right, then tell me this—are the Zakos killing and the attempt on your life connected?" He was fumbling, grasping for straws.

Surprisingly, Wally's head moved slightly up and down: yes.

Encouraged, Tate pressed on. "All right, you don't know who had you hit. You don't know who killed Spiro Zakos. But they're connected." His brow wrinkled. It didn't make sense. But the man was dying. Dying men don't lie. It *had* to make sense. He pulled another random question out of the air.

"All right. What's the link?"

This time Wally's lips moved slightly. Perry leaned forward. "He's trying to say something."

Annoyed, Tate motioned Perry to be quiet.

"What are you trying to say? Nicky Pappas' name?"

Wally shook his head no and continued trying to form a single word.

"Then it's Papa Pappas," Tate said. "That's what you're trying to say, isn't it?"

Again Wally moved his head from side to side slightly, then he managed to make an unintelligible sound.

"Again," Tate said, his ear close to Wally's mouth. "Again. Try harder!"

When Wally uttered the sound, it was only a whisper. "H-Haw-Hawley."

Tate sat back in his chair, a look of astonishment on his face. "Hawley. He said Hawley."

"I know," Perry said. "I heard him too."

"Hawley," Tate repeated, his mind working, his surprise gradually turning to acceptance, then anger.

"Hawley," he said, furious now. "And that bastard Baroni, he knew it. He's known it all the time! That stinking, no good goddamn Baroni!"

Perry wasn't able to accept it all so quickly. "It can't be Hawley. Hawley's a nobody—a nothing—"

"Nobody?" Tate retorted. "Nothing? Perry, that's why you're only a sergeant and I'm a lieutenant. Hawley's not a nobody at all. He's a real somebody, and that bastard Baroni knew it from the start. That's why he's kept after him. Not because he might have killed his wife, but because he knew he was on to something really big!"

He looked at Wally, lying motionless on the bed, his eyes closed, his face blank.

"Wally," Tate said, leaning forward again, "listen to me. You've got to tell me everything you know about Hawley. Who he is, what he is. Everything."

Wally didn't stir. His eyes remained closed.

229

"Wally," Tate prodded. "Listen to me. This is very important. I've got to know everything about Hawley. I've got to have evidence."

Wally's eyelids fluttered and his head turned slightly toward Tate.

"Lou," Wally whispered. "Lou. . . . Ask Lou. . . . He has all—"

The effort of talking seemed too much. For a moment Wally seemed to stop breathing, then his eyes closed and his chest began to rise and fall rhythmically.

Perry, standing near Tate, watching him sitting beside the bed, stricken, dismayed, his face ashen, kept his own expression noncommittal. But he was enormously pleased to see Tate in trouble. The lieutenant had just fired the one man who had the evidence to break the Zakos-Pappas case!

Tate stood up abruptly. "Come on," he said, and he and Perry started for the door.

"Where are we going?" Perry asked. "After Baroni?"

"Like hell," Tate replied. "After Hawley."

Neither bothered to look back at Wally as they left. If they had, they would have seen a small smile on the wasted face.

It was still there the following night when he died.

14

WHEN Tate left Wally's room he pushed by the nurses and interns in the corridors and shoved his way into the elevator.

The two men rode down in silence. Perry knew it wasn't wise to say much when Tate was in a foul mood. And Tate was preoccupied making plans.

As they were leaving the building, Tate said finally, "Don't tell anybody about this. Understood?"

"Right."

"Especially about Baroni," Tate added.

Perry couldn't help adding, "But he has the evidence—"

"I know," Tate snapped, "but I'll be damned if I go to him begging."

Perry kept his face straight.

"Baroni might go to the chief."

"I'll get the evidence myself first."

"How?"

"I'm going to search Hawley's apartment."

Perry was surprised. "You'll need a warrant."

"I'll get a warrant."

"But what about sufficient probable cause?"

"We have Wally Blue's statement."

"It's not enough—" Perry began, but Tate cut him off. They were in the parking lot, approaching their car.

"It's enough. A dying man's last statement. I know a judge who always goes for that."

Perry continued to enjoy Tate's consternation. "There

231

might not be anything left in the apartment. Blue said Baroni has it all."

"If he has it," Tate said grimly, "I'll get it from him somehow." He turned to scowl at Perry. "Everybody wants something. But first I'm going to try to get it myself. Understood?"

"Understood."

They reached their car. As they got in, Tate said, "While I'm getting a warrant, I want you to watch Hawley's apartment. I want to know if Baroni goes near it or takes anything from it."

"Right."

"And be clever about it. Don't let him see you. Find someplace off the street from which you can watch—a roof, maybe, or a window."

Perry thought immediately of Laurie's apartment. It was a pleasant thought. "I know just the place."

When Lou left the hospital he drove directly to his apartment. He had no reason to go to the station. He didn't work there anymore. And Hawley was at his own job. Anyway, he was tired.

Fully clothed, he lay on his bed, his eyes closed against the bright sunlight that managed to seep in around the windowshade, and tried to sleep.

But his mind wouldn't let go of his problem. It seemed overwhelming. If Tate could make his suspension stick—and with his brownnosing he probably could—it meant the end of Lou's pension and there didn't seem to be much he could do about it.

He could appeal it, of course. He could go to the chief himself. But he was a realist and he knew he didn't have much of a chance against Tate. Unless he could come up with something new.

He sighed and rolled over onto his side, cradling his face in the crook of his arm, his hand shielding his eyes from the light. The main trouble, he thought, was that he was so tired of it all—Tate, the chief, the department, everything.

232

He wished there was some way he could say the hell with the whole damn thing, but he knew there wasn't.

He thought of Edward Hawley, their plan to share an apartment. That was out now. That idea had included his pension. Without it, he'd have no way of paying his share.

He rolled over onto his back and pulled a pillow down over his eyes. The future looked grim—years of looking for some kind of a job that would enable him to live the way he wanted to. And while he was looking, he'd have to live with his daughter.

As he finally fell asleep, a half hour later, he was still trying desperately to think of a way out.

Laurie was sitting in the sunlight on her balcony, studying the part of a saloon girl, when she glanced down at the street and saw Perry arriving. She studied his posture and his gait as he entered her building, deciding that here was a man with something on his mind. Something besides sex, she meant—though she didn't doubt that was there, too.

When she opened her door to his knock she was pleased to see she was right—his eyes went first to her balcony and the view of Hawley's apartment before they shifted to her denim shorts and halter.

"Hi," she said, smiling. "I didn't expect to see you here at this time of day."

"Any time's the right time," he said, his eyes still following the lines of her figure.

She laughed and deliberately moved away from him. She had decided to play coy. He was there for more reasons than one and she wanted to know what the others were.

"Want some coffee?" she asked.

"I'd rather have you," he replied. Laurie felt like wincing. She'd heard that line in her first year of high school.

"I meant first," she said teasingly. "We've got lots of time, haven't we?" She stood at the stove in her kitchen-alcove, her back to him, preparing the coffee.

"No," Perry replied, "only a couple of hours."

She turned to see him move to the balcony.

233

"Why only a couple?" she asked conversationally. "What happens then?"

"Tate arrives with a warrant," Perry answered.

"Who's Tate?"

"My lieutenant. You know, I told you about him."

He had. So had Lou.

"But why a warrant?" she asked. "What's it for?"

Perry laughed. "That guy across the street. You're not going to believe this, but he turns out to be a king of crime."

"You're joking!"

Perry shook his head. "A very reliable snitch told us."

"A snitch?"

"An informer. A hype named Wally Blue."

Laurie left the coffee to perk and joined Perry on the balcony.

"I don't understand," she said. "You're really going to arrest him? I mean, you've got evidence?"

"Not yet. That's what the warrant's for—to search the place."

"Search it?" Laurie said in surprise, trying to put the pieces together. "But—I mean—what makes you think there's evidence there?"

Perry shrugged, took Laurie's hand, and led her to the sofa where he pulled her down beside him.

"Baby, I don't think there's any evidence there at all. I know exactly where it is and so does Tate. But he's desperate. He's spinning his wheels."

Laurie allowed Perry to put his arms around her bare waist.

"But if you know—I mean," she said, "where the evidence is, why don't you just go there and get it?"

Perry smiled. "You're not going to believe this either, but Baroni's got it. That detective I told you about—you know."

"But I don't understand. If he's got it, why do you and Tate have to search—"

"Because Tate fired Baroni—that's what's so funny."

234

"Fired him?" Laurie didn't have to feign surprise.

Perry nodded. "Before Wally told him about Hawley. Now the only way Tate's going to get it is by finding it himself or by crawling to Baroni."

Laurie nodded and allowed Perry to finger her navel, her mind working. She didn't understand it all, but the outline was there. She wondered if Lou knew about it.

Perry put one hand on her thigh, moving the other to her breast. "Let's have the coffee after," he said and nodded toward the bedroom.

Laurie loosened his tie and began undoing his shirt. "But I'm expecting a call from my agent. I wouldn't want him to phone in the middle of things—would you?"

"You call him then," Perry suggested. "Now."

It was just what she had wanted him to say. She smiled seductively. "All right. You go into the bedroom and get ready."

Perry didn't have to be told twice. The moment he was gone Laurie placed the phone on her lap and dialed Lou's number.

Lou was asleep when the phone rang. It took him a moment to remember where he was and longer to realize who was calling and why.

He only interrupted Laurie's hushed recital once, and that was to exclaim, "Wally told them what?"

Later, after he hung up, he exclaimed "Jesus!" to the room, and in his mind cursed Wally for being such a damn fool. He didn't doubt Wally had meant to help him, but when he thought of the trouble it was going to cause Hawley he exclaimed "Jesus!" again, getting up from the bed to pace the length of the room, thinking frantically. If Tate reopened Evelyn Hawley's case, even as an excuse to investigate, he might find out about the money in the joint account. If he went to that personnel manager at Hawley's office, Hawley would be fired for sure. And even if Hawley could beat the rap, he'd have to spend some time in jail, hire

235

a bondsman, pay a lawyer. He'd go broke. But Hawley wouldn't beat the rap. Not him. He'd admit to Tate, as he had to Lou, that he had slapped his wife. That would be enough for a manslaughter conviction if a smart DA went to work on it.

As Lou's thinking processes slowed down, he began to see other ramifications to the case. Laurie had quoted Perry's remark about Tate having to crawl to him for the evidence he didn't have. The mental picture it presented appealed to Lou and he began to play with it.

In the kitchen, he opened a can of beer, took it back into the living room, sat down in his easy chair, and began to go over the possibilities. Slowly the frown on his face gave way to a grim smile. Wally Blue hadn't realized it, but the dying hype might actually have handed him a way out—if only he could find a way to make it work. He glanced at a calendar. That part of it was fine. It was the morning of the twenty-seventh.

He sat there thinking about it for another quarter of an hour. It seemed longer—his mind covered so many ploys, so much strategy—but at the end of it he had formulated a plan, one that could possibly work and was certainly worth a try.

He made several phone calls. The first was to Ed Hawley. He didn't have any trouble convincing him to do what he suggested, even though his suggestions sounded wild. Hawley responded to the note of urgency in his voice and said yes to almost everything. There was only one thing he questioned—drawing the $5,800 from the bank—but even so, in the end, he agreed to do it.

The second call was to Miller at the station. Their conversation began with Lou asking if Tate were there.

"Yeah. He's doing the workup on some kind of warrant. He's doing it himself, too."

Then Lou proceeded to ask him for a big favor. He was prepared to remind Miller of all the favors he had done him, but it wasn't necessary. When Lou had gone through the whole thing, detail by detail, he agreed readily. It appealed to him.

The conversation ended with one final instruction. "Stress today," Lou said. "Make it sound off the cuff, but make sure he gets the idea that it has to be today!"

Finally he called Laurie Knight back.

"You couldn't have called at a worse—or better—time," she told him, "depending how you look at it." There was laughter in her voice.

Lou was puzzled for a moment until she added, "I was just in the middle of something—with a friend."

"You're not alone?"

"No. I'm being interrogated by a policeman, but don't let it bother you, Sam. He's a nice policeman." Sam was the name of her agent.

Lou thought for a moment and then asked, "Can you get rid of him or leave him there? I want you to buy some stuff for me and then meet me at my place."

"What's happening?"

"All or nothing," Lou answered. "Cross your fingers."

"Oh, I will."

Then Lou told her what he wanted her to buy—and do.

At the other end of the phone she opened her eyes wide in surprise. "What in the world do you want all that for?"

"Tell you later," Lou promised as he hung up. Puzzled, Laurie put the phone down.

Perry, standing nude in the bedroom doorway, said, "Come on, let's get back to it."

She turned to him, her expression one of complete dismay. "Oh, darling—I'm sorry, but I can't. That was my agent. I've got to report to a studio right away—a really big part—the chance I've been waiting for. I'm to star in a major mystery!"

It was almost three hours later when Lieutenant Tate finally arrived at Hawley's apartment building. Perry, alone in Laurie's apartment, saw him approach on foot, walking

237

furtively across the driveway of the adjacent building. He hurried downstairs to meet him, crossing the street in full sight of anybody who might be watching.

Tate, standing out of sight beside a hedge, scowled at him. "You must be out of your mind. He probably saw you just now."

"Who?" Perry asked, puzzled.

"Hawley, of course. What's the matter with you?"

Perry had trouble keeping his anger in check. He was in a bad mood. "Nothing's the matter with me. Hawley didn't see me. He's at work this time of day."

"No, he isn't," Tate replied. "I've checked. He walked out. Without a word."

"Well, he didn't come here. I've been watching."

"He could have come in the back way. He could be up there right now."

"No," Perry lied. "I haven't taken my eyes off his windows for a second. If there was anybody up there, I'd have seen him."

Tate didn't want to discuss it. "We'll assume he's there and act accordingly. If he isn't, we'll search the place. I've got the warrant."

Perry followed Tate, hugging the walls, to the entrance of the building and then darted inside after him.

They were in the elevator when Perry remarked, "I'd just about given you up. What took you so long?"

Tate ignored the reproach. "I had things to do."

"I thought you'd have trouble getting that warrant."

"It wasn't the warrant," Tate told him. "Remember I told you everybody wants something? Well, I found out what Baroni wants."

The elevator reached Hawley's floor and Tate said no more. Stepping out, he drew his gun. For the first time Perry realized that if Hawley really was who Wally Blue said he was, they might be in trouble, and decided to draw his gun.

238

"What about backup?" he asked. "We should have men—"

Tate cut him off. "We're doing this ourselves."

"But—" Perry persisted.

"You said he wasn't here, didn't you?"

"Yes."

"Then we don't need backup. Come on."

Unhappily, Perry followed him down the corridor toward Hawley's door. Tate motioned to him to take up a position on one side and he moved to the other. Silently they flattened themselves against the wall in the approved police manner, holding their breath, listening for any sound inside.

After a moment, Tate whispered to Perry, "You're absolutely sure you saw nobody, nothing?"

"Absolutely," Perry whispered in reply. Since he had lied before, he had to continue.

"Then go ahead."

Perry felt like protesting but he didn't. He was the junior officer. He moved out in front of the door while Tate crouched beside it, gun ready. Then, raising his foot, Perry drove it into the door beside the lock. Wood splintered as the door flew open.

Tate, still crouching, rushed into the room, his gun held in both hands before him. Perry followed, darting left away from the doorway.

Both froze, holding their stance, as their eyes took in the room. Neither liked what they saw. Lou Baroni was sitting on Hawley's sofa, his feet on the coffee table, sipping a can of beer.

Tate was the first to overcome his surprise. "Goddamn it, Baroni, I expected to see you today, but not here!"

Smiling, Lou took another sip of beer before he replied. "He wasn't at work, was he?"

Tate and Perry were still crouching. Straightening up, they lowered their guns.

239

"You know he wasn't at work," Tate said. "Where is he?"

Lou shrugged. "At this moment, it's hard to say."

Tate turned to Perry. "Search the place."

Perry nodded and left to look through the apartment.

"For what it's worth," Lou said, "Hawley didn't kill Zakos or even have him killed. He hasn't anything to do with the Pappas family."

Tate glared at him. "I don't believe you."

Lou took another sip of beer. "I didn't think you would."

From the bedroom came the sound of drawers being opened and closed.

"He won't find anything," Lou said.

"How can you be so sure?"

"There's nothing to find."

"How do you know?" Tate demanded.

Lou didn't answer. His smug smile infuriated Tate.

"You know because you've got the evidence somewhere yourself, haven't you?"

"Have I?"

"Yes! I've got the statement of a reliable witness."

"Wally Blue's not a reliable witness. He'd say anything he thought I'd like him to say."

Tate grew livid. "Baroni, you're going too far!" He shook a finger at Lou. "Too far!"

"What are you going to do?" Lou asked casually. "Take away my badge? You've already done that."

Tate was about to reply angrily as Perry appeared in the bedroom doorway and shook his head. Tate looked at Lou, who was sitting self-assuredly on the sofa.

Tate seemed to wilt. Then, after a moment, he forced a comradely sort of smile and sat down on the edge of Hawley's easy chair opposite Lou.

"Lou, Lou—what are we fighting about? We're a team, you know—a team—and you're a very important part of it. You always have been."

"Yeah?" Lou said sarcastically.

Tate sighed. "All right, Lou, all right. I admit it and I

240

apologize. I treated you badly and I won't deny it. But, Lou, you've got to understand how it is. I've been under a lot of pressure lately. The chief's been on my back for weeks. Every day he expects me to walk in with the evidence to put the Pappas away for good. If I don't deliver soon—well, you know what it means."

Lou nodded. He knew.

"But you can change all that, Lou," Tate went on, leaning closer, earnestly. "You have all the answers."

Lou raised his eyebrows. "I do?"

Tate ignored the remark. "And there's enough recognition in it for both of us. I'll make it known you've been instrumental. You'll share in the glory."

Lou drank the last of the beer. "You're forgetting something. I'm a civilian. You fired me."

"No, Lou, no. I didn't mean that. I was worried. Upset. I lost my temper, that's all." His smile was sheepish.

"You mean you didn't put my suspension papers through?"

"Of course not. I never intended to."

"Bull," Lou said. "You just happen to think I've got you by the short hair and that's why you're crawling. But it won't do you any good. I haven't got anything to tell."

Tate's eyes became cold, his body rigid. "All right, if you won't cooperate willingly, we'll do it another way."

"There is no other way," Lou said.

Tate got up and stood looking down at him. "I happened to have a talk with Miller this morning—about you. He told me about a conversation you had. It didn't mean anything to him, but I'm a better judge of character than he is." His expression changed to one of smugness. "I saw right away the real meaning behind everything you told him. He wasn't just telling me about a conversation he had with you. He was telling me, without even knowing it himself, your price!"

Lou said nothing, waiting for Tate to go on.

"He was telling me your price, wasn't he?"

241

"You're doing all the talking."

"You're right, I am," Tate said. "And I'll say this—your price is too damn high."

Lou sighed deliberately and started to get up. "Guess I might as well be going—"

Tate cut him off. "Sit still. The price is too high—I meant that—but since it won't cost me anything, I'm prepared to pay it."

Perry, still standing near the bedroom doorway, was completely confused. "What price?" he asked. "Money?"

"No, not money," Tate told him scornfully. "Our friend here wants something else much more than money. He wants to retire right away. But he wants a promotion first. He wants to retire with a sergeant's pension."

There was silence as both Tate and Perry looked at Lou.

"Is that what Miller told you?" he asked.

Tate smiled mirthlessly. "You know damn well it is."

"I've talked to a lot of people about it," Lou admitted. "I guess I could have mentioned it to Miller, too."

"You mentioned it, all right," Tate responded. "And, as I said, I'm willing to pay it."

Lou looked at him questioningly, "Promotion and early retirement now—you can't arrange them both, can you?"

"I not only can, I have. I had to use all my influence. I had to pull a lot of strings, but it's done." He took a sheaf of papers from his inside jacket pocket and held them enticingly in front of Lou.

Perry looked from Baroni to the lieutenant and then at the official documents in Tate's hand. Listening to every word, drinking it all in, memorizing it, he was seeing his own future being made.

Lou stared at the papers hungrily for a moment. Then, suspiciously, he asked, "What do I have to do for them?"

"Come off it!" Tate snapped. "You know damn well what I want. Tell me everything you know about Hawley's connection with Zakos and the Pappas family. Turn over all the evidence you have."

"That's all?" Lou asked.

"That's all."

Lou paused as though he were thinking. Then he looked at Perry, who was standing near the sofa, and then back at Tate. He indicated the documents in Tate's hand.

"You know you're trying to bribe me, don't you?"

"The word is reward," Tate corrected. "That's how it reads in here. A reward for long and faithful service."

Lou allowed himself to smile. "How do I know those papers are real? How do I know you won't cancel them tomorrow?"

Tate's smile was cold. "I knew you'd think of that. But I won't rescind them because I can't," Tate said. "Both copies are here and I'll give you both. One you'll keep and the other you can mail in to administration yourself. My signatures are all over them both. I'd look like a fool if I tried to negate them. I'd have to admit I made a mistake, not only to the chief, but to all the commissioners as well. You can be sure I won't do *that*."

Lou nodded. "No, you're right. You'd never do that." He reached for the papers.

Tate drew them back quickly. "Oh, no," he said. "Not until I have the evidence."

Lou snorted and got up. "Forget it." He started for the door. "Shove your papers!"

"Wait!" Tate exclaimed. "I've shown my good faith. You have to show yours."

At the door Lou said, "Like hell I do. I don't even have to talk to you. I can go to the chief myself. He can promote me. He can arrange the retirement."

It was the flaw in Tate's sales pitch and Tate knew it. He had known it from the beginning, hoping Lou wouldn't realize it.

"All right," he promised, "we'll do it your way. I'll turn over the documents first. But you've got to promise in front of a witness"—he indicated Perry—"that you'll tell me everything you know about Hawley's connection with the Za-

243

kos killing and the Pappas family, that you'll turn over all the hard evidence you have."

"All right, I promise."

Reluctantly, Tate handed over the documents. Lou took them and put them into his inside jacket pocket, but only after making sure both signed copies were there.

"Now, Lou," Tate said eagerly, "tell me what you know."

"Sure," Lou said with a straight face. "That's easy. I don't know anything."

Tate didn't seem to comprehend the words at first. "What did you say?"

"I don't know anything," Lou repeated.

Tate's face went white. "You promised—"

Lou nodded. "I said I'd tell you everything I knew about Hawley's connection with Zakos and Pappas—and I will. Everything is nothing. There is no connection."

Anger suffused Tate's face. "I don't believe you! You said you'd give me hard evidence."

Lou shrugged. "I said I'd give you all the evidence I had. And I will. Nothing. I don't have any. There isn't any."

Tate refused to accept it. "But Wally Blue said you had it."

"Wally Blue lied. I told you that."

"He did," Perry said, trying his best to keep from laughing. "That's exactly what he said." He failed. He laughed out loud.

Tate was livid now. He turned on Perry. "Shut up!" he yelled. "Shut up!"

Lou took that moment to open the door. Tate saw the move and lunged at him. *"Give me those papers!"* he screamed.

But Lou was too quick. He moved aside as Tate crashed against the wall. Before Tate could recover, Lou slipped through the door. He could hear Perry's laughter and Tate's screams following him, and that was the only topper Lou needed. With all Perry had seen and heard, the two were wedded forever. And, in his opinion, they truly deserved each other.

15

LOU drove straight home, hoping the rest of the day would also go according to plan. Laurie was the next step. He had told her to meet him at his apartment. As he parked his car in front of the building, he wondered if she had made it. She had. He knew that as soon as he walked into the lobby. Much of the material he had asked her to buy was piled in a corner.

When he entered his apartment he found her sitting cross-legged on the sofa, wearing an Indian feather head-dress and holding a peace pipe. Both accessories went well with the brass-studded denim jeans and shirt she wore.

"How," she said.

"How yourself," Lou replied, crossing to the bureau.

"I've just figured out what you want with all this stuff. You're planning an uprising."

Lou shook his head. "Wrong. I'm going to put one down." He began rummaging through one of the bureau drawers.

Laurie watched him for a moment and then made a mock gesture of despair. "Lou, if you don't tell me why you had me buy all that stuff, I'm going to scream."

Lou enjoyed being mysterious. "You'll know soon enough."

He finally found what he was looking for—an envelope.

He wrote the address of the police department's administration office on it and then put one copy of Tate's document inside, as well as a brief note which authorized the

245

payroll department to send his pension checks to his bank. Then he went to the door.

Laurie, still sitting on the sofa, watched him and shook her head sadly.

"What's the matter?" Lou asked, opening the door.

"The way you licked that letter. A dénouement deserves more flare." She pantomimed the way he should have done it, exaggerating it.

Lou chuckled and Laurie liked the sound of it. "You know, that's the first time I've heard you laugh."

"Come on. We've got things to do."

Downstairs they loaded everything Laurie had bought into the back seat of the car, as it wouldn't fit in the trunk. That was already full of suitcases. Then they drove away, but not before Lou had paused to take a long, lingering look at the apartment building.

Watching him, Laurie said, "I've got a funny feeling."

"What's that?"

"I've got a hunch I'm going to have mixed emotions about something pretty soon."

They drove to Toni's home. On the way Lou talked about his daughter. He spoke mostly of the years when she had been a child, a time when she had yet to learn to use love as a club.

When they parked in front of Toni's house, Laurie remarked, "You sound like you love her very much."

Lou grunted his assent. "That's why I don't want to live with her."

They began to unload. Laurie said, "You know, I'm looking forward to meeting your daughter."

"You won't today," Lou told her. "She's downtown on a wild-goose chase. She thinks she's meeting me."

"That's mean."

"No, it isn't. If she were here, she'd try to change my mind." He hoisted the largest item, a number of wooden poles wrapped in a multicolored canvas, onto his shoulders and carried it into the house. Laurie followed with an armful of bows and arrows.

246

Once in the house, they moved aside the formica-topped table that still occupied the center of the large room, and along with it, the chrome chairs padded with vinyl, the plastic flowers, and the mass-produced prints that hung on the walls.

As they worked, Laurie commented, "From what you said, I wouldn't have thought your daughter would like this stuff."

"She doesn't," Lou replied.

They unrolled the canvas and set up the poles in the center of the room, spread wide at the bottom, but tied together at the top. Then they placed the canvas around the poles and stood back to inspect the result of their work.

"Now that," Laurie said after a moment, "is the nicest tepee I've ever seen."

Lou grunted his agreement and went to work hanging tomahawks and bows and arrows on the walls. Laurie spread out the squaw's buckskin dress, the brave's loincloth and leggings, and the chief's feathered headdress.

When it was all done, Lou asked, "How does it look?"

Laurie stood by the door to see it from the point of view of someone who had just entered. "All it needs is a campfire in the middle of the floor."

Lou nodded. "They'll see to that." Then he joined her at the door.

"Lou," Laurie asked, "what's it all for?"

Lou took one last look around the large room before he answered. It looked exactly like something he might have found on one of his dinner visits. "I'm just setting things back to normal," he said at last.

When they were driving away, Laurie leaned back in her seat and asked, "Where to now?"

Lou, concentrating on threading his way through traffic, answered briefly, "To a restaurant."

"Oh, good. I'm getting hungry." But then, looking at Lou's profile, she winced. "That's not why we're going there though, is it?"

"We're meeting Hawley."

247

"I've been wondering about him. If the police believe he's mixed up in something—and Perry said—"

Lou interrupted. "He's not."

"I know, but if they think he is, life could get pretty difficult for him, couldn't it?"

Lou nodded. "Damn difficult."

Laurie studied him for a moment. "You're not worried about it at all, are you?"

"No way."

Laurie sighed and stared through the windshield. "All right, don't tell me why. I don't mind. I like drama better anyway—the gradual unfolding, the sudden revelations, the abrupt recognitions, the startling reversals—they all make life more interesting."

"I'm not worried about it," Lou said, "because Hawley won't be in the country tomorrow."

Laurie turned to look at him again. "But that doesn't make sense! You two were going to share an apartment so neither of you would be alone—" She broke off when she realized he really was smiling now. "You don't care?"

Lou shook his head, obviously enjoying the moment.

Laurie considered the possibilities. "He's going away," she said, thinking aloud, "and you don't care. The question is, why wouldn't you?" Suddenly her face lit up. "Talua! I don't believe it!"

"Believe it," Lou told her. "If he managed to do what I told him to do, he'll be leaving on the *Mary J* tonight."

But Laurie was still puzzled. "But how? And why? I thought you were going to work out something together? If he goes, you'll be here by yourself—" She interrupted herself as a new thought struck her. "You won't be by yourself! Neither will he! You're both going!"

Lou shrugged. "Why not?"

Laurie smiled, but her eyes were moist. "I knew I was going to be happy and sad at the same time," she said at last.

Ed Hawley was sitting at one of the red-checkered tables in Giovanni's waiting for them when they arrived. There

248

was anxiety on his face, but it was the kind that comes from a belief that something wonderful might possibly happen—maybe.

When Lou and Laurie sat down he placed an envelope on the table. "I got them. Two tickets on the *Mary J,* sailing to-night."

Laurie laughed with pleasure, but Lou knew it wasn't going to be that easy. Hawley's expression had already told him there were problems to discuss. But the discussion had to wait, for Giovanni came over with three glasses of beer.

"I sense a celebration," he said. "Drink up."

"I want to eat up, too," Laurie said. "I'm starving."

She ordered, but neither Lou nor Hawley was hungry.

Hawley could hardly wait to hear what Lou had to say. Even before Giovanni walked away, he began to speak. "Lou, I got the tickets as you said. I drew out all the money. But I still don't understand what's happening. How do you expect us to live once we get there? It's cheap, yes, but—"

Lou withdrew his copy of his promotion and retirement papers from a jacket pocket and placed them on the table beside the tickets. It took him only a few minutes to explain what the documents were and how he had gotten them. Laurie enjoyed every moment of the monologue, but the worried look never left Hawley's face.

"It doesn't seem possible." He was looking down at the retirement papers as if they might suddenly vanish.

"You see," Laurie said. "You see? Your dream really is going to come true!"

Hawley looked up at Lou. "Can you really leave, today, just like that?"

Lou nodded.

"But don't you have to notify somebody? Give two weeks' notice or something?"

Lou shook his head. "Only my immediate superior—and that's Tate."

"What about the chief or the police commissioner?"

"There are thousands of men in the department. Most of the commissioners don't even know I'm alive—and the

chief knows it only when he happens to think about me."
He reflected for a moment. "I'll have to send him a letter,
though. He's all right."

"Everything really is okay then," Laurie said, looking
from Lou to Hawley.

Hawley slowly shook his head. "I'm afraid not."

"But why? What else do you need? You've got the pension, you've got the tickets—" She broke off as she thought
of something. "Passports!" she exclaimed. "You don't have
passports!"

Lou reached into his pocket and took out two passports.
"I got mine three years ago for an extradition case, but I
never got a chance to use it. Some young hotshot talked the
department into sending him."

He placed it on the table along with Hawley's, which he
had located in Hawley's apartment while waiting for Tate
to show up. Hawley picked his up and leafed through its
blank pages.

"I applied for this more than fifteen years ago, when I
still thought Evelyn and I might get a chance to go together." He sighed. "I've been renewing it ever since."

Laurie was still puzzled, troubled. "Well, if it isn't passports, what is it?"

"Cash," Hawley replied. "We haven't got enough cash."
He indicated the boat tickets. "They cost sixty-two hundred
dollars. I had to add some of my savings. I've only got three
hundred left and that's not enough. We'll spend most of it
before we even get there. There'll be fees for landing per-
mits and we might need certain inoculations along the way.
All kinds of expenses could turn up. And then, when we get
there, we'll need some money until we get settled."

Laurie put down the breadstick she had been nibbling
on. "You can't let that stop you. You mustn't!" She turned
to Lou. "You can find a way to manage, can't you?"

Lou didn't answer directly. "I should be able to get elev-
en or twelve hundred for my car, and lots of people owe me

250

money—ten here, twenty there. If I start right now, maybe I can collect some before the boat leaves."

Hawley didn't seem relieved. He was still worried. Actually, Lou was too, and it showed.

"All right," Hawley said at last. "We'll have enough to get there and maybe enough to live on until your pension starts coming through. But what if it doesn't? What if Tate finds a way to stop it?'

"He can't," Lou said.

Hawley shook his head slowly. "You're not sure of that—not one hundred percent sure."

Lou leaned back in his chair, drained the last of his beer. "No, I'm not even fifty percent sure, but it's worth a try, isn't it? It's worth a gamble. I'm willing to take the risk and I'm not even sure I'll like living on an island. So it's up to you. Whatever you say."

Laurie, who had been looking from one face to the other, exclaimed, "Say yes! You've got to. It's your dream. Yours. You'll never get another chance!"

Hawley stared down at the tablecloth, thinking. Finally he looked up at Lou. "It's not really such a gamble, is it? We really haven't got that much to lose, have we?"

Laurie clapped her hands with delight, making a mental note that years later she would tell her children how wonderful it was to see a dream coming true.

A waitress brought Laurie a plate of spaghetti. Hawley, hungry now, ordered the same. But Lou didn't have time to eat. With Hawley's help he unloaded the suitcases from the trunk of the car—his and Hawley's, which he had packed while waiting for Tate—and then, after leaving the luggage in the restaurant, he left. He had a lot to do. He had to sell his car and collect as many debts as he could and he didn't have much time to do it.

He didn't get far. He had just turned a corner, heading north along a narrow street toward the freeway, when a

251

white Chevy pulled across the street and screeched to a stop directly in front of him. Acting almost instinctively, Lou hit the brakes and skidded to a stop, shoving his transmission into reverse. But he had no chance to back up. A green Ford pulled directly behind him.

It all happened in seconds, but even so, Lou had one hand on the door handle and the other reaching for his Police Special. But he didn't draw the gun. He couldn't. Four men surrounded his car, each aiming a weapon through its windows. Three weapons were revolvers, one was a sawed-off shotgun.

Lou sighed, thinking of Hawley and Laurie waiting for him back at Giovanni's, and slowly placed both his hands on the dash where they could be seen.

Two of the men got in the car with him. One was a small-time punk, just muscle, whom Lou recognized. The other he had never actually met, but knew by reputation. He was Papa Pappas' friend, companion, bodyguard and chief lieutenant, Demetri.

Demetri, who sat beside Lou, told him where to drive, but said little else. When Lou asked him what it was all about, he refused to answer.

The route took them away from the city. They switched from one freeway to another and then, more than an hour later, when they reached the desert, they left the main highways entirely to travel along deserted secondary roads. By this time the sun was low on the horizon and the tall, twisted Joshua trees around them cast grotesque shadows on the land.

Lou, whose mind had never stopped searching for a way out, was forced to admit that whatever was scheduled for him would happen in the utmost privacy. That became more and more apparent as the miles passed. It was an unpleasant thought.

Finally, as Lou was about to drive by a small shack that

stood beside a deserted corral, miles from anywhere, Demetri told him to turn in and then directed him to park in back.

Another car was already parked there, an expensive-looking chauffeur-driven limousine.

Demetri guided Lou into the shack without saying a word. The muscle was left outside on guard duty.

Once inside it took Lou only a moment to adjust to his surroundings. A propane gas lamp hanging from a rafter illuminated a single room, revealing an old table, a chair, a briefcase sitting on the floor. Nothing else—except the old man who sat in the chair at the table—Papa Pappas.

Papa made a motion to Demetri, who nodded, turned, and left. Lou stood in front of the table and waited.

After the door closed behind Demetri, Papa sighed.

"Mr. Baroni, you have caused me a great deal of worry."

"I have?" Lou asked. He wasn't being sarcastic, but Papa took it that way.

"Please," he said. "Please. I know all about your activities."

Lou decided to be cautious, sensing he shouldn't let Papa realize he didn't know what he was talking about. He said, "You know all about 'all' of my activities?"

Papa nodded. "A certain Negro was almost killed last night. You managed to prevent it."

Lou nodded. It was common knowledge on the street by now, anyway.

"I also know," Papa went on, "that Negro—who might possibly recover—is very grateful to you for other favors you've done him in the past."

Lou remained silent.

"He's so grateful, I am told, that he feels he owes you a debt of honor—a debt you might use to convince him he should tell you certain things I'd rather have left untold."

Lou listened carefully. So Wally did know something about Nicky Pappas and the Zakos killing. He had never

253

really been certain of it before. Well, he thought, it didn't make any difference to him now. He wasn't a cop anymore. Officially, he was retired.

"I also know," Papa continued, "you recently caused a detective named Perry to sit in a car near my home evening after evening for reasons I have not yet been able to discover."

Lou smiled. There was no point in denying it. Obviously Hoyle had talked. He hoped they hadn't hurt the little man too much.

"I don't suppose you'll tell me why you had him sitting there for so long?"

What could Lou tell him? That he had arranged it to get Perry out of the way so he'd be free to follow Hawley?

"You'd never believe me," Lou said.

Papa sighed. "There's a great deal more, too, isn't there, Mr. Baroni? There's a great deal you're doing I know nothing about. Perhaps you're reopening old crimes of mine. Perhaps you're looking for witnesses who weren't available before. Perhaps you're gathering evidence to convict my son or, at least, to convince a grand jury to indict me."

Lou didn't know what the old man was talking about. "Perhaps."

"I'm glad you don't deny it," Papa said. "Too many of my people have said you're the only one in the Police Department I should fear. 'Watch out for Baroni,' I am told. 'The others do not matter, but watch out for Baroni.'"

Lou grinned. It was flattering in a way.

"But now, Mr. Baroni, we come to the point where a decision must be made."

"I figured we'd come to it before long," Lou said grimly.

Papa spread his hands on the table, pushing himself to his feet. "You're a threat, Mr. Baroni, a threat to me, to my son, to my legitimate businesses, to my achievements. What am I to do about you?"

Lou felt like saying he should be allowed to sail off to the South Seas, but he was sure Papa wouldn't take that suggestion seriously, so he said nothing.

"I'm told you should be killed, Mr. Baroni. Removed once and for all." He paused, studying Lou. Lou waited. Papa sighed, then moved to a small, broken window. Through it Lou saw the sun had set and the desert was dark.

With his back to Lou Papa said, "I don't want to have you killed, Mr. Baroni. Killing always creates problems. I'm old and tired and I don't want any more problems." He walked back to the table. "But what am I to do? I don't want you to go on with your investigations. I don't want you to go on building cases against me and my son. How can I convince you to stop besides having you killed?"

For a moment Lou was ready to tell him he didn't need to worry, to explain he hadn't been building cases against him and his son, that he wasn't even a detective anymore, that he was through with it all, retired. But some instinct, some sixth sense, told him to keep his mouth shut.

"Maybe," Papa said, "killing you is the only answer, but I hope there's another."

"So do I."

"Maybe," Papa suggested, "you're tired, too. Maybe you long for a little peace as much as I do."

"Maybe," Lou said.

"Maybe, in that case, Mr. Baroni, you'll accept an offer I have in mind."

"What offer?"

Papa reached down beside the table and picked up the briefcase. Opening it, he placed it on the table in front of Lou.

"Fifty thousand dollars," Papa said. "For you."

A bribe, Lou thought wildly. A bribe! A bribe to stop an investigation he had never begun, and never would, now that he was no longer a cop! He threw his head back, laughing so hard it was some time before he could pick up the money.

There were tears in Laurie's eyes as she stood beside Lou's car on the dock, waving good-bye.

It was dark around her although a full moon sparkled on

255

the water. The huge warehouses were black shapes in the night. So were the barges and freighters moored to neighboring wharves. But out in the bay the *Mary J* was anything but a shadow. She was bedecked with a myriad of lights, and so were the tugs that nudged her gently out toward the open sea. Laurie knew she was just an old tramp steamer, but never before had she seen anything that looked so beautiful.

On board the *Mary J,* Lou and Ed Hawley stood on the deck, leaning on the rail, watching the lights of the city slowly receding; watching Laurie, standing beside Lou's car, vanish into darkness.

"It was nice of you to give her your car," Hawley said.

Lou shrugged. "She's a good kid."

They were silent for a moment. Already the absence of smog, the smell of salt air, seemed to put them in another world. Lou shook his head.

"What's the matter?"

"This seem real to you?" Lou asked, his gesture indicating the ship, themselves, the ocean.

Hawley nodded. "Yes. Yes. Much more real than all that." He pointed to the shoreline, the city lights beyond.

"Well," Lou replied, "it doesn't seem real to me. No matter how many times I tell myself it's true, I just can't believe it."

Hawley was puzzled. "What is it then?"

"It's me!" Lou exclaimed. "I'm on a ship bound for the South Seas. Me! Lou Baroni! Sailing off into the sunset! Christ!"

On shore Laurie stood beside Lou's car, watching, until the lights of the *Mary J* disappeared over the horizon.

256